Belzhar

Belzhar

A NOVEL

MEG WOLITZER

DUTTON BOOKS FOR YOUNG READERS
AN IMPRINT OF PENGUIN GROUP (USA) LLC

DUTTON BOOKS FOR YOUNG READERS
Published by the Penguin Group
Penguin Group (USA) LLC
375 Hudson Street
New York, New York 10014

USA * Canada * UK * Ireland * Australia
New Zealand * India * South Africa * China

penguin.com
A Penguin Random House Company

CIP Data is available.
ISBN 978-0-525-42794-0
Printed in the United States of America
1 3 5 7 9 10 8 6 4 2
Design by Kristin Smith

For my sons, Gabriel and Charlie

PROLOGUE

I WAS SENT HERE BECAUSE OF A BOY. HIS NAME was Reeve Maxfield, and I loved him and then he died, and almost a year passed and no one knew what to do with me. Finally it was decided that the best thing would be to send me here. But if you ask anyone on staff or faculty, they'll insist I was sent here because of "the lingering effects of trauma." Those are the words that my parents wrote on the application to get me into The Wooden Barn, which is described in the brochure as a boarding school for "emotionally fragile, highly intelligent" teenagers.

On the line where it says "Reason student is applying to The Wooden Barn," your parents can't write "Because of a boy."

But it's the truth.

When I was little I loved my mom and dad and my brother, Leo, who followed me everywhere and said, "Jammy, *wait.*" When I got older I loved my ninth-grade math teacher, Mr. Mancardi, even though my math skills were deeply subnormal. "Ah, Jam Gallahue, welcome," Mr. Mancardi would say when I came to first period late, my hair still wet from a shower; sometimes, in winter, with the ends frozen like baby twigs. "I'm tickled that you decided to join us." He never said it in a nasty tone of voice. I actually think he was tickled.

I was in love with Reeve in a fierce way that I'd never been in love with anyone before in all my fifteen years. After I met him, the kinds of love I'd felt for those other people suddenly seemed basic and lame. I realized there are different levels of love, just like different levels of math. Down the hall in school back then, in Advanced Math, a bunch of geniuses sat sharing the latest gossip about parallelograms. Meanwhile, in Mr. Mancardi's Dumb Math, we all sat around in a math fog, our mouths half open as we stared in confusion at the ironically named Smart Board.

So I'd been in a very dumb *love* fog without even knowing it. And then, suddenly, I understood there was such a thing as Advanced Love.

Reeve Maxfield was one of three tenth-grade exchange students, having decided to take a break from his life in London, England, one of the most exciting cities in the world, to spend a semester in our suburb of Crampton, New Jersey, to live with dull, cheerful jock Matt Kesman and his family.

Reeve was different from the boys I knew—all those Alexes, Joshes, and Matts. It wasn't just his name. He had a look that none of them had: very smart, slouching and lean, with skinny black jeans hanging low over knobby hip bones. He looked like a member of one of those British punk bands from the eighties that my dad still loves, and whose albums he keeps in special plastic sleeves because he's positive they're going to be worth a lot of money someday. Once I looked up one of my dad's most prized albums on eBay and saw that someone had bid sixteen cents for it, which for some reason made me want to cry.

The covers of my dad's albums usually show a bunch of ironic-looking boys standing together on a street corner, sharing a private joke. Reeve would have fit right in. He had dark brown hair swirling across a pale, pale face, because apparently there's no sunlight in England. "Really? None? Total darkness?" I'd said when he insisted this was true.

"Pretty much," he'd said. "The whole country is like a big, damp house where the electricity's been turned off. And everyone's lacking vitamin D. Even the queen." He said all this with a straight face. There was a *scrape* to his voice. And though I don't have any idea what people thought of him back in London, where that kind of accent is ordinary, to me his voice sounded like a lit match being held to the edge of a piece of brittle paper. It just exploded in a quiet burst. When he spoke I wanted to listen.

I also wanted to look at him nonstop: the pale face, the brown eyes, the flyaway hair. He was like a long beaker in chemistry class, and the top was always bubbling over because some interesting process was taking place inside.

I've now compared Reeve Maxfield to both math and chemistry. But in the end the only class that came to matter in all of this was English. It wasn't my English class at Crampton Regional; it was the one I took much later, at The Wooden Barn up in Vermont, after Reeve was gone and I could barely live.

For reasons I didn't understand, I was one of five students tapped to be in a class called Special Topics in English. What happened in that class is something that none of us have ever talked about to anyone else. Though of course we think about it all the time, and I imagine we'll think about it for the rest of our lives. And the thing that amazes me the most, the thing I keep obsessing about, is this: If I hadn't lost Reeve, and if I hadn't been sent away to that boarding school, and if I hadn't been one of five "emotionally fragile, highly intelligent" teenagers in Special Topics in English, whose lives had been destroyed in five different ways, then I would never have known about Belzhar.

CHAPTER 1

"JESUS, JAM, YOU'D BETTER GET UP ALREADY," SAYS my roommate, DJ Kawabata, an emo girl from Coral Gables, Florida, with "certain food issues," as she put it vaguely. She looms over my bed, her black hair hanging in my face. Because of DJ, our room is a treasure hunt of hidden food: Twizzlers, granola bars, boxes of raisins, even a squeeze bottle of some off-brand of ketchup called, I think, *Hind's*, as if the company hoped that people would get confused and buy it. All of it has been planted strategically for so-called emergencies.

I've been living at The Wooden Barn for only one day, and I haven't witnessed one of my roommate's emergencies yet, but she assures me they're coming. "They always come," she'd said, shrugging, when she first tried to explain what it would be like to share a room with her. "You're going to see some shit you wish you'd never seen before. But don't worry, I'm talking *figurative* shit. I'm not seriously unhinged."

"Seriously unhinged" doesn't get admitted to The Wooden Barn. This place isn't a hospital, and they make a big point of how they're against giving out psychiatric medication. Instead, they insist that the school experience is meant to bring people together and help them heal.

I can't imagine that this can be true. They don't even let you have the Internet. They ban it completely, which just seems cruel. They also confiscate your cell phone. There's one ancient pay phone in the girls' dorm, and one in the boys'. There isn't any accessible Wi-Fi, so you can use your laptops for writing papers, but you can't research anything. You can listen to music, but you're out of luck if you want to go online and download new songs. You're cut off from everything, which makes no sense at all, because everyone at this school is already cut off in one way or another.

Although no one comes right out and says it, The Wooden Barn is sort of a halfway house between a hospital and a regular school. It's like a big lily pad where you can linger before you have to make the frog-leap back to ordinary life.

DJ told me she'd previously been in a special hospital for eating disorders. The patients there were all girls, she went on, and they were constantly being weighed by nurses who wore those pediatric nurse blouses that had patterns of cutesy puppies or panda bears on them. Sometimes when their weight got too low, the girls were force-fed through tubes.

"That happened to me once," DJ said. "One of the nurses held me down, and her boobs were smashed into my face, and when I looked up, all I could see was an ocean of tiny golden retrievers."

By the time I arrive at The Wooden Barn, DJ has been here for two years. And this morning, on the very first day that classes begin, as she hovers above me with her hair hanging in my face like a curtain, I just want her to go away. But she won't.

"Jam, you already missed breakfast," she says, as if she's my parent or something. "It's time for class. What've you got first?"

"No idea."

"Haven't you looked at your skedge?"

"My '*skedge*'? If you mean my schedule, no."

I'd arrived the day before, having made the six-hour drive up with my parents and Leo. My mom was sort of crying the whole way but pretending it was allergies, and my dad was listening to NPR with a strange intensity. "Today," said the woman on the radio, "we are going to devote our entire show to the voices suppressed by the Taliban."

My dad turned up the volume and nodded his head thoughtfully, as if it were the most fascinating thing, while my mom closed her eyes and cried, not about the voices suppressed by the Taliban, but about me.

My brother, Leo, was just being himself, sitting beside me pressing buttons on the grimy little handheld in his lap. "Hey," he said when he'd beaten a level of his game and caught my eye.

"Hey."

"It'll suck without you in the house."

"You'd better get used to it," I said to him. "Our childhood together is pretty much over."

"That's mean," he said.

"But it's true. And then eventually," I went on, "one of us will die. And the other one will have to go to the funeral. And give a speech."

"Jam, *stop*," Leo said.

I immediately felt sorry about what I'd said, and didn't even know why I'd said it. I was in a bad mood all the time. Leo didn't deserve to be treated this way. He was only twelve, and he looked even younger. Some kids in his grade looked like they were ready to have children; Leo looked like one of the children they might've had. Occasionally he got tripped in the hall, but nothing really bothered him because he'd found a way not to care. From the time he turned ten, he'd been obsessed with the alternative world of a video game called *Dream Wanderers* that has to do with magic cubes and apprentices and characters called driftlords.

I still have no idea what a driftlord is. At the time, I didn't even understand what an alternative world was, but now of course I do. And so I get what my little brother has known for a while: Sometimes an alternative world is much better than the real one.

"I wasn't trying to be mean," I told Leo in the car. "I get like this," I added.

"Mom and Dad told me that when you act this way I should just let it go, because—"

"Because why?" My voice had an edge.

"Because of what you've been through," he said uneasily. He and I had barely talked about it. He was so young, and he couldn't possibly know what I'd been through, what I'd felt.

The conversation had nowhere to go, so we each looked out our separate windows, and finally Leo closed his eyes and went to sleep with his mouth open. The car was enveloped in the smell of the cool-ranch-flavored chips he'd been eating. I felt sorry for him that he was like an only child now. That he no longer had a normal older sister. That instead he had one who'd become destroyed enough to have to go live at a special school in another state six hours away.

Drop-off at The Wooden Barn was highly tense. My

mom kept trying to arrange my room, while DJ lounged on her bed, silently watching the whole scene, clearly amused by it.

"Be sure you give your study buddy a couple of big punches every day so the filling stays even," my mom said to me as I put things in drawers.

From my trunk, I took out the jar of Tiptree Little Scarlet Strawberry Preserve, the jam that Reeve had given me the night we first kissed, and I held the cool glass cylinder in my hand for a moment. I knew I'd never open this jar. It was almost like an urn that had Reeve's ashes in it. The seal would remain unbroken forever. The jar was sacred to me, and I deposited it in my top dresser drawer and covered it carefully with a mess of bras and underwear and an old Tweety Bird nightshirt.

"Just reach out and hit it, okay, Jam?" my mom continued. "Just hit it like it was a predator who's jumped you in an alley."

"Mom," I said, while DJ kept watching, not even pretending she wasn't. She annoyed me so much, and I couldn't believe I was going to have to live with her.

"I mean, just give it a good slug all around the bottom and the sides," my mom continued, demonstrating how I should attack the so-called study buddy, that big pillow with arms that she'd insisted we buy for my room at the Price Cruncher back in Crampton.

The woman at the checkout counter had smiled at us when we managed to hoist it onto the moving belt. And then she'd said in a singsong voice, "Is someone going to Fenster Academy?"

Fenster Academy is the snotty boarding school not too

far from my house in New Jersey where the girls have horses and everyone wears a sky-blue uniform, and sings these corny songs with bad rhymes like, "Oh Fenster, dear Fenster, we will ne'er forget our semesters . . ." Mom and I both awkwardly shook our heads no.

The study buddy was enormous, orange, and corduroy. I hated it in the store, and I hated it again when it sat on my bed in The Wooden Barn with its arms out. I even hated the name "study buddy." Everyone knew I was still in no condition to study.

Apparently, though, it was time to "knuckle down," or "get with the program," as people said. And since I couldn't do that, then it was time for me to enroll at The Wooden Barn, where supposedly a combination of the Vermont air, maple syrup, no psychiatric medication, and no Internet will cure me. But I'm not curable.

The other thing that makes the name "study buddy" awful is that I have no "buddies" anymore. Before I met Reeve and wanted to be with him all the time, my closest friends in Crampton were two other low-key, nice girls with long, straight hair—girls like me. We worked hard at school but weren't nerds, and had done a little weed but weren't stoners. Mostly we were all considered cute-looking and sweet and sort of shy.

Actually, I don't think anyone thought about us all that often. We were the kind of girls who braided one another's hair when we were younger, and practiced synchronized dance moves, and slept over at one another's houses every single weekend. On those sleepovers we talked very frankly about a lot of topics, including "relationships," of course, though among us only Hannah Petroski had an actual, long-term boyfriend, Ryan Brown. The two of them were really serious, and had almost had sex.

"We are a *millimeter* away from actually doing it," Hannah had revealed one weekend. And though I didn't exactly know what that meant, I nodded and pretended I did. Hannah and Ryan had been in love since Mrs. Delahunt's kindergarten class. They'd had their first kiss on a carpet remnant in the nap corner.

After I lost Reeve, my friends came around a lot at first, dropping solemnly by the house. I could hear them from my bedroom when they stood in the front hall and talked to my parents. "Hi, Mr. Gallahue," one of them would say. "Is Jam doing any better? No? Not at all? Wow, I don't really know what to say. Well, I baked her some snickerdoodles . . ."

But when they knocked on my bedroom door I never wanted to talk to them for very long. "I just wish you'd get over this already," Hannah finally said one day, sitting on the edge of my bed. "You didn't even know each other for very long. What was it, a month?"

"Forty-one days," I corrected.

"Well, I know you're having a hard time," she told me. "I mean, Ryan is my life, so it's not as if I can't appreciate it in *some* way. But still . . . ," she added, her voice trailing off.

"But still *what*, Hannah?"

"I don't know," she said. Then she added, miserably, "I have to go, Jam."

If Reeve had been there I would've said to him, "Don't you hate the way people say, 'But *still,* dot-dot-dot' and let their voices kind of drop away, like they've actually finished the sentence? 'But still' doesn't mean *anything*, right? It just means you can't explain what you feel."

"I do hate that," Reeve would've said. "People who say 'But still' have *Satan* in them."

He and I just tended to see the world the same way. After I lost him, I stayed in my room, drowsing on my bed. Once I wore my Tweety Bird nightshirt for five days straight. My friends stopped coming. No more visits, no more snickerdoodles. My parents made me try to go back to school, but everyone there stared at me because they knew how much I'd loved Reeve. I just sat in class with my eyes shut, hardly listening to anything being said.

"Hello in there," a teacher would say. "Jam, *hello*?"

Sometimes, in the middle of a school day, I'd be standing in a patch of red light under the exit sign by the gym, or sitting on a beanbag chair in a corner of the library. And suddenly I'd remember that this was a place where I'd been with Reeve, and I'd go into a total panic. The breath would fly out of my chest, and I'd run down the hall and out through the fire doors and keep going.

At first, some teacher or staff person would always run after me, but after a while they got tired of running. "I'm too old for this!" the school nurse once bellowed at me from across the playing fields.

"If Jamaica can't bring herself to stay at school during the day," the principal said to my parents, "then perhaps you ought to make other arrangements for her."

So they tried homeschooling. They brought in a former history teacher who, we'd all heard, had been fired for coming to class wasted on vodka shots. He was a nice guy with a sad, creased face like one of those Shar-Pei dogs, and though he was never drunk when he came to tutor me, I just couldn't pay attention. Again, I drifted off. "Oh, Jam," he said. "I'm afraid this isn't working."

Now, after my mom and dad and my brother, Leo, have said their good-byes to me in my dorm room—all of them so upset, and me sort of empty and thick inside—and after I've sat through baked chicken, green beans, and quinoa in the dining hall, overwhelmed by all the new faces and voices around me, but staying separate and not talking to anyone, and after a night spent barely sleeping, I lie curled in bed on the first morning of classes at The Wooden Barn.

And DJ, already fully dressed and with her hair in my face, demands to see my "skedge." I motion vaguely toward the desk, where some of my non-clothing belongings are piled in no particular order. DJ paws through them and finally pulls out a folded piece of paper. Her expression changes as she looks at it.

"What?" I ask.

DJ looks at me strangely. She's half Asian, half Jewish, with straight, shining dark hair, and freckles tossed across her face. "You have Special Topics in English?" she says, her voice rising up in disbelief.

"I don't know." I haven't checked my classes. I really don't care.

"Yeah, you do," she says. "It's your first class of the day. Do you know how unusual it is that you got in?"

"No. Why?"

DJ sits down on the bed at my feet. "First of all, this is a legendary class. The person who teaches it, Mrs. Quenell, only teaches it when she wants to. Like, last year she decided it wasn't going to be offered at all. She said there wasn't the right 'mix' of students, whatever that means. And even when she does teach it, almost *nobody* gets accepted into the class. You go through this whole effort of applying for it, but basically they always give you another class instead.

"This summer I even wrote a special sucking-up note to her saying how important it was to me to be allowed to take the class this fall. I said that when I got to college I wanted to be an English major, and that 'if I was lucky enough to be accepted into Special Topics, it would surely send me on my way.' I actually used those ass-kissing words. But they didn't work. I got put in regular English, just like almost everybody else. It's a total joke."

"Well," I say, "you're probably lucky that you didn't get in."

"That's the same thing people always say," DJ says, irritated. "And it just makes me want to be in it more. By the way, it's one semester long. It ends right before Christmas break. And you only read one writer."

"One writer the whole semester?"

"Yeah. It changes each time. Mrs. Quenell is really old," DJ goes on. "She's one of the only teachers at The Wooden Barn who's called 'Mrs.' On the first day of class, every other teacher says 'Call me Heather' or 'Call me Ishmael,' in this we're-your-best-friends-and-you-can-tell-us-anything way. But not Mrs. Quenell. And here's another weird thing: Some people get into her class who didn't even *apply*. Like, apparently, you. There are usually only five or six people in it. It's the smallest, most elite class in the entire school."

"Feel free to take my place," I say.

"I wish I could. During the semester, everyone in the class acts like it's no big deal. But then when it's over, they say things about how it changed their lives. I'm dying to know in what way it changed their lives. But it's not like you can ask anyone about it now, because no one who was in that class is still at school. It's mixed grades, but the last of them graduated or left. I swear, it's like one of those secret societies." DJ looks me over with an expression that's partly impressed, and partly hostile, and says, "So. Tell me. What's so special about you?"

I think about this for a second. "Nothing," I say. Reeve was the most special thing that ever happened to me. Now I'm just an apathetic, long-haired girl who doesn't care about anything except my own grief. I have no idea why I was chosen to be in Mrs. Quenell's Special Topics in English. I don't even *want* to be in an advanced class where you obviously have to work extra hard to do well. I'd rather be allowed to hang out in the back of a classroom all year and get some sleep while the teacher gets all worked up and about to have a stroke over whether or not *Huckleberry Finn* is racist.

Instead, I'm probably going to have to "participate." But I don't want to participate in anything. The world can go on without me and just leave me alone to close my eyes and rest during the school day. Apparently The Wooden Barn didn't get that message.

But DJ, who doesn't get the message that I want to be left alone either, makes me get out of bed and get dressed. "Up," she says, making getting-up motions with her hands. Her nails, I notice, are painted grayish green.

"What are you, my mommy?" I ask.

"No, your roommate."

"I didn't know that getting me up was your job," I say coldly.

"Well, now you know," says DJ. Despite her appearance and the snaky way she behaved when my parents dropped me off, she seems very involved in being a roommate. She manages to get me out of bed, and even insists that I eat a little something before Special Topics in English begins. "You want your mind to be sharp," she says.

"Not really."

"Believe me, you do. Here. Eat." This, of course, is deeply ironic—the food-issues girl urging her non-food-issues roommate to eat—but DJ doesn't seem to notice. She's reached under her mattress and pulled out a flattened s'mores-flavored granola bar.

I take the bar and wolf it down, though it tastes like old compacted dirt shot through with little bits of gravel. I don't ask her why I ought to listen to her when I don't know her at all, except to see that she must be a genuinely screwed-up person to have landed at The Wooden Barn. But then again, I must be one too.

"It's for the best," my dad had said a few nights earlier, when I was packing the trunk that I used to take to Camp Swaying Spruce every summer.

Then my mom, who always blurts out the truth when she's under stress, added, "We don't know what else to do with you, babe!"

So now, having been banished to The Wooden Barn, and having eaten a flattened, tasteless granola bar, my roommate, DJ, hustles me outside. The leaf-bright campus is actually pretty, though I still don't care. Fine, so instead of living in a pale blue suburban ranch house at 11 Gooseberry Lane in Crampton, New Jersey, my half-dead self now lives on the campus of an abnormal New England boarding school that's made to look like a normal one. There are plenty of trees, winding paths, and kids with backpacks.

"See this building?" DJ says, pointing to a big red wooden structure. "It used to be a barn—that's where the school got its name, *duh*—but now it's where a lot of classes are held. It's the nicest of all the buildings. Of course, Special Topics is held here." She leads me inside and takes me down a long hall. The old, polished wooden floors creak and groan under our feet. People are wandering around, killing time before class.

"Yo, DJ, you in Perrino's section A physics?" a boy calls to her.

"Yeah," she says suspiciously. "Why?"

"I'm in it too."

"What a staggering coincidence," she says.

DJ seems popular here, which would never have been the case in Crampton. Then again, it was pretty surprising that I got to be popular there, having spent so many years as one of those interchangeable, long-haired nice girls. But when I started spending time with Reeve, some people in the group of kids that decided which other kids mattered began to pay more attention to me. Everyone noticed the way Reeve sat with me during art class once, and how I sketched him. We sat very close that day, and word got around that there was something between us.

Which explains why Dana Sapol, the girl who probably mattered most at Crampton, and who was never nice to me, had actually looked up from her locker and said, "My parents and Courtney the brat are going to our grandparents' this Saturday, so it's par-tay time. You should come. The hottie exchange student will be there."

I pretended not to think it was a huge deal that she had said this. But of course it was. Dana had had it out for me since the day in second grade when she forgot to wear underpants to school. I only found this out because she hung upside-down on the jungle gym that day, though luckily I was the only one who saw. "Dana, you forgot your *underpants*," I hissed, blocking her from everyone else's view.

You'd think she would have been grateful. I saw it before anyone else could see. But instead it was like I suddenly knew something scandalous about her that I could hold over her forever. Not that I ever would have, of course, but it was what she thought. Years passed and Dana's underpants incident might've become something funny that we could have joked around about, but we never did. She just treated me cruelly or ignored me—until now, when suddenly I was invited to her party.

I'd twirled my combination lock and made an expression of only the vaguest interest. As if I didn't care that I was invited, or as if I didn't care that Reeve would be there. As if maybe I had something else to do on Saturday night besides some sleepover at Hannah's or Jenna's, or a trip to the mall to look at skinny jeans, or a family game night with my parents and Leo. I hadn't really minded those nights before—I'd even liked them—but all of a sudden I couldn't believe I'd spent so much time that way.

I just wanted to be with Reeve now. He was all I thought about. He'd said that the Kesmans, his host family, were concerned about him making the "right" friends. This was sort of understandable. The previous year, the Kesmans had hosted a girl from Denmark who did nothing but wear clogs and smoke weed. So when Reeve came to live with them, they went through his luggage looking for illegal substances.

"Or clogs," Reeve added.

But he wasn't into substances, and neither was I. "If I want to get all paranoid and scarf down an entire Cadbury Dairy Milk bar and a bag of crisps, I don't need something herbal to make me do that," he once said, which I thought was pretty funny.

"'Cadbury Dairy Milk bar,'" I said. "'Crisps.' And pronouncing the 'h' in 'herbal.' Those British things you say—I love them."

"'In hospital,'" said Reeve, continuing to try to amuse me. "'Flat.' 'Bloody hell.' 'That'll be twelve quid.' 'Duke and Duchess of Fill-in-the-Bloody-Blank.'"

Standing in the hallway outside my classroom at The Wooden Barn, I'm swimming in thoughts of Reeve—his voice, his face—but DJ puts an end to this. "*Focus*. Class is about to start. You'd better tell me all about it later," she says, and then she pushes me inside.

CHAPTER 2

"WELCOME, EVERYONE," SAYS MRS. QUENELL WHEN all of us are seated around the table. "All of us" is only four people. The class is even smaller than DJ said it would be. To my surprise, there's no loud, in-your-face bell here to signal that class has begun. I guess people at The Wooden Barn are so fragile that a ringing bell could send them over the edge. Instead, our teacher glances at the extremely small face of the gold watch on her long wrist, and frowns slightly, the way people do when they look at the time.

Mrs. Quenell is like someone's elegant, graceful grandmother, with hair the color of faded snow, swept back off her face. She must be in her late seventies. She looks up and around at us and says, "I had hoped that everyone would be here promptly at the start of class, but I guess that's not the case. We have a lot of work to do, so I'd like to begin, even with one student absent."

I wonder who that student is. Maybe she's new like me, and doesn't have a roommate who will get her out of bed and push her into the classroom. She could still be fast asleep right now, wanting everyone to go away, just like I do.

"As you are all well aware, this class is called Special Topics in English," Mrs. Quenell says. "And now I'd like to go around the room and have you all say your names and a few things about yourselves. Even if you already know one another, remember that I don't know any of you. Except on paper."

The three other kids sitting at the oval oak table in this small, bright room include a neatly-pressed type of boy with freshly cut black hair and a striped button-down shirt; a beautiful African American girl with a head of braids with bright little beads at the ends like optical fibers; and a boy whose face is obstructed by a gray hoodie. Not only is the hood up, but he's got his head resting on his crossed arms, his face turned away from everyone.

Suddenly, as if he knows I'm looking, hoodie boy turns in my direction. The movement is sharp and surprising, like when one of the giant sea turtles at the zoo suddenly decides to turn its head. Unlike a sea turtle, hoodie boy is good-looking, but in a hostile way. You can tell he'd rather be anywhere but here, which is how I feel too, though I hide my feelings better than he does. Detachment is my style, not hostility.

Then the boy yanks down his hood, letting loose his long blond hair. I can imagine him surfing, snowboarding, doing something daring while his hair blows in the wind. So he's one of *those* people, I think, the reckless kind I've never liked. Reeve never liked that kind either.

"The *dudes* have arrived," Reeve said one day when a few of those boys hulked into the cafeteria together. "They're here to get their recommended daily allowance of dude protein."

"Eight million grams of raw shark flesh," I said.

Now, as I find myself looking at the boy in the hoodie, he gives me a glance that seems to say, "Move along now."

Flustered, I look elsewhere, gazing out the window and half expecting to see a lone student hurrying late to our class.

Mrs. Quenell motions to the African American girl, who sits to her left. She's the kind of girl who, when she walks down the street in a city, people from modeling agencies probably come up to her and hand her their business cards, saying, "Call me anytime." She sits up straight in her chair with the best posture I've ever seen on a creature that isn't a sea horse.

"Why don't we begin here," says our teacher.

"Okay," says the girl after an uncomfortable pause. "I'm Sierra Stokes." She stops, as though we have all the information we need.

Mrs. Quenell says, "Can you say a little more?"

"I'm from Washington, DC. I've been at The Wooden Barn since last spring. Before that," Sierra adds in a slightly stiff voice, "I was out of school for a while. That's all, I guess."

"Thank you," says Mrs. Quenell, and then she nods to the serious-looking boy. He has one of those square, masculine heads that have probably been square and masculine since he first emerged from his mom's birth canal.

"I'm Marc Sonnenfeld," he says, and I think, *debate team*, possibly captain. "I'm from Newton, Massachusetts," he continues, "and I live with my sister and my mom. I was president of the student council. Also, captain of the debate team."

Yes.

"But then everything got kind of horrible, and I don't really know what I'm into anymore." He pauses, then says, "I guess that's all."

"Thank you, Marc," says Mrs. Quenell. She turns to the

blond boy in the hoodie and says, "All right, why don't you introduce yourself next?" His silence goes on so long that it seems rude, as if maybe he were pretending he didn't hear her. Then finally he speaks in a voice so soft and flat that I can't even hear it across the table.

Mrs. Quenell says, "One voice. That's all we're given." No one has any idea what this means, but she seems content to let us remain confused, and wait.

"Um, what?" says Marc.

"We each have only one voice," says Mrs. Quenell. "And the world is so loud. Sometimes I think that the quiet ones"—she nods toward the rude boy—"have figured out that the best way to get other people's attention is not to shout, but to whisper. Which makes everyone listen a little harder."

"That wasn't what I was doing," says the boy in a suddenly louder voice. "I was just talking the way I talk. I used to always get told to use my *inside* voice. So now I did. And, what, instead you want my *outside* voice?"

Mrs. Quenell smiles so slightly that I don't even know if anyone else sees it. "No, just your real voice," she says. "Whatever that is. I hope we'll find out."

Who *is* this teacher? I can't tell whether she's being playful or serious. I feel awkward sitting here, and the class is so small that there's probably no way to hide my awkwardness. There's no way to hide anything at all when there are so few of us sitting around a table. A whole semester of this will be excruciating. Looking around, I'm pretty sure everyone else feels the same way.

But our teacher acts as if she doesn't notice that we're uncomfortable. She's still looking at hoodie boy, waiting for him to introduce himself properly. When he finally does, it seems to take all his effort. "I'm Griffin Foley," he says.

Then he stops. That's *it*?

"Welcome, Griffin," Mrs. Quenell says, and she waits.

"I'm from a farm a mile and a half away," he continues. "I always get bad grades in English. I'm just warning you." Then he sinks back down.

"Thank you," says Mrs. Quenell. "I'll consider myself warned."

Just then the door bangs open, the knob slamming so hard against the wall that I worry it'll leave a crater. Startled, we all turn at once to see a girl in a wheelchair trying to push herself into the classroom. "Oh, fuck," she says as her backpack catches the edge of the doorframe.

Everyone around the table, including Mrs. Quenell, jumps up to help, though right away we're all clearly a little embarrassed at our own extreme show of helpfulness. Sierra gets there first, and she lifts the backpack off the wheelchair and out of the way, and the girl zips inside. She's small, red-haired, delicate, but she's in a real state, and the word that comes to mind now is *blazing*.

"I know there's no excuse for me being late," the girl says in a nearly hysterical voice. "I don't want to play the cripple card—oh, excuse me, I mean the *disabled* card. And I don't want you to tell me it's perfectly all right that I'm late," she goes on.

As I look over at our teacher, though, I can see that it's not all right. The thing is, this girl doesn't understand it yet. She's probably heard that all the teachers at The Wooden Barn are really easygoing and gentle with their students, afraid that a single stern word might make them disintegrate. But Mrs. Quenell says, "I won't tell you that. I would like for it not to happen again. We have a lot to accomplish. I don't want to waste a second."

The girl seems startled. I bet usually no one has wanted to upset her, just the way no one has wanted to upset me either.

"I'm sorry," she says. "I haven't figured this out yet."

"I understand. But you'll have to, somehow," says Mrs. Quenell, which seems a little harsh. "If you go through life like that, you'll miss out on too much."

And then I realize—and maybe all of us realize, because as it turns out this girl is new too, like me—that she wasn't born disabled, and that her wheelchair must be a pretty recent addition. I suddenly really want to know what happened to her. I don't see a cast on either of her legs, so it's not a broken bone. But the legs don't look shriveled up, either, like the Wicked Witch of the East's right before they disappear under the house. They look like normal legs packed in blue jeans, except they're clearly not functional.

"But it's just so hard," the girl says in a voice that makes her sound very young.

"I know that," says Mrs. Quenell, more gently now. "*Hard.* You've used the perfect word. And I'm a big believer in finding the perfect words. I've been that way as long as I can remember."

She closes her eyes, and I think that she is literally remembering something, dragging up a specific image in her mind from long ago. I wonder if maybe she's too old to be teaching. Her personality seems a little unpredictable—shifting between impatient and sympathetic.

Mrs. Quenell opens her eyes and says to the girl, "You've already learned two things since you've been here. One: Lateness—your teacher doesn't like it. And two: Perfect words—she likes them very much. And now maybe we can all learn something about *you*."

The girl looks unhappy with this idea. "Like what?"

"We've been going around the table and the students have been saying their names and a little something about themselves. Now it's your turn."

"I'm Casey Cramer," the girl says grudgingly. "Casey Clayton Cramer. All Cs," she adds.

"What?" says Marc. "Your grades?"

"No. *Casey. Clayton. Cramer*. They're all *C* names."

"Oh," he says. "Right."

We all sit there, each of us feeling awkward and incredibly sorry for Casey Cramer, who can't walk and has already been scolded by our teacher. But we're also kind of waiting for Casey to say, "The reason I'm in this wheelchair is . . ." But she says nothing like that. She's done.

Which means, I realize with a light sensation of nausea, I'm the only one who hasn't spoken.

I don't have to tell them anything big, I remind myself. Anything about Reeve, or what happened to me. I just have to say the barest little nothing, like everyone else. I just have to throw them a bone.

Mrs. Quenell looks at me with her clear, interested eyes and says, "All right, it's your turn now."

She waits. I have no choice in the matter. I can't say that I'm not in the mood; I'm sure Mrs. Quenell would never put up with that. I gaze downward at the wood grain of the table, which suddenly seems as interesting as Casey Cramer being in a wheelchair. I just stare and stare at it, and finally I look up and start, "Okay, let me see. My name is Jam Gallahue." Then I stop, hoping that that's enough to satisfy Mrs. Quenell.

But of course it's not.

"Go on," she says.

"Well," I say, looking down again, "my name is actually Jamaica, which is where my parents went on their honeymoon. And where I was *conceived.*" Marc laughs in embarrassment. "My brother called me Jam when he was little, and it stuck. Oh, and I'm from New Jersey."

Then I'm done, and I look around, and other than Mrs. Quenell no one seems all that fascinated by what I had to say. We're all so pathetically awkward: five mismatched students and the teacher who chose us.

And though this would be a good time for her to tell us why we've each been chosen—for her to say something like "You may be wondering why you're here. Well, on your standardized tests, you each showed a special aptitude for reading comprehension"—she doesn't even try to explain. Instead, she turns her head slightly to take each of us in; it's as if she were studying us, trying to memorize our faces.

I have rarely felt anyone pay this much attention to me before, outside of my parents and Dr. Margolis and, of course, Reeve. I wonder what she thinks is so interesting. If I were her and I had to sit here looking at us, I would be bored out of my mind.

But Mrs. Quenell glances at me, and then at the rest of the class, as though we've all been riveting, and says, "Thank you,

Jam, and thank you, everyone. It's only fair for me to tell you a little bit about myself. My name is Mrs. Quenell. Veronica Quenell, actually, but I prefer being called *Mrs.* If any of you prefer being called *Mr.* or *Miss*, I am happy to oblige." There's silence. No, none of us prefer that. "I've been teaching at The Wooden Barn since long before you were born," she continues. "I have certain demands that I place on my students, and I do ask that you meet them. Punctuality, of course, but not just that. Also, hard work, honesty, and openness. Now, you might well be thinking to yourself, *Yes, yes, Mrs. Quenell, I will meet all your demands.* But sometimes the mind shuts itself off, and no learning takes place. Reading does not get done. Assignments do not get met. And when that happens, well, there is no point to our being here.

"But if you do all that I ask of you, I think you will find it very rewarding. I am passionate about teaching this class, which is the only class I now teach, because I am no longer a spring chicken. By which I mean I am no longer *young*. In case, somehow, you hadn't noticed." She pauses and looks around at all of us again. "Oh, so then you *have* noticed," she says with a very faint smile. "Alas. Age is one of those things that none of us can do anything about." Another pause, then she finally does say, "Some of you are perhaps wondering why you've been invited into Special Topics in English."

"No shit," bursts out Griffin Foley, and there's startled laughter around the table. Marc shakes his head. "You made a big mistake with me," says Griffin.

"Like anyone, I do make mistakes," says Mrs. Quenell. "I am certainly not perfect. But I have reviewed your files carefully, and I have no doubt that you are in the right class. Even you, Griffin." She glances around at us once again. "Between now and late December, when class ends, I'll be extremely interested in hearing what you have to say about yourselves." Then she says, "I don't expect you to understand anything that I'm trying to tell you."

We all just look at her. No, we don't understand it at all.

"But it's all right," says Mrs. Quenell. "You will. Of that I am certain." She peers at her watch again and says, "I see that time is flying by, the way time tends to do. I'd like to introduce the first writer we'll be reading this semester. She also happens to be the last writer, because she's the *only* writer we will read. Whenever I've taught this class, I've focused on a single writer, and it always changes. I like to keep the conversation fresh." In a quieter voice Mrs. Quenell adds, "I guess I can also tell you now that you are my last students."

We're confused. Sierra raises her hand and asks, "What do you mean?"

"Raised hands aren't necessary in here, Sierra. Only raised minds. What I mean is that I'm going to retire after this class ends," says Mrs. Quenell. "I've been here a very long time, and it's been magnificent. But I believe it's time for me to take my leave. So I've sold my house, and I plan to take a world cruise—one of those enormous ships stuffed with old people like me waiting in line for dessert—before I decide where to settle down. By the time the semester is over, I'll be packed up and saying good-bye to The Wooden Barn." Emotion pokes through as she speaks, though she clearly doesn't want it to. "The school is giving me a retirement party at the end of the semester," she adds. "Of course you'll all be invited."

The end of the semester seems so far away; I can't even

imagine how I'll get from here to there. It will be agonizingly long. She may think that time flies, but I think it stands still.

"But enough about me," Mrs. Quenell continues. "I'm not important to this discussion. You are. So let's get on with the last Special Topics ever."

She reaches below the table and pulls out a stack of five identical books, which she passes around. It's *The Bell Jar*, by Sylvia Plath. I remember Hannah Petroski telling me it was incredible, "but so depressing."

Marc Sonnenfeld raises his hand, then remembers what Mrs. Quenell said, and quickly lowers it. "I know that book," he says. "It's supposed to be really dark. I think I remember something about the author." He pauses, not sure if he should go on.

"Go ahead, Marc," says Mrs. Quenell.

"Well," he says uneasily, "I guess she . . . you know . . . killed herself, is that right? She turned on the gas and put her head in the oven?"

"Yes, that's right."

"No offense," says Marc. "I'm sure you're a good English teacher and all, but is that . . . appropriate for us? I mean, aren't we all sort of—" He breaks off in the middle of the sentence, embarrassed.

"Go on."

"*Fragile*," he says, with a little bit of irony in his voice. "Like it says in the brochure. We're all supposed to be so, so fragile. Like porcelain."

"Yes, I believe it does say something like that in the brochure," says Mrs. Quenell. "Marc, do you feel as if reading a book about a young woman's emotional problems—by a writer who finally succumbed to her own emotional problems—would be too much for you?"

Marc considers it. "I don't *think* so," he says. "I know it's supposed to be a classic."

Mrs. Quenell looks around the table. "Is there anyone here who feels uncomfortable about reading *The Bell Jar*?"

We all shake our heads no. But I wonder what my parents would say. Maybe they'd worry about me reading such a depressing book. I imagine going to the pay phone when class gets out and calling them to say that I'm reading *The Bell Jar*, and that it's making me feel upset. "We're pulling you out of that school," my dad would say, outraged. And then I'd get to leave here tomorrow, and return to my own home and my own bed, and not have to deal with this odd, new environment and all these people with problems.

"All right, thank you," says Mrs. Quenell, as if she'd barely noticed before now that her choice of book and writer, at a school like this, is kind of unusual. Marc is right; suicide has to be a touchy issue here. A lot of students at The Wooden Barn are probably depressed. But it's almost as if Mrs. Quenell were going right for the gut by picking Sylvia Plath. It's like she's doing whatever she wants, because she doesn't care what people think of her. And for the quickest second, I'm almost impressed.

"If anyone's feelings change," she goes on, "please come talk to me. I chose the curriculum with care. Just the way I chose all of you."

Maybe she did choose us with care. But who knows how the choices were made. None of us in the class seem to have much in common.

"For those of you who aren't familiar with *The Bell Jar*," she says, "it was written over fifty years ago by the brilliant American writer Sylvia Plath. The book is autobiographical, and it tells the story of a young woman's depression and, I suppose, her descent into madness. Does anyone know what a bell jar is?" We shake our heads. "It's a bell-shaped glass jar used for scientific samples. Or to create a little vacuum. Anything that's put under a bell jar is isolated from the rest of the world," she says. "It's a metaphoric title, of course. Sylvia Plath, whose depression made her feel as if she herself were in a kind of bell jar, cut off from the world, took her own life at age thirty."

No one says anything; we just listen. "This is the one novel she wrote in her lifetime. She was a very fine and accomplished poet, and she wrote some of her most powerful work—the poems in her collection *Ariel*—at the end of her life. We'll be reading them, too, of course. Oh, and she also happened to be a prolific keeper of journals over the years. Which is why," she says, "I'm also giving you *these*."

Mrs. Quenell reaches below the table again and pulls out a stack of five identical red leather journals, passing them around. When I get mine I open it and the book makes a slight creaking sound, its spine tight. It's a well-made object, I can tell at once, and it's also clearly very old, the pages slightly yellowed, as if it's been sitting in a box in a closet for decades. The pale blue lines on the paper are closer together than I'm used to, and I know that I'd have to write a lot to fill up even one page.

"Whoa, this is an antique," says Griffin.

"Yes. Just like your teacher," says Mrs. Quenell with a smile. She folds her hands and looks at us. "For tonight," she continues, "in addition to reading the first chapter of *The Bell Jar*, you will also begin thinking about keeping your own journal. Try to imagine what you might write. Begin writing, if you can. But at the very least, think about it. It's your journal, it belongs to you, and it will be a representation of you and your inner life. You can write anything you like."

But all I can think is, sarcastically, *ooh, how exciting*. Because there's nothing I want to write. I'm hardly going to put down on paper the things I think about all the time, night and day. The person I think about. That's only for me.

"Once the spirit moves you," says Mrs. Quenell, "you will write in the journal twice a week. And you will all hand your journals back to me at the end of the semester. I won't read them, I never do, but I *will* collect them, and keep them. Like the writing itself, this is a requirement. I'm a firm believer in my students moving forward and not dwelling on what might be less than productive." She takes a moment, then says, "You will be doing close reading all semester, and also what I call close writing. And you will all be asked to participate in class discussions. Some days this will be harder than others, no doubt."

She looks around the room again, very seriously, and says, "And there's something else that I require for this course. Though I don't like to put it like that. It's something that I would like to *ask* you to do, human being to human being. Which is that you all look out for one another."

I'm not sure any of us really knows what she means, but we all agree that we'll do what she's asked of us.

"Thank you," says Mrs. Quenell. "Are there any questions?"

"Are you sure it's okay to write in this?" Marc asks. "It looks like it should be in a museum."

"It's perfectly all right," she assures him.

"But what should we write?" he presses.

"Marc," says Mrs. Quenell. "You're not a young child anymore, are you?"

"No," he says.

"I didn't think so. If I told you *what* to write, then I would be treating you as if you were. I believe your birthday was in the summer, yes? And you turned sixteen?" He nods. "That's a fine age to be. An age at which you can make certain decisions on your own, and one of them is what to write in your journal. You don't need some old woman giving you prompts. I know that there's a lot going on in your brain."

But Marc still looks stressed. "Mrs. Quenell, I don't mean to be annoying," he says. "But I do best in school when teachers give me instructions. I'm sorry," he adds.

"No need to be sorry. Just a moment, let me think." She takes a few seconds, and then she tells him, "I would say that you should write whatever best tells the story of you. I hope that helps."

I look at Marc. No, it doesn't seem to have helped at all, but Mrs. Quenell doesn't appear to notice. She stands up then, and I see how tall she is. She towers over us with her white head and elegant silk blouse.

"Everyone," she continues, looking around at all of us, "has something to say. But not everyone can bear to say it. Your job is to find a way."

CHAPTER 3

"SO WHAT WAS IT LIKE?" DJ ASKS ME THAT EVENING during study hours. This is a two-hour period when we have to sit in our rooms or in the common room downstairs in our dorms and do homework. I've actually decided to use my ugly orange study buddy for the occasion, and to my surprise it's sort of comfortable to lean against the corduroy surface and rest my human arms on its thick, inanimate-object arms.

"What was what like?"

"Special Topics in English, *obviously.*"

"It was fine, I guess," I say. The truth is that Special Topics in English was a little strange. It alternated between being uncomfortable and oddly interesting.

"You didn't learn an obscure language?" DJ asks. "Or go through an initiation rite involving essential oils?"

"Nope."

"Maybe those kids in the class the year before last were yanking everybody's chain," says DJ. "At the end of the semester, they acted like it was the biggest deal in the world."

"It was hardly much of anything. She handed out copies of *The Bell Jar.*"

"Sylvia Plath? That's who you're reading all semester?" DJ says with light superiority.

"Yep."

"Nice choice for this place."

"Exactly," I say. "I guess she thinks we can learn from it or something."

"I read *The Bell Jar* ages ago," says DJ. "Well," she adds in a pleased voice, "it's probably for the best that I'm not in the class, since it would've been tedious to have to read it again."

"Oh, and we have to keep a journal," I add. "We can write whatever we want. But we have to hand it in at the end, and then she keeps it. She swears she isn't going to read it."

"*Journals.*" DJ snorts. "What a cliché."

DJ settles back onto her bed comfortably, clearly happy that Special Topics in English doesn't seem so great. My first day at The Wooden Barn hasn't been horrible, but it's been no better than any of the days I've been living for almost a year. The hours have gone by pointlessly; only the difference is that my parents are no longer hovering in my doorway, worrying about me, wondering when I will "snap out of it."

I lean against my study buddy and quickly read the first chapter of *The Bell Jar,* and then the second chapter, even though I'm not supposed to go that far. The book is all about a smart, hyperambitious college student named Esther Greenwood, who wins a magazine contest and gets invited to spend the summer in New York City to work at a fashion magazine with a group of other prizewinning girls. And while she's living at an old hotel where men aren't allowed above the first floor, Esther starts to feel really unhappy and peculiar.

The book takes place back in the 1950s, when the world was different. People wore hats, and went on dates.

According to a stapled handout Mrs. Quenell gave us, Sylvia Plath herself had won a contest and worked for a magazine one summer during college. And while she was there she started to feel detached and isolated. Just like Esther, when she got home after that summer she swallowed a lot of sleeping pills and hid in the crawl space under her family's porch, waiting to die.

But she didn't die. Instead, Sylvia Plath went into a coma, and then came to consciousness days later; her family heard her moaning and called an ambulance and saved her life. Then, after being put in a psychiatric hospital and given a lot of regular therapy and also shock therapy—where they attached electrodes to her and turned on the voltage—Sylvia Plath recovered. And so did her character Esther. In real life, the author went on to become a writer, and she had a troubled marriage to another writer, an English poet named Ted Hughes. They had two children, a boy and a girl.

But when she was thirty years old and living in London, she made another suicide attempt, turning on the gas and putting her head in the oven, just like Marc said in class. This time she succeeded.

DJ snaps her history book shut and stands up. "I am so done," she says. "I'm going to go downstairs to see if I can bum a Mint Milano off Hayley Bregman. Want to come?" This is the first vaguely social invitation I've received at The Wooden Barn, but I can't work up any interest. Besides, DJ and I are spending plenty of time together already.

"Nah," I tell her. "I should probably write in my journal. Not that I have anything to say."

"Just go the bullshit route," DJ says. "That's what I always do when someone asks me to write something about myself."

When she's gone, I pick up the journal from where it lies on my desk. So far tonight I've spent absolutely no time sitting at that desk. Instead, I've done all my homework in bed, and my efforts have been really feeble. My grades are not going to be good, but I just can't bring myself to "try," like my parents begged me to do before they sent me here.

"Just try, Jam," my dad said. "Give it one semester, okay? See how it goes."

Far from home now, sitting in this bed with the wind shaking the old windowpanes of my dorm room, and the distant *thump* of dubstep from the girls across the hall, I lean back against the study buddy and open the journal.

I'm only going to write a few lines, nothing more. *Just go the bullshit route*, DJ had said. I'll write something bland and boring so at least at the end of the semester, when Mrs. Quenell says, "Everybody hand in your journals," she'll see that I seemed to have made an effort—even though she's not going to read what I wrote. I realize that for some reason I don't want to irritate or disappoint her.

But I've really got nothing to say. The only thing I ever think about is Reeve.

It's funny how you can go for a long time in life not needing someone, and then you meet them and you suddenly need them all the time. Reeve and I had met in the first place because we had gym class together. A few years earlier, my school created an alternative to regular gym called "co-ed gym," which involved a lot of yoga and badminton. So on the first day, in the middle of badminton, this dark-eyed boy showed up, wearing long, wrinkled shorts and a red T-shirt that said Manchester United. Someone whispered that he was one of the new exchange students.

This English boy didn't even try during the game, but just let the birdies whip past him. I gave up trying to play too, preferring to observe this person who muttered "Bloody hell" as little plastic things came within inches of his face.

Then gym class was over, and as the girls and boys headed off into their separate locker rooms, I did something totally out of character. You have to remember that I was one of the quiet, shy, nice girls. I wasn't someone who went out of her way to make a big impression on anyone.

But for some reason I said to this boy, "Good strategy." It took all my nerve even to say something to him as dull as that.

He looked at me with a squint. "And what strategy was that?"

"Avoidance."

He nodded. "Yeah, it's basically how I've gotten through life so far."

We half smiled at each other, and that was the end of it. I saw him around school throughout the week, and I made excuses to talk to him and he made excuses to talk to me.

"My host family, the Kesmans," he said one day in the cafeteria, "enjoy singing rounds. Do you know what rounds are?"

"'Rounds'?" I said. "Oh, like 'Row, Row, Row Your Boat.'"

"It's excruciating. After dinner, we all have to stay at the table, and we sing rounds for *hours*. Or maybe it only seems like hours. This is the most wholesome family I've ever met. Are all American families like this?"

"No," I said. "Mine isn't."

"Lucky girl," said Reeve.

I was so excited by him, but I told myself to stop it, to not be excited, he's just a friend. Still, I hoped he would become more than that. But really, why would he be interested in *me*, when there were so many more obvious choices? But I could swear he was interested. I told none of my friends, but just quietly felt what I felt.

One afternoon our art class was sent off to do landscape drawing, and I was sitting with my pad and charcoal on the hill overlooking the parking lot with the trees in the distance, when Reeve appeared beside me.

We sat in stillness, shoulder to shoulder, not touching. Our shoulders were so near each other's, encased in sweaters, but they hadn't even accidentally banged. I'd only known this boy a couple of weeks then, and I barely knew anything about him. Our entire relationship consisted of smiling, smirking, and saying funny things to each other.

But I *wanted* our shoulders to touch. It was as if I thought our shoulders could almost communicate. My shoulder, under the sky-blue wool of a sweater that my grandma Rose had knitted before she died, could have a little conversation with *his* shoulder, which was under the chocolate-brown wool of a sweater that had probably been purchased in a shop somewhere in London. And if our shoulders managed to touch, I knew I'd feel a thrill beyond anything I'd ever known. Which made me realize that I'd never felt *thrilled* before.

In ninth grade, I'd kissed Seth Mandelbaum exactly four times. It was okay, but *thrilling* is the wrong word. The second time it happened, we'd stood behind the drapes at Jenna

Hogarth's fourteenth birthday party ("It's Jenna's Sweet Fourteen!" her mother kept going around saying, annoyingly), and Seth put his hand up my shirt and on my bra and whispered in a serious voice, "You are very womanly." Which made me crack up. Seth, hurt, had to say, "What's so funny?" And I had to say, "Nothing."

That relationship didn't really end, but just sort of faded away. Soon it was as if it had never happened at all.

But Reeve and I were different. I felt so much when I was with him that I had to play it down. There was no touching at all at first; there was barely even much eye contact. Every morning I'd quickly scan the hall, and my laser-beam focus would pick him out from among the dozens of people in the big morning-breath crush at the lockers.

And the day after art class, where I ended up drawing an impressive likeness of Reeve, and everyone saw that he and I had a real connection, Dana Sapol invited me to her party. I couldn't believe it, and I was so excited, though I forced myself to act ultra-low-key. Reeve and I would be seeing each other outside of school for the first time, and who knew what would happen.

The idea of just sitting beside this boy who was visiting for a few months from London, or even being in the same room with him at a party, made me feel like I might pass out and fall down with a loud *clunk*.

On Saturday night my parents dropped me off at the Sapols'. Leo was in the car, because he and my mom and dad were going to the mall for pizza and a movie. As we drove through town, I looked out the window at the stores in the shopping center, and I saw the little purple horsey ride that my dad used to take me on when I was little. He'd keep putting quarters into the slot, and I'd ride and ride like it was the most exciting thing in the world.

But really, I'd never done anything exciting. I'd barely been far away from Crampton, except once to go to Disney World, and every summer to visit my grandparents in Ohio. Reeve was from a whole other place, where they spoke differently, and had different words for things. He'd had experiences I couldn't even imagine, but wanted to. The world was huge, I thought as I was driven to the party that night. Just unimaginably huge, and sometimes thrilling, and Reeve was part of it.

"Have a great time, babe," my mom said as I got out in front of Dana's McMansion in the rich neighborhood in our town, where the houses are spread far apart. There were white columns out front, and an enormous picture window, but the drapes were closed.

My parents had no idea about the significance of this evening. They didn't know this was a different kind of party from the ones I'd gone to before. They imagined that all the kids at Dana Sapol's house were sitting on the rug playing Bananagrams. And, of course, they didn't know anything about Reeve, because I'd never mentioned him to them.

The Sapols' living room was dark when I walked in, and smelled of cigarettes and pizza and beer and weed. The music was loud and thumpy. I didn't see Reeve, and I said hi to a few people but didn't stop to talk. He was the only one I wanted to talk to, so I made my way through the crowd until a British accent drifted out, and I was like a dog who snaps to attention at its master's voice. Then I followed that voice, and there was Reeve Maxfield in a wrinkled button-down shirt.

Sometimes it seemed as though he still hadn't unpacked since he'd arrived in the US. His sleeves were rolled up and he held a grocery bag in one hand, and a beer bottle in the other. He saw me, and abruptly stopped talking to a group of guys right in the middle of a sentence.

"Finish what you were saying, bro," said Alex Mowphry, who was holding his beer bottle by its neck and trying to look older than he really was. In sixth grade Alex had projectile-vomited on the bus during our grade's overnight to Colonial Williamsburg.

"Nah," said Reeve, and he put down the beer and headed right toward me. "You're going to have to imagine what I was about to say."

"Douchebag," muttered Alex.

"Douchebag?" said Reeve, holding a hand to his ear. "Sorry, I'm not familiar with that as a name to call someone. I only know that it's a device for female hygiene. And I do like hygiene. So I'm assuming it means . . . something *nice.* We don't usually call people 'douchebag' in the UK."

Alex flipped him the finger, but Reeve just laughed. Then he came over to me and said hi. My face went hot; I could feel it even in the warm room. The other guys began to joke with us about how I'd drawn Reeve's portrait in art class. He and I joked right back. Then he said to me, "Want to go somewhere and talk?"

"Sure," I said, and we walked down the hall toward the bedrooms. The first door we opened revealed two people in a tangle on top of a pile of coats. They looked up at us without much interest. I recognized the girl as Lia Feder, who'd been in last year's Dumb Math with me. She nodded and said, "Hey," then went back to kissing a boy I'd never seen before, and who maybe Lia hadn't either.

We closed the door and kept walking. The next room had a group of kids sitting on the floor playing what seemed to be the early stages of strip poker. They all looked up and snickered.

Finally Reeve and I were in Dana's little sister's bedroom. Courtney Sapol was five, and she and her parents were away for the weekend, leaving Dana here with her sixty closest friends, plus me. Courtney's bedroom was pink and white, and the bed had a canopy over it. It seemed wrong to sit down on this bed; it seemed like a cliché, as though we were saying, We are a teenaged boy and girl who like each other. And because no parents are on the premises of this suburban teenaged party, it's time to hook up on a child's bed.

But I didn't want to do that. I was overwhelmed by what I felt for Reeve, and besides, what if he just thought I was "sweet" and "nice," and he liked my long hair but wasn't really interested in me?

I looked around the dim room. The carpeting was spongy and synthetic, and in the darkness I couldn't even tell what color it was. It's a weird thing about color, the way darkness just drains it all away. Reeve put down the bag he was carrying.

"Groceries?" I asked.

"Yeah, English ones," he said, and when I peered into the bag I saw a small jar, which I pulled out.

"'Tiptree Little Scarlet,'" I read on the label. "Strawberry. It's a kind of *jam*?" I asked. Reeve nodded.

And then I realized: Oh my God. He's brought the jar of jam *because of my name*. Of course. It was a present for me, a little in-joke just between the two of us, and I was so touched by it that heat sprang to my face again. I waited for him to tell me that it was for me, but he was shy.

"So can I have it?" I asked quietly.

"Sure. It's good stuff."

But I knew I would never open that jar. Instead it would be a memento of this party, this night. I closed my hand around it and let it fall deep and safe into my purse.

On the floor by our feet was a large, elaborate dollhouse, one of those insanely expensive ones that the Sapols had had specially designed for their daughter. It resembled their actual house—a miniature McMansion inside a life-size McMansion. The rooms were decorated with fancy doll furniture that you probably had to order from a special catalogue. There were framed paintings that actually had teeny lights that lit up over them if you pulled a little chain. The mother doll's dressing table had a set of matching silver combs and brushes. The bristles were as tiny as a baby's eyelashes.

In the den were clustered all the members of the doll family. Reeve crouched down, and I crouched down beside him. "Here you go," he said, solemnly handing me a blond wooden mother doll in a retro dress and apron. "This is you." He picked up the father doll, who wore a suit and tie, fresh from his job. "And this is me," he added. Together we trotted the male and female dolls around the house, having them make dinner in the granite kitchen and sit together in the den to watch TV.

"*Britain's Got Talent*," Reeve announced. "That's what they're watching."

"No, *America's Got Talent*," I insisted.

"Britain."

"America."

"Our first fight," said Reeve.

Our doll selves were side by side on the couch, and the dolls' shoulders were touching, which was what I had wanted our real shoulders to do. Reeve dropped the male doll, so I dropped the female one. The two dolls lay side by side, and in the soft, colorless light we turned to each other. I could feel my heart working so hard, but I tried to ignore it.

Our eyes closed, and our faces moved together in that awkward way that I remembered from Seth Mandelbaum. Our shoulders touched too, and I felt the rustle of his creased cotton shirt.

This was nothing like Seth Mandelbaum.

Reeve's soft lips stuck to mine for a spongy second, then unstuck with a little click. Feelings were gathering in me very fast. He pulled back and made a sound, like *ohh,* and then I did too; neither one of us felt self-conscious. Only thrilled. We kissed endlessly in the space above the dollhouse.

This turned out to be the night we fell in love. We'd known each other for sixteen days. We'd have only twenty-five days left.

I open the journal now and pick up the pen, but I can't bring myself to write a word.

CHAPTER 4

JUST PAST MIDNIGHT, SHRIEKING AND CRYING wake me up. "DJ, what's *that*?" I say, suddenly surfacing.

She grunts from across the room. It takes her forever to get out of bed and stagger into the hall, but I'm out there right away along with a bunch of other girls, all of us in nightshirts or nightgowns, saying, "What's going on? What's happening?" No one knows. Jane Ann Miller, the history teacher who's also our houseparent, appears in her hot-pink shortie bathrobe and strides down the hall. She takes the stairs in the direction of the noise, while all of us follow behind her like ducklings.

The sound is coming from one flight up. Room 43. Beside the door is a nameplate: JENNY VAZ AND SIERRA STOKES. Jane Ann bangs hard and Jenny, who I've never spoken to, appears. The screaming and crying—mostly crying now—continue, so it's Sierra who's in distress.

Jane Ann turns to all of us and says in a stern voice, "Go back to bed. There's nothing to see." But even after she goes inside and shuts the door we all linger, and soon the crying calms down, and finally there's silence.

In the morning everyone feels kind of hung over from being awakened in the night, and at breakfast I'm standing on the oatmeal line, my eyes half closed, almost swaying, when I see Sierra two people ahead of me, talking to a girl I haven't met.

"Yeah, I know, of course it *seemed* real," the girl is patiently telling her. "You wouldn't *believe* the one I had this summer. I was taking a big exam, like the SAT or something, and all of a sudden I realized I'd forgotten to bring a pencil—"

"It was nothing like that," Sierra interrupts.

"Oh, I know, they always feel like they're actually happening," says the girl.

"Just forget it," Sierra says, turning away.

At the table during breakfast, DJ tells me, "It's no surprise that Sierra Stokes had a really bad dream, given what she's been through."

"What's she been through?"

DJ looks at me, uncomprehending. "Oh. You don't know. Right." She has three grapes and a piece of almost black toast—emo toast—on her plate. She takes a bite of the toast, swallows, then says, "I'm actually not supposed to talk about it. It goes against Wooden Barn policy. People are supposed to reveal their own stories to other people here only if they want to. You know her?"

"She's in Special Topics in English with me," I say.

"She got in and I didn't? Oh, whatever. Well, all I'll say is that she arrived here last year in a real *state*, and maybe the nightmare means that she's not doing much better."

"This 'thing' that she went through," I say. "Is it something really bad?"

"Yes," DJ says. "The worst." I feel myself clench inside, though of course I don't know what "the worst" means.

We go off to our first-period classes, and during Special

Topics in English I glance across the oak table at Sierra, who seems upset, distant. Casey's late again, and she bangs into the room in her wheelchair in the middle of a discussion of the first-person narration in *The Bell Jar.*

There's a long pause, and I think we're all nervous. "Casey," Mrs. Quenell finally says. "The world will not wait."

This is the *world*?

"Sorry," Casey mutters.

Mrs. Quenell turns back to the class. "As I've said, the book was written over fifty years ago," she says. "But can any of you relate to it today?"

"Sure," says Casey. "You could say I'm trapped in my own little bell jar on wheels."

Me, I think, I've got my own version too. I think about how, after Reeve died, I used to lie in bed all day hearing my family and friends talk about me out in the front hall or the living room. I began to feel as if my bed were its own island, and I was floating farther and farther away from everyone with only my thoughts about Reeve to accompany me.

"The isolation is just so hard," I say, and right away I'm embarrassed that I've spoken.

Mrs. Quenell looks at me. "Yes," she says. "And you're all so young. Plath's protagonist is young too. To be on the verge of your life and not be able to enter it . . . that ought to be prevented whenever possible."

Everyone is paying very close attention to her. We're talking about the novel, right? But maybe we're not. We're talking about ourselves. And I guess that's what can start to happen when you talk about a book.

I remember reading *Charlotte's Web* with my mom when I

was little. I was sitting next to her on the brown couch in the den when Charlotte died. And it was as if that little barn spider was my actual friend. Or even as if she was *me.* I guess I suddenly knew that I was going to die someday too. I really, really knew it for the first time, and I was shocked, and I cried.

Just the way Sylvia Plath's character Esther's depression now makes me feel: *Oh, I get it.* And her isolation reminds me of how I've been feeling since the whole thing with Reeve.

"Yeah," says Griffin, nodding. "It's like you can't talk to other people. What do they know about what you're going through? Nothing."

"Nothing at all," I agree.

"So other people know nothing at all," says Mrs. Quenell. "And Esther seems to feel that way too, and she's alone inside her despair. Nothing changes for her. Which, I guess, is the opposite of life."

"Isn't death the opposite of life?" asks Sierra. It's the first time today she's joined the conversation.

"I think *not changing* is sort of like dying," says Griffin, and I can tell he's uncomfortable actually taking part in a vaguely literary discussion. I bet he's never done that before in his life. "But maybe I'm wrong, Mrs. Q," he adds quickly.

Mrs. Q! A couple of people laugh nervously. Yet right away the name fits, and it *stays,* just the way Leo started calling me Jam, and it stayed.

"You know much more than you think, *Mr. F,*" she says. "Change can be crucial. Everything is changing all the time. Your cells are changing this very minute. The view from that window is slightly different from how it was a few seconds ago."

I automatically look toward the window, and almost as if

Mrs. Quenell planned it, a leaf blows off the tree and slaps the glass. It clings for a second, before spinning away.

"We can't be afraid of change," she tells us. "Or else we'll miss out on everything."

Class is almost over. Mrs. Quenell peers at her watch, seeming to want to bring herself back into the moment. We've all been far away, thinking about Sylvia Plath, and her alter ego, Esther Greenwood, and, of course, ourselves. This class is like one of those twenty-four-hour convenience stores, except the only thing this one sells is depression. If it were actually a store, it would be called Bleak Mart.

And I do feel bleak. That discussion has worn me out, I realize after we're dismissed and I'm walking slowly across campus. Maybe I'll just sleep during physics class today. There's no point in being awake anymore. Without Reeve, I'm hardly even a person.

I turn the corner and I'm alone on the leafy path, walking in silence among the trees. I know the colors here in Vermont in the fall are supposed to be a big deal, and yet I just don't care. The colors actually seem to be taunting me, saying, Here we are, Jam, all the colors of the spectrum. Roy G. Biv, remember? And yet you can't appreciate us one bit. *Ha-ha-ha-ha-ha.*

I shove my hands deep into my pockets, finding a dime that's coated with lint. As I turn it over and over between my fingers, I notice Sierra up ahead hurling stones against a tree. Again and again she winds up and then torpedoes a stone against the tree's surface, using all her force. She's driven, focused, as though throwing stones is some kind of release for her.

"Hey," I call, breaking her rhythm.

She turns and looks at me, suddenly self-conscious. "Hey," she says back.

"You've got a good arm." I come closer.

"Thanks."

We stand awkwardly together, and I say, "You must be really pissed at that tree. Did it give you a communicable disease or something? Dutch elm? Root rot?" But she doesn't even smile at my pathetic joke.

Instead she says, "I had a rough night. I guess you know that."

"Yeah. Sorry."

Sierra studies me, as if trying to figure out whether it's okay to talk to me or not. Then she says, "Have you ever had an experience that made no sense?"

"I'm not sure."

"I mean an experience that's so surreal that if you told anyone, they'd be like, 'What the hell is wrong with *her*?'"

My heart is quickening. I did go through something intense after I lost Reeve. And some people did look at me funny because they weren't used to seeing that kind of intensity, and that kind of grief, in someone my age. But Sierra means something else. I'm not about to reveal the story of Reeve right now.

All I say is "Could you say more?"

"Never mind," she says. "It doesn't matter." She picks up her backpack, looping it over her arms, and turns away, done with me. She'd tried to see if I was a kindred spirit, and apparently I'm not. I was put to a test, and I'd failed it.

On Friday night there's a social. This is about the saddest idea in the world: a bunch of psychological misfits gathered awkwardly in a gym at night with house music playing as if this is some normal "teen time" get-together, while on the edges of the room a few bored teachers chaperone. Like everything at The

Wooden Barn, this social is probably supposed to be "healing," and we're meant to actually get something out of it. Like, learn how to be social.

"Oh God, these things are the worst, I should've warned you," says DJ, who stands beside me, surveying the grim room.

"How long do we have to be here?" I ask.

"Until the next millennium."

"But what's the *point*?"

"That is the million-dollar question."

DJ's hair is so deeply in her face that it's more like a wall of hair now than a curtain. She wears a pink miniskirt and Doc Martens and an army jacket, and somehow it all pulls together and looks cool on her. She stands with her arms folded across her chest. I'm in my usual jeans and sweater and Vans.

Suddenly I remember Reeve's brown sweater, the soft chocolate wool and the particular sweet-and-sour smell of him. And though I'm forced to remain at this social, in my mind I start doing this thing I sometimes do, which is to go back over the forty-one days of our relationship in detail. The forty-one days that I've memorized, and that in times of stress or boredom I replay in a loop in my head, like a movie on repeat. I start to remember every single thing we did together:

The morning he showed up in gym class for the first time.

The afternoon in art class when I was drawing on the hill, and he came and sat beside me.

The night we kissed above Courtney Sapol's dollhouse.

The time he showed me a DVD of his favorite old Monty Python sketch about the dead parrot.

And there were other things we did too, but as the thoughts start to bunch up in my brain, my throat feels kind of choked.

And if I don't stop thinking of the forty-one days, then I might start to cry right here in the middle of this stupid-ass social.

Stop thinking about him, I tell myself. *Be social.*

But it's too hard. There's no point to being here; it's insane that they force us. Casey Cramer has shown up late again, parking her wheelchair beside the exit. It doesn't matter that she can't dance. No one else here is dancing either. The music blares, and there's even a disco ball spinning pathetically overhead. What, was someone on staff sent out to a place called Vermont Party Supplies to buy one? But the twirling shards of light from the disco ball only call attention to the fact that we're all standing around like emotionally fragile lumps.

"Someone could take a photo of this scene," Casey says, "and call it 'Tragedy.'"

Griffin is standing not too far away. In the low light of the gym at night, with his hood off, his face looks even more sullen than usual, and I wonder why he's this way—whether he was always like this, or whether it's the result of whatever brought him here.

"What are you looking at?"

Griffin's voice startles me. "Nothing," I say, but I *was* still looking at him without even realizing it.

"Yeah, you were," he says. "You were looking at me."

"I wasn't," I insist, and I don't even know why it's so important to me to deny it. It's like the way little kids say to each other, "Was not!" "What did you think," I say to him, "I was desperate to discover the soulful self inside your hoodie?"

"Well, whatever," he says, the most meaningless response in the world. Then he turns and lopes out the door of the gym.

"What was that about?" Casey asks as we watch him go.

"No idea."

Around us, a few kids have started to move onto the dance floor, and to distract myself from the bad moment with Griffin, I try to focus on the scene. Even though the people here are obviously kind of a mess, some of them still want to take part in these basic human activities. I have no idea why.

The music gets a little louder and the room fills. Kids form couples or clusters and begin to dance. "So you're just going to leave him out there?" Casey asks.

"Who?"

"Griffin. He went outside."

"So he went outside. Fine."

"I'm just thinking about what Mrs. Quenell said. About how we should look out for one another. And we all said we would."

I don't really want to deal with Griffin any more than I have to. My feelings would have to be pulled apart and examined. Sometimes in the summer my mom or dad would give me and Leo a job in the kitchen shucking corn. We'd have to remove the silk from between the mosaic of kernels. Pull it out, strand by strand, and it always took forever. This would be like doing that, but with my feelings instead of corn silk, and who wants that?

In the doorway behind Casey, the outer doors to the gym are open onto the night. And under the outdoor phosphorous light, with his hood up again, Griffin stands hugging himself in the cold.

Casey's right, I ought to go out there and say something to him.

But I take too long to decide what to do, and by the time I'm out on the porch, Griffin is gone. We're not supposed to leave the social until it's over, but unlike Marc Sonnenfeld, Griffin isn't big into rules. If I had my way I'd leave the social too, *and* the school. I'd get on a Greyhound bus late tonight, leaving behind all these people and their sad pasts, and I'd head back home to New Jersey and climb into bed for the rest of my life.

Behind me under the buggy, yellow porch light someone says my name, and when I turn around, Casey's there, looking so tiny in her wheelchair outside at night.

"Thinking of making a break for it?" she asks.

"It's not a bad idea."

"It won't be so terrible here for someone like you," Casey says.

"Like me?" Casey Cramer doesn't even know me.

"Someone who can walk," she explains. "You know what we call you guys? TABs."

"I don't know what that is."

"It stands for temporarily able-bodied. No one ever knows when something might happen to them, right? I mean, look at me. I never expected this. So live it up while you can," says Casey. "Go hook up with angry young Griffin."

"I wasn't going to hook up with him," I say primly. "Only be nice to him."

"Sorry," says Casey. "I get a little bitter. It's not like anyone's ever going to be attracted to *me* again."

"That's not true."

"Yeah, right, Jam, a guy's really going to be into me when I can't even move half an inch. And he's going to just *love* carrying me to the bathroom and putting me on the toilet. That's a big turn-on, right?"

I start to say something, but it would just be pointless babble. There's nothing I can tell her to make her feel better. I know this from experience. Both of us are lost and fragmented. We stand in the cold, shivering a little and saying nothing at all.

CHAPTER 5

FINALLY, LATE ONE NIGHT, I GO TO BELZHAR FOR the very first time. I don't call it Belzhar right away; none of us does. After I go there—after "it" happens to me—I'm naturally terrified to let anyone know. At first it seems too wild and incoherent and absurd to tell anyone.

One time in ninth grade when Jenna Hogarth and I got high on her uncle's medical marijuana, I imagined that the cat-shaped lamp in her parents' den *meowed.* That flipped me out for about thirty seconds, until I was able to calm down and laugh it off. (To this day, I am not particularly into smoking weed, or losing control.)

But there's no way to laugh off Belzhar. It's too huge for that. Belzhar comes out of nowhere and changes everything for all of us in Special Topics in English. Before we go there for the first time, we're all just innocently wading into the semester at The Wooden Barn, following the monotonous rhythm of homework and dorm life and meals. I miss Reeve with a deep bone ache that doesn't go away, no matter how I try to distract myself.

The night I first go to Belzhar feels like any other night. Casey and DJ and I are in our T-shirts and sweatpants doing homework in the first-floor common room of our dorm. The three of us have started hanging out, though we never discuss anything personal. Instead, we all just sit around in the evening studying and talking about nothing much. Sierra never joins us.

"So now that you've been in it a while longer, what's the big deal about Special Topics?" DJ asks when Casey and I start to talk about the upcoming Plath presentations we have to give. No matter how many times I've assured DJ that the class is very ordinary, she still can't let go.

"Who says it's a big deal?" asks Casey.

"Everyone," says DJ. "But Jam says it isn't. Maybe she's keeping something from me."

"DJ, you are insane," I say.

"Jam's right," says Casey. "It's no big deal. Mrs. Quenell is kind of interesting, though. All the other teachers here handle us oh-so-gently. And I love the reading."

I do too. But I'm not crazy about any of the other students besides Casey.

Griffin and I have mostly avoided each other since the social, and Sierra has been quiet and distant to everyone. Marc has looked surprisingly wiped out for a day or two. I overheard him at dinner telling another boy he's been having trouble sleeping. So, the class is a bad mix, but at least reading Sylvia Plath is worthwhile.

"Okay, time for me to rock and roll," Casey finally says when it starts to get late. "Especially roll."

She wheels herself to the door, and we open it for her, and help her leave the room and go into her first-floor double. A little while later, DJ and I make our way back upstairs, and once we're in our own room for the night, without asking me if it's okay, she reaches over and suddenly snaps off the light, leaving us in total darkness.

"Thanks a lot, DJ," I say.

"You're welcome."

"Did it occur to you that I might like to keep the light on a little longer? So I can finish my useless homework without needing to do it in Braille?"

"Then go back downstairs, Jam," DJ says from under the covers.

"I don't want to go back downstairs. I want to stay here."

"So stay. I'm going to sleep."

I think about getting up and snapping on the light, but of course all DJ would do is snap it right off again. And besides, I just don't care enough. In a way, the darkness suits me; it suits my mood tonight and every night. I don't really care if I spend the rest of my life in a pitch-dark room.

And here's where it all begins. I'm sitting in the darkness, staring at the form of my rude roommate who's under the covers across the room, and I think about how trapped I am in this place, and how sad it is that everything's ended up like this. I'm supposed to be living in New Jersey, walking on the playing fields behind the high school with my boyfriend, Reeve Maxfield, our arms around each other. That's supposed to be my life, but it was taken from me.

I sit on my bed now with my study buddy behind me. I remember that at the end of class the first day, when we were talking about our journals, Mrs. Quenell had said that everyone had something to say, but not everyone could bear to say it. Our job was to find a way.

In the darkness, I go to my desk and root around for my journal and the little book light that my mom made sure I took with me to school. "You never know when you might want to read in the middle of the night," she'd said. As if reading was still a top priority of mine.

Sitting back down on the bed, leaning against the study buddy, I open the journal. Maybe it's time to write about Reeve for real. Maybe it'll help, even a little. I click the pen, and the first words I write are these:

> *Reeve Maxfield was the person I'd been waiting to meet since I was born, but of course I didn't know it.*

And, then, having written that, I feel the arms of the study buddy start to soften and bend.

The corduroy material seems to change texture, the ridges getting filled in, the whole thing becoming more like wool.

The arms start to feel like human arms.

I must have fallen asleep, and now I'm dreaming about the boy I loved, who died.

And yet I'm sure that I'm awake, and that something's happening to my thoughts.

Turn around, I tell myself.

But I can't bring myself to do that, because the arms that hold me have become confident and familiar, and the thing I want more than anything—the thing that's impossible—seems to be happening. And if I'm wrong, I'll be devastated.

Turn around.

I do, and he's there. I take in a sharp breath as I look at his sleepy eyes and rumpled brown hair. This isn't a dream sequence, and I'm not doing what's known as lucid dreaming. Instead, my boyfriend Reeve, who has been lost to me, is just simply there, *here*, with me.

We're not in my room at The Wooden Barn now; instead

we're outside somewhere on a neutrally gray day. Where exactly are we? For a few seconds I can't figure it out. It's cold where we are, and I look around and realize there are no tall Vermont trees with leaves on them or collected around them in drifts. Instead, we're standing on the vast stretch of playing fields behind my old high school in Crampton, New Jersey.

"You're back," I say to him, my voice cracking, and then I begin to cry. It's not that I haven't cried since the last day I saw him—I've cried constantly, boiling my eyes, inflaming my face, keeping my family awake at night, worrying everyone sick.

But this crying is different. It's *relief* crying. The last time I cried like this, I think I was five years old and had gotten lost in Price Cruncher. Suddenly I saw my mom come around the corner of the aisle with her cart, and I began to sob, as if she'd returned home from war.

"Oh, *shh,* Jam, *shh,*" Reeve says, and he pulls me against him, letting me cry as he strokes my hair.

"Thank you" is all I can think to say. "Thank you."

"The lingering effects of trauma," the phrase my parents wrote on my school application, have kicked over into a new state. I'm like the demented old lady in Crampton who sometimes sits on a bench at the bus stop, babbling at people who walk by, saying to them, "Angela, when are you coming home? Angela, my little girl, I'll leave the light on for you."

But unlike that old lady, I feel suddenly happy. Her daughter Angela will probably never come back to her, but Reeve has somehow come back to me. And because of that, this new state isn't such a terrible thing.

"Jam," he finally says. "Are you all right?" His voice is the same as always: the English accent, the *scrape.*

"You're asking *me*? How about you?" I say. "Are *you* all right?"

He nods. "Now I am."

"I can't believe you're here," I say, and I start to cry again.

"Where else was I going to go," he says with a sad smile. "Back to the Kesmans' house to sing rounds?"

I'm unable to get over how he's simply been returned to me like a lost object that I'd long ago misplaced. Maybe the trick is that you have to grieve hard enough—you have to make yourself absolutely sick with crying—and then your mind finally just *blows* and takes on magnetic properties, and you can actually make someone come back to you.

"It's been horrible," I tell him.

"I know. But please don't cry anymore, Jam," he says. "Because I'll cry too. And we don't have a whole lot of time. Do you really want to spend all of it crying like one of those teenaged girls in an American PG-13 movie?"

"I'm not like one of those girls. And what do you mean, we don't have a whole lot of time?" I ask, wiping my eyes. "Aren't you *back*?"

"Not entirely." Reeve shakes his head apologetically, and that's when I see that though this is definitely him, down to the sweet face and beautiful mouth and the elongated place between his lips and his nose that I know is called the philtrum, because he once told me—"It's in the OED, the *Oxford English Dictionary*; go look it up"—he looks a little more delicate, as if he's been washed with watercolor.

"I mean, I'm back, yeah, but only for a while," he says. "I think you probably already know that," he adds. And I guess he's right; I do seem to know that.

"But what *is* this place?" I ask. "I get that it's the fields behind the school, but it just goes on and on. It looks different."

"I think you already know that too," he says.

He takes my hand in his—I feel the long fingers, the calluses, the dry, curving cup of his palm—and we walk along the hard, brown playing fields, which now seem to be the place where you can go if you've lost someone and desperately need him back. If *not* having him back has just caused you too much sorrow.

And it's true that I fell apart when I lost Reeve, and was sent into a state of flatness, a kind of agonizing, dead-inside *Bell Jar* state.

This wide-open space, all gray sky and flattened, dry grass, is as bleak as anywhere I've ever been, but it's also a wonderful place, because he's in it. I wonder what we should do in this limited time we have together. Kiss? Touch each other? Talk? Crack each other up? Lie very still on our backs, each of us with one iPod earbud in an ear, listening to the opening chords of a song by Wunderkind, the British indie band that Reeve loved?

"Come here, Little Scarlet Strawberry," he says, and I cry in gasps against his shoulder, my tears falling on his brown sweater.

"I'm sorry, you're going to smell like a damp dog," I say when I can speak.

"I think damp dog smell is underrated," he answers. "I just hope people don't start, you know, following me around to sniff my arse."

"*Arse!*" I say. "You're the same."

But we both know he isn't, not totally. And when he said we didn't have a whole lot of time, he was warning me not to get too comfortable. Are you *ever* allowed to get comfortable with love? My mom and dad always seem really comfortable, sitting on the old brown couch in the den after dinner. Rubbing each other's feet after a long day at the office where they're both accountants. Not dwelling on the fact that one day one of them will die and the other one will be heartbroken.

Reeve and I don't have a lot of time even now; maybe no one ever does. We lie on the ground together, and though it's a little too cold, we kiss, and he tells me stories he's already told me, like about how he always wanted to grow up and be in a Monty Pythonish comedy troupe. I'm happy to hear everything all over again.

I want to ask him, Have you been thinking about me all this time, the way I've been thinking about you? But I don't. If we lie together like this, so light and tender, maybe somehow we'll never have to get up, and it'll never have to end.

But it does end, suddenly. The sky gets sharply dimmer, and Reeve says in a strained voice, "You should get back." He stands up, and I look him over, seeing the skinny-boy body, the unmanageable brown hair, the face that's smooth and kind and too exposed.

He kisses my hands and then my mouth, and I don't have the chance to ask how I can see him again. I don't even know how I got here in the first place. All I know is that I've left my unbearable inner life for a little while, and I'm starting to panic at the idea of being without him again.

I close my eyes for the barest second, a blink's length, and when I open them I'm sitting in bed again in my pitch-dark dorm room at The Wooden Barn. The old red journal is open in my lap. But although I remember writing only one line, page after page has now been filled up with my handwriting, telling the story of Reeve and me and how we first met. And also the story of us now, when we've found each other again.

At various places the ink is smeared and running, as if someone has been leaning over the page, crying and crying.

CHAPTER 6

"*DJ*," I HISS INTO THE DARK ROOM. THERE'S NO answer. "*DJ*," I try again, urgently.

After a few seconds I hear her turn over in bed, and then she says, "What's the matter, Jam?"

I'm about to tell her what just happened to me, but I stop short. Somehow, I know I shouldn't say anything.

"Nothing," I finally say. "I couldn't sleep."

"You couldn't *sleep*? You actually woke me up to tell me you couldn't sleep?"

"Yeah" is all I can say.

"Why don't you try counting little images of me jumping over a fence to slap you," she says. Then she mutters something I can't hear and rearranges herself in her bed. Within seconds her breathing has changed and she's asleep again.

I sit unmoving in bed in the dark room. Probably I ought to go confess everything to Jane Ann, the houseparent, and she can call the nurse, and I'll have to sit shivering in a bright room in the middle of the night and explain everything to those kind, concerned women.

"I saw my boyfriend," I'd say while the nurse looked into my eyes with a little light.

“Mm-hmm,” she’d say, humoring me.

“No, I was *with* him again, don’t you get it? We were together. It really happened. I’m not making it up.”

Because the school doesn’t believe in medication, no one would try to sedate me unless it was an absolute emergency. But they might decide I was too unbalanced to stay here, and I’d wind up in a mental hospital like Sylvia Plath did, with electrodes sending shuddering impulses through my brain.

So I’m not going to tell anyone at all.

Somehow I manage to fall asleep, but in the morning when I wake up I immediately remember what happened the night before, and I reach onto my desk and grab my red leather journal to make sure it really did happen. Five full pages are filled in with my handwriting. There’s a long description of Reeve on the day we first met in gym class, and another description of the moment when I saw him again in that strange version of the playing fields behind my old high school.

It happened.

“You seem weird today,” DJ says as we get dressed. She strips off the big My Chemical Romance T-shirt she slept in, and puts on a bra and boys’ plaid boxers. “I mean weirder than usual,” she adds.

“You should talk.”

“I’m well aware of how weird I am,” she says.

I feel out of it this morning, the way Sierra seemed after her bad dream. At breakfast I sit in a corner by myself, facing the wall eating a banana muffin that’s as solid as a doorknob, not wanting to talk to a single person. Everyone seems to know enough to leave me alone. People get into funks here, and everyone is respectful.

I eat in silence, slowly gnawing off the muffin top, allowing myself to go over every minute of what happened last night, to remember how the arms of the study buddy morphed into Reeve's arms, and then we were together again. I might have stayed lost in this for the entire breakfast, but suddenly there's a crash.

"Shit!" I hear. Casey has backed her chair away from a table straight into Marc, whose tray has flown to the floor. His cereal bowl wobbles like a top, then finally goes still. "For fuck's sake, Marc," says Casey. "Look where you're going."

Marc, pinned between the wheelchair and the next table, says, "It was an accident. Cool your heels."

"They're cooled."

"You know what I mean."

Without even thinking, I hurry over and grab the handles of the wheelchair to help Casey move.

"Leave it, Jam," she says, as if talking to a disobedient dog. And then, with great difficulty, she extricates herself, and all I can do is watch her go. When she's gone, Marc crouches down to start cleaning up the food and scattered silverware, and I help him.

"I don't know why she got so upset," he says. "She's really on edge."

"She's not alone."

He gets a dustpan and a broom, and we finish cleaning up, then we leave together and walk toward English class in silence. I predict that class isn't going to go very well today, and when

I get there I'm proven right. Casey's in a crap mood, and so are Marc and Sierra, and so am I. Griffin's always in a crap mood, and today's no different.

Mrs. Quenell looks at us from her place at the table and finally asks, "What's going on?"

No one has an answer for her.

"I see," she says, but of course she can't possibly see.

I'm bursting out of my skin. If there's a teacher on earth who I would want to tell what happened to me last night, Mrs. Q is the one. After all, I'd been writing in my journal when it happened. Maybe somehow she'd understand. But I couldn't possibly explain something that I can't even figure out myself.

"Shall we pick up where we left off last time?" Mrs. Quenell asks. "I believe Sierra was—"

"No offense, Mrs. Q," says Sierra. "But I just can't focus on this."

"Me neither," says Marc. "Sorry."

"It's like the words on the page mean nothing," Griffin says.

Mrs. Quenell looks around at us. Will she be irritated and say, "It doesn't matter whether you can focus or not. You are here to learn." Or will she be understanding?

Then she really shocks us all, saying, "You know what? I'm going to dismiss you early today."

"Really, are you sure?" says Marc. He looks panicked, like, *Isn't it against the rules?*

"You heard Mrs. Q," says Griffin.

"Go get a little mountain air, all of you," she says. "Mrs. Q here insists. It's pointless trying to teach you when your beautiful brains are all somewhere else far, far away. Go see if you can focus on nature."

But the mountain air can't help me sort this out. What I really want to do is call my parents and confess what happened to me last night. Before I met Reeve, I used to tell them so much. Something would happen at school when I was a little kid—like, Dana Sapol would "accidentally" bang into me as we walked past each other, or else push me out of the lunch line—and I'd come home and unburden myself to my mom and dad at the dinner table. They'd always be so supportive.

There's a pay phone on the first floor of the dorm, and I have a calling card. You almost never see pay phones in the world anymore, which is probably a good thing. I read that somebody did a study and found that the receivers are swarming with millions of disgusting bacteria. *Fecal* bacteria, if you must know. But here at The Wooden Barn, which is like living in Amish country, pay phones are the only way to connect to the outside world.

It's the morning of a school day, a workday for my mom, so I call her office number. She answers, saying, "Karen Gallahue," in her businessy voice.

Just hearing her makes my throat tighten and my eyes flood. "Oh, Mom," I say.

"Jam?" she says. "Is that you?"

"Yep, it's me. Can I come home? There's a bus. And maybe you and Dad could even get a tuition refund."

"Now, babe," she says, "we talked about this. Remember that family meeting with Dr. Margolis? We all agreed you needed to try it for at least one semester. To get away from home, to get out of your bed. To be someplace where they're good with adolescent—"

"But, *Mom,*" I say. "You don't understand."

"I think I do, Jam. You feel homesick—"

"That's what you think?"

"Well, yes. Because you're outside your comfort zone. Thrown into a new situation, after being in a cocoon for so long."

"Listen, Mom, it's not like that at all." I gather in a breath and then, in a quiet voice, I say, "I was with *Reeve* last night, okay? We were *together,* and he was right there, and we were holding each other—"

"*Jam,*" my mother interrupts sternly. "You know that isn't true. If you remember, Dr. Margolis said we were likely to see certain behaviors, but that we shouldn't validate them."

"Certain behaviors?" I cry into the receiver, and immediately I feel bad for speaking so sharply to my mom. But I just can't take it. "You don't even know what you're talking about! You've got to let me come home. I'm starting to unravel here—"

"*Jam,*" she interrupts again. "You have to give it time. One semester at least." She is serious. I am really and truly not allowed to come home.

When I hang up, I'm shaking hard. Should I go to the infirmary and try to sleep it off? Or go upstairs to my room and try to get back to Reeve?

I start to head blindly out of the dorm now, and I run into Sierra, who's just coming in. We've been sort of awkward with each other since we had our moment in the trees. When I saw her that day, she'd wanted to know if I'd possibly had an experience like hers. If I'd experienced something "surreal." I hadn't known what she was talking about then. But maybe now I do.

I block her way in through the front door, and I say, "I have to ask you something."

Sierra looks at me without much interest. I'd had my chance, and I blew it. It's like she can't imagine that what I'm going to ask her now can be very interesting; she thinks she's all alone. But maybe I can pull her back from her isolation. Or else maybe I'll just seem unhinged.

"The thing you were trying to ask me that day when you were throwing rocks," I say. "Was it about something you saw? But something that you really couldn't have seen?"

Sierra keeps looking at me. "What do you mean?" she asks.

I look around to make sure we're alone. "I *saw* things last night," I say, knowing I'm going really far here. "There's no good explanation. It didn't feel like I'd been drugged. It wasn't like that."

Sierra quickly pushes me into the front hall, then off into an alcove. "Here's the thing," she whispers. "If something like this happened to you too, then maybe . . . I don't know. But, yeah, it's exactly what I was trying to ask you over by the trees. And I didn't have anyone to talk to."

"You can talk to me."

"Where were you going just now?" she asks.

"Just for a walk. I had a bad phone call with my mom."

"I could come with you," Sierra says.

So we walk, not saying anything more about it. It's like we both know it would be too intrusive to ask, "So what exactly did you *see*?" Of course I'm dying to know the specifics of Sierra's hallucination or whatever you call it. Maybe it's connected to what DJ said happened to Sierra—the "really bad" thing. And maybe she's dying to know what *I* saw and who *I* am too. And to find out what landed me at The Wooden Barn.

There's so much to say, but instead we say almost nothing, except to tell each other how relieved we are to have someone who went through a similar, shocking experience. Sierra and I continue to walk, mostly in silence. I'm still buzzing inside about everything, but I'm also relieved. Finally we wind up at the steps of the library, where she needs to pick up a book. Heading into the stacks with her, I look across the main reading area and see everyone with their heads dipped down in concentration or daydream or nap.

One boy sits alone at a study table, his head in his hands. It's Marc, and even from across the room I can tell that something's wrong. He glances up and sees Sierra and me. A look passes between us, a silent communication.

Something's happened to Marc, not only to Sierra and me.

Maybe something's happened to all of us in Special Topics in English.

Marc stands up, shoves his papers into his backpack—neatly, of course—and heads over to us. "*Hey,*" he whispers.

"Outside," Sierra says.

On the wide stone steps of the library, we confront him in as vague but direct a way as we can. "You look wrecked," Sierra says.

"Haven't slept," says Marc.

"Too much work?"

"Nah. Workload's pretty light here."

"Seeing things?" I ask.

Marc looks from me to Sierra, trying to figure out what's going on.

"It's okay," says Sierra. "You can say it, Marc. We just admitted it to each other."

"What if someone slipped us drugs?" he says tensely. "Did that ever occur to you?"

"It's not that, and you know it," says Sierra. "This is something else. What's your best guess?" she asks him.

He looks at her helplessly and says, "I just don't know. And I usually have answers for everything." Then Marc asks, "So, when did it happen to both of you? Exactly what were you doing? Because I was sitting at my desk writing in my journal."

I tell him I was writing in my journal too, and Sierra nods. So: the journals.

"Is it the whole class? Casey was upset at breakfast," I say. "Griffin's harder to read."

"We could get everyone together and ask them," says Sierra.

"And what if the two of them don't know what we're talking about?" Marc says. "They could tell the administration what we said."

"Oh, come on, they're not going to do that. Anyway, I'm willing to take the risk," Sierra says. "I don't know what else to do."

So we agree to hold an emergency meeting in our classroom that night at ten o'clock, in the brief slice of time between study hours and lights-out. "The classroom buildings are kept unlocked," Sierra says. "So it shouldn't be a problem."

The classroom is a good spot, she explains, because the trees outside the window will protect us from being seen when security makes its nightly rounds.

We decide that Marc will be responsible for getting Griffin there, and Sierra and I will be in charge of Casey. We make our plan, and then we wait.

During the rest of the school day I sit in classrooms and look out over trees and mountains and sky, recalling how it felt to be with Reeve last night. Thinking that, maybe, when I write in the journal next, I'll be swept up to be with him a second time.

That night, everyone shows up at ten. Marc brings Griffin, who appears to be in a quiet, controlled state of annoyance, his hood up as usual. But Griffin would probably be in that state if you woke him up and told him he'd won Powerball. Casey seems relieved to be here. We can't turn on the overhead light in the classroom because it might be seen through the trees. Instead, Sierra lights the big, fat, hazelnut-scented candle she's brought, and Marc unfolds a comforter with a Marc-like geometric pattern, and we all sit on it on the wooden floor of the classroom with the candle casting a dim glow around us.

The hazelnut smell is strong and artificial, but I like it. I remember going to the Yankee Candle Company with Hannah and Jenna when we were thirteen. We walked around the store picking up every single candle and sniffing it. "Smell this one!" we said to one another. "Now this one!"

It's cold in the classroom, and I loosen the wobbly knob on the old radiator. Maybe we can get some food from the teachers' lounge, I suggest, so Sierra goes out and returns with the best she can find: a half-empty box of Wheat Thins, and an almost-full liter of diet root beer. Probably neither one will be missed.

The heat starts to seep in and the room grows warmer, and we sit on the comforter passing around the soda bottle and taking unhygienic swigs. We're all on the floor except for Casey, who looks down upon us from her wheelchair.

"So what *is* this?" Casey finally asks. "Why are we here?"

"Don't you have any idea?" Marc asks.

"Maybe," she says. "But I want someone else to say it, not me."

"Yeah, what the hell is this?" asks Griffin. "It better be good."

Sierra says, "Just listen, okay?" Then she asks him, "Have you been having visions? Because we have."

Griffin is sitting very still with his arms wrapped around himself. Casey's the one who finally nods. "All right, sure," she says. "I did have an experience that I guess counts as a 'vision.' And I was worried that it could happen again. And that someone could find out and say there was something seriously wrong with me, and then I'd have to leave The Wooden Barn. But I don't want to leave. I couldn't take it if they sent me home."

Me, I'd begged my mom to let me leave. And yet I also know what Casey means.

"So are you all actually saying that this happened to you too?" she asks, and we nod. "But it can't be the same thing that happened to me," she says. "That wouldn't make sense. What I saw—it has to do with *my* life. I'm assuming what you all saw has to do with yours." She looks around at us, her eyes bright in the stuttering candlelight. "Okay, somebody say what happened to them," Casey says. "Just say what you saw. I can't be the one to go first. I'm not good at that. Somebody else go."

We all sit stiffly, and no one wants to speak. I notice that Griffin is listening as closely as the rest of us. The silence goes on and on.

"All right," Sierra finally says. "I'll start."

CHAPTER 7

"YOU'LL NEED SOME BACKSTORY," SHE BEGINS. "THE first thing you have to know is that André was eleven when he disappeared."

I don't know who André is or was, but I can guess, and I get a little panicky.

"I was fourteen," she goes on. "It was three years ago, so he'd be a teenager now. But back then he was a kid."

I studiously stare at a point just to the left of Sierra's head. This story can't be going anywhere good.

Sierra and her brother were extremely close, she says. Their relationship was obviously very different from the one I have with Leo. I love Leo, even though we've never had anything in common. But Sierra and André were both dancers at the Washington Dance Academy, where they'd been taking classes for a long time.

Sierra's talent was ballet, and André's was jazz and hip-hop. Three days a week after school they rode the city bus together to their dance classes, and then they rode it home.

Nearly three years before we all sat in the dark classroom at night at The Wooden Barn, Sierra and André Stokes were on the bus heading home from dance class. "It was that time of day in late fall, right before dinner," Sierra explains, "when it's gray and cold and really depressing out. I had a ton of homework, and I wanted to get down to it.

"So when André asked me if we could make chocolate chip cookies tonight, I told him we didn't have any cookie dough in the house, and that I couldn't go to the store because I had to get home and work on my history report. He started whining, so I told him he was welcome to go buy a roll of cookie dough himself. There was a convenience store in our neighborhood called Lonny's. It was four blocks from our apartment, and for the past few weeks our parents had been letting André go there alone.

"So he got off the bus at the stop near the store, while I stayed on for the two remaining stops. I went home, and my mom was there, but my dad was still at work. I set the table and then sat at my desk to do my report. When I heard a key in the door I assumed it was André, but it was only my dad. He said, 'Where's your brother?' And I said, 'At Lonny's.'

"And time passed, and dinner was ready, and now it was dark out, but André wasn't home yet. Finally my dad and I put on our coats and went back outside. We speed-walked to Lonny's, looking into every store window along the way, because this is the route André would've walked, and some of it's not great, though of course he knew not to talk to strangers, et cetera. The guy behind the counter at Lonny's knew him and said he'd been in a while ago, and that, yeah, he'd bought a roll of cookie dough. So my dad and I hurried back to the apartment thinking my brother would be there by now, but he wasn't.

"Then we had to break the news to my mom that we couldn't find him. She was hysterical. We called all of André's friends, but no one had seen him. My dad called the police, and two of them came to the apartment, and then they sent a patrol car out. A while later the doorbell rang, and when my mom answered it, another policeman said something like, 'We found this on the sidewalk near the convenience store.' And he held out a clear plastic bag with a roll of chocolate chip cookie dough inside.

"My mom just gasped and reached for it, but the policeman said, 'No, sorry, we have to take it in for fingerprinting. It's evidence.' And my mom collapsed and gashed her head, and there was a lot of blood. Blood and tears and a roll of cookie dough. That's what I remember from that night."

All I can think, listening to this, is that I need to know the ending right now, and I need it to be okay. Maybe it isn't as bad as I'm afraid it is. Maybe André was found a few hours later, having been roughed up by a few older, thuggish kids, but not seriously. And although Sierra is still emotionally shaky because of that experience, and other experiences we haven't yet heard about, maybe her little brother is okay, and back in Washington, dancing.

But of course Sierra started off this story by saying "He'd be a teenager now." If he'd been found, she meant. Or if he was alive.

"What happened to him?" Casey gets up the nerve to ask. "Did you ever find out?"

"No," says Sierra. "He became one of those missing child cases. A task force was set up. The detective, Sorrentino, gave us his card and told us to call him if anything occurred to us, even in the middle of the night. So I tried to think about what I'd seen that day after class, anything I could remember or anything that occurred to me about people in the neighborhood. Whenever I phoned him with a detail about a bike messenger who looked suspicious, or the old man with the purple birthmark on his face who'd once yelled at André and his friend for littering, he always took the call, no matter what time of day or night. I once woke him up at two a.m., and he was really nice about it.

"But after a while, he told me I had to stop calling so much. He thought I was the girl who cried wolf, but I wasn't. And I'm not. He started taking longer and longer to call me back. He said he had other cases too, and that, no offense, I was being a nuisance.

"But I was just doing what he'd told me, and I'll keep on doing it as long as I have to. Sometimes I even call him from the pay phone in the dorm and leave a long message on his voice mail, asking if they've looked into this thing or that. I'm desperate, and so are my parents. We can't bear being without André, and not knowing what happened to him."

"Oh, Sierra, I'm so sorry," I say with a cry, and there are similar sounds coming from all around me. Sierra puts her hand up to her eyes as if trying to shield her vision. Marc loops an arm around her, and Casey reaches down to pat her shoulder. Griffin looks shell-shocked, and he just sits grimly. None of us really knows one another, yet here we are, all intimate all of a sudden, in a little improvised huddle.

"How do you get through it?" I ask Sierra. I need to know how she wakes up every day and gets out of bed and takes a shower and eats a waffle and goes to class and behaves like a human being. Does she actually care about anything she's doing? Does the water from the shower feel good when it pounds down on her head? Does the waffle even have a taste or a texture? Does the world hold anything of interest now?

Sierra says, "I've barely gotten through it. Same with my

parents. But I guess there's some part of me that just keeps going. The only reason I'm at The Wooden Barn is a scholarship fund that pays for the whole thing. The fund sends everyone else to really academic boarding schools. I'm the only one at a boarding school for people who are messed-up." Then she adds, "And if they knew about what I've seen, they'd probably take away my scholarship and send me home."

"So what have you seen?" Casey asks, but we all know the answer.

"You saw André," I say.

She nods. "Yes," she says. "And after I did, after I had the 'vision,' everyone in the dorm insisted it was a dream. Jane Ann made me some Sleepytime tea and told me about a very realistic dream *she'd* once had, about losing her teeth. But I knew I'd seen my brother, even though I couldn't explain it."

"Do you remember what you were doing?" Casey asks. "I mean, when it started?"

"Writing in my journal."

Casey's face changes slightly, and I know that the journal was the way in for her too. For all of us. Even, I bet, for Griffin.

"I was sitting at my desk in the middle of the night, with only my little lamp on," Sierra tells us. "I'd been awake for hours, lying in bed, but I couldn't sleep, so I got up. My roommate, Jenny, was asleep, and I opened the journal and wrote a line. And it was like the whole desk suddenly started to *vibrate.* And then I wasn't at my desk anymore. I was on the bus in DC again, and it was moving, and I was heading home from dance class. I know that, because I had my dance bag with me; it was banging against my leg. I was sweating in the cold, the way I often do after practice. It was the end of the afternoon, and right beside me on the crowded bus was my little brother. He was still eleven, the age he'd been the last day I'd seen him.

"At first I just stared. My heart was beating so hard! He was leaning his head against me, half asleep. We were somewhere between dance class and home. And I just kept staring. I could practically feel my blood going through my arteries. I thought I might have an aneurysm. Finally I shook him awake really frantically, and said, 'André!'

"He opened his eyes and in a crabby voice he said, 'What, Sierra? I was *napping.*'

"And I said, 'You're *here.*'

"And he said, 'No shit, Sherlock.'

"And I said, 'But that's just amazing, you do know that, right?' And he mumbled something about how there were other things that were more amazing. Like *Sojutsu*, which is apparently a kind of Japanese spear-fighting. And black holes.

"I realized that I didn't need to argue with him. He was *here,* and he knew he was here, but he was still André, just a regular eleven-year-old, so he wasn't going to get all sentimental. And then I asked him, real casually, 'How long do you think this can go on? Me being here with you. Or you being here with me. However you want to look at it.'

"He said, 'I don't know, probably not too long,' and he opened his mouth and yawned, and I could see his two fillings.

"'Can you tell me what happened to you?' I asked him.

"He looked up at me and said something that I'll never really get over. He said, 'I don't want to talk about it. Please don't make me.'

"'Are you sure, André?' I said. 'Sometimes talking about

things is better.' Believe me, I'd been hearing that one for quite a while.

"I just needed to find out whether in real life—and not just in this weird other-world—he was *alive* somewhere. Or whether, you know," she said, her voice catching, "he wasn't. I needed to know, but he didn't want to talk about it. It was too hard for him.

"'Let's just sit here on the bus for the rest of the ride, okay?' André said.

"And I told him okay. So we sat like that, both of us with our backpacks and our dance bags, my little brother and me. We used to have this whole fantasy story going about how we'd grow up and become a famous dance team called Stokes & Stokes. The name would have an ampersand in it. That's the 'and' symbol. We'd play huge arenas and charge a fortune for premium gold-circle tickets that would include a champagne reception with us afterward. Our YouTube videos would get millions of hits. It was such an idiotic fantasy.

"And what I wanted now was so much simpler than that. I wanted to stay beside my brother, riding that bus, sitting there with him in this other reality. I was *relaxed* there. All the terrible feelings I'd had since the day he disappeared were gone."

In the dim classroom, Sierra shifts position and rolls her shoulders, the way dancers sometimes do without even thinking, and says, "So we rode together for a long time, just feeling the vibrations of the bus. And after a while I looked out the window, and I wasn't looking at a street in DC any longer. I was looking at the view from my dorm window here at The Wooden Barn. I was back at my desk, and André was gone, and that's when I started screaming. To have found him and *lost* him again, it was just grotesque—and the entire dorm woke up and came to see what had happened. I told a few girls that I'd seen my brother, really *seen* him, spent *time* with him, but everyone just said it was a dream. And they told me about teeth dreams, and test-taking dreams, and going-onstage-naked dreams. They wouldn't shut up about all their stupid dreams."

Beside her, Marc nods. "I had my version of that. And when it was over and I told my roommate, he insisted I was dreaming."

"In *my* case," I say, "I tried to tell my mom, but she wouldn't listen."

"We'll listen," Casey says.

"Okay," I say. "Thank you."

But I don't like talking about Reeve. It's so much easier to go over the story in my head, instead of having to say it out loud. I'm not going to go into detail, like Sierra. But I have to tell them at least a little of it so they'll understand the basic outline of what I've been through.

"I had a boyfriend," I say in a quiet, careful voice. "His name was Reeve Maxfield. He was an exchange student from London, and we fell in love." I can hardly say anything more, though everyone is listening closely, and waiting.

"What happened to him?" asks Sierra. It's amazing that she's concerned about me and my story, even right after telling us about André. But she's waiting. All of them are. There's a circle of glittering eyes in the dark room.

"Oh my God, he died, didn't he?" says Casey, when I don't reply to Sierra's question. "Jam, I'm so sorry."

I can't bring myself to speak. I feel my mouth start to pull downward into that pre-crying expression.

"What you're telling me is a story of loss," Dr. Margolis had said to me in his office, the first time my parents made me go see him. There was a dead cactus on the windowsill behind his head. I didn't know cacti could die. I thought it took almost nothing to keep them alive. If a psychiatrist couldn't keep his cactus alive, how was he supposed to help his patients?

He wasn't a bad guy, though. He tried to help, but he couldn't. After that first time, telling him what he called a "story of loss," I stopped trying to explain anything to him. Instead, I sat there twice a week and said very little, but of course my mind was basically jabbering with thoughts about Reeve. And here now, in the classroom at night, even after so much time has passed, it still is.

"Falling in love with someone and losing him like that," says Marc. "That must have been devastating, Jam."

"It was," I say. *Devastating.* I prefer that word to *trauma.* What happened was devastating. And because of it I was *devastated*, and I guess I still am.

"Was it sudden?" Casey asks. "If you don't mind my asking," she quickly adds.

"Yes, very sudden," I say.

We sit, everyone reflecting on what's happened to us, and what's been said tonight. Marc looks at his watch—one of those thick, technical-looking silver ones where you can read not only the time, but also probably how many nautical knots you are from somewhere. He says, "The houseparents are going to start bed check soon, before lights-out. We have to get back in . . . four and a half minutes."

"Remember, nobody tell anyone anything," Sierra says anxiously. "Not even your roommates. Everybody promise."

Everybody promises. Then Marc says, "And everybody also has to promise that they won't write in their journals again until we've gone over things carefully, okay?"

"Why?" Griffin asks. "What's going to happen?"

"No idea," says Marc. "Which is why I said it. We just don't know enough yet."

I can tell that all of us are scared of that other place, yet we also want to go back to it. But who knows if it would even be the same next time? For all we know, when we write in the journal again, something entirely different might happen.

Or nothing might happen at all.

We're supposed to write in the journals twice a week; we all know that. But despite what Mrs. Quenell asked us, we all decide not to write in them "until further notice," as Marc puts it. Then we arrange to meet here again tomorrow night at the same time.

Griffin leans forward and blows out the candle with one sharp blast, leaving us in the dark.

CHAPTER 8

BACK IN MY DORM ROOM AFTER OUR LITTLE nighttime meeting, DJ says to me, "Where were you?" and all I tell her is "Out."

"With who?" she asks.

"Whom," I correct her, which is a stupid thing to do.

"*Ooh,* Miss Special Topics in English," she says in a sarcastic voice. "Is that what you learn in that class? When to use 'whom'?"

"Something like that."

Jane Ann pokes her head in. "Hey, guys, homework done, et cetera? You're both good to go?"

"We're fine," I say, though, no, I'm not at all good to go.

DJ turns off the light and we just lie there. After a long, uncomfortable silence she says, "Jam?"

"Yep."

"Can I talk to you about something?"

Oh God, now she's going to confront me. She's going to say, "Something's going on with you, something totally over the top, and I want to know what it is."

"Sure," I say, and then I wait.

There's another long, stressful silence. We both just keep lying there, and finally DJ says, "Did you happen to notice anything unusual about me at the social?"

"What?" I ask, surprised. The social? I try to remember. "Well, you were *dancing.* I guess that was kind of not what I expected."

"Oh, you think I don't dance, I just sulk?" DJ says, and she snorts lightly. Then she continues, "No, I meant who I was dancing *with.* Did you happen to notice that?"

She isn't asking me anything about myself at all, and I'm so relieved. I vaguely remember that she was dancing with a girl that night, the way that girls do, just for the hell of it, or to show off.

"A blond girl, is that right?" I say. "Her name's Rebecca?"

"Yeah, Rebecca Fairchild. I think she's very cute. Hot, I guess I'm saying."

"Oh!" I say. It's never occurred to me for one second that DJ might like girls. Or that dancing with Rebecca Fairchild meant anything at all. "It's fine, of course," I quickly reassure her.

"'*It's fine*'? Gee, Jam, thanks for your approval," she says. "Now I don't need to feel like such a circus freak anymore, or worry about being *shunned* by you."

"Oh, shut up, DJ. I just said that because I know I sounded surprised. And, okay, I was."

"I surprised myself too," DJ admits. "Calling another girl hot. I've never said anything like that in my life. I sort of still can't believe I said it out loud." This is the first time DJ has made herself vulnerable in front of me in any way. Usually she hides everything so carefully. The real, true DJ Kawabata is kept buried like the junk food she's placed out of sight around our room.

We lie in silence for a while, but it feels less tense now. "You've liked other girls before?" I ask.

"Oh, sure," she says.

"Boys too?"

"Not like that."

"Did you always know?"

DJ rustles around for several seconds and then says, "The first thing I remember is that I loved my third-grade teacher, Miss Clavel. Seriously, that was her name, like in *Madeline.* She wasn't a nun, though. She was sort of a leftover hippie who put wildflowers in her hair. She quit her job at the end of the year to move to California with her boyfriend, and when I found out, I cried so hard."

I lie in my bed picturing DJ as a freckled little girl, yearning for her pretty, young teacher. It's easy to imagine, actually. "That's sad," I say.

"And you know what? My food issues began that spring."

"Really?"

"No! Jesus, I was joking."

"Oh!"

We laugh together a little. Then she says, "What about you?"

"What?"

"Who was, like, your first big love?"

I get very uncomfortable suddenly. "Oh," I say, trying to sound vague, "it's complicated. But anyway, we were talking about you, not me."

"Actually," DJ admits, "Rebecca is the first time I've ever, you know, *liked* someone and felt she might actually like me back."

"Well, that's a big deal."

"But I honestly have no idea if she feels the way I do. That night at the social, I thought there was something between us. We kept catching each other's eye. And now she keeps giving me these *looks,* like we have this private joke going. But if I'm wrong, then we're stuck in this tiny little incestuous community, where everyone eventually knows everyone else's business, and how would I deal with that?"

My eyes have gotten used to the dark now, and I can see that DJ is facing me on her bed, straining toward me as she tells me things that are important to her.

"I think you should say something," I say.

"Even if it could screw everything up really bad?"

"Trust me, life is short. Someone gets taken away from you, and then you can never say anything to them again."

"Wow," says DJ. "That's true. I'll have to think about it. In the meantime, when I see her next I'll be, like, 'Hey, Rebecca, what's going on?' I'll just be normal."

"Normal for you," I say with a little laugh.

"Yeah, normal for me."

We yawn, one after the other, because yawning is so contagious. Soon we're each turning over, facing away from the other person, and then, like two people jumping off a rock into water, I guess we both fall helplessly into sleep. I'm not sure which of us gets there first.

In the morning, it's hard to believe that the sunlit classroom is the same place where, the night before, all five members of Special Topics in English sat by candlelight trading stories of trauma and hallucination. Mrs. Quenell greets us as if today is just a regular morning, and she doesn't seem to notice the few little droplets of candle wax that spatter the floor.

"I hope everyone's feeling lively and rested today," she says. "Who'd like to kick off the in-class presentations?" She looks around the room. "Jam," she says. "Why don't you begin?"

I am so not up for this.

Everyone looks at me. I could be wrong, but Griffin seems amused. I'm going to try not to let him bother me. I'd gone to the library in the past couple of days and read up on Plath's life, and I'd also read a few of her poems. It's not like I put a lot of time into the assignment, because I just don't care enough, but still I understand the main ideas, I think. Now, for some reason, I'm actually nervous. What if everything I'm about to say is wrong?

They keep looking at me, waiting, and I flip through my pages of notes, not really wanting to make eye contact. "Sylvia Plath's father kept bees as a hobby," I start. "He was this huge figure in her life, and he died when she was eight. This was really upsetting to Plath, who was left with her mother and her brother, and I guess a feeling of, you know, *sorrow*.

"Look at the poem called 'Daddy,' where she curses her father, and the power he has over her, even though he's been dead for a long time. I mean, she's *furious* at him in the poem. I don't know that it's *him* exactly," I go on, "or even if it's her. It's a lot bigger than that, and it uses images of Nazis, and makes these points about history, and World War Two. It's really angry, and really complicated. And I think that even though the poem is filled with incredible rage, it's also got, like, heartbreak in it."

I shuffle through the papers I'm holding, and I find the poem. "'Daddy, I have had to kill you / You died before I had time,'" I read aloud. And then I recite another line, from later in the poem: "'At twenty I tried to die / And get back, back, back to you.'"

I lower the page. "I think that's what she wanted," I say. "To get back to him."

Mrs. Quenell asks, "Do you think Plath's depression is a kind of unfinished grief?"

"Well," I say nervously, "I'm not an English teacher. Or a psychiatrist."

"But you're a thinking person, Jam," says Mrs. Quenell. "And besides that," she says, "you've had experiences that qualify you to weigh in on these matters. You all have. Don't be afraid to use them. Use whatever it is you bring to the table. *Literally,* in this case," she adds, knocking on the oak surface of the oval table where we sit.

"I guess I feel like grief is this huge part of everything," I say in a burst. "But you're supposed to act like it's not. Like, if you lose someone, how are you supposed to go on caring about stupid day-to-day things? Like whether a test will be hard, or whether you have split ends, or had an argument with your friend. How is Sylvia Plath, or Esther Greenwood in *The Bell Jar,* whose father died too, supposed to just *be* in the world?" I ask.

What I really want to know is: How are any of us in this room supposed to care about anything, when we're constantly being pulled back by unbearable thoughts and feelings?

"Those are good questions," says Mrs. Quenell. "Anyone want to answer?"

At first no one does. And then Griffin says, "This isn't an answer. But sometimes maybe it's not exactly a person you're missing, you know? It could be anything that meant something to you."

I wonder what happened to him, what hurt him and shut him down.

When class ends, Griffin walks out ahead of everyone else

in his clomping bad-boy biker boots; this time he doesn't even make a show of trying to help Casey, the way the rest of us do. As we leave the building, he's already way up ahead on the path alone, his hood back on, his hands jammed into the pockets of his coat.

That night at ten, when we all meet up again in the darkened classroom, I'm a little surprised that Griffin shows up. I thought maybe he was going to disconnect from us. But he's there, sitting on Marc's comforter. We all arrange ourselves, and Sierra lights the candle, and the faux-hazelnut fragrance makes the place smell like a cutesy, overpriced café. Casey says, "If anyone feels like helping me out of this contraption, I might actually be able to sit on the floor with you guys."

We all sort of stare at her dumbly, as if it hadn't occurred to us that she could *exist* outside the wheelchair. Marc goes to stand in front of the chair and lifts Casey out, saying, "Is this okay? I'm not gripping you too hard?"

"I'm not going to *break,* Marc," she says. "I already broke, right?"

"Just checking. I've never done this before."

Sierra has created a little place for Casey to sit where she can be supported, and finally she's in the circle with the rest of us, though her legs are out in front of her, with her small, delicate feet in stylish ankle boots flopping to either side.

The candle sends its campfire glow around our circle, and this time we've come prepared with food that's been snuck out of the dining hall at dinner, so we don't have to steal anything from the teachers.

"Who's going to go first?" Marc says.

Casey, leaning against the wall, raises a hand as if it were morning and she's in class.

"Raised hands are not necessary in here," Marc says, imitating Mrs. Quenell's voice, and there's a little laughter. "Only raised minds."

"I'll go," Casey says. "Anybody want to hear how I got like this?"

CHAPTER 9

"I GREW UP RICH IN NEW YORK CITY," CASEY TELLS US. "I don't want to sound obnoxious, but my family's apartment was featured in *Architectural Digest.* Yeah, one of *those.* It's a duplex on Park and Seventy-First. We have a housekeeper who keeps everything running smoothly, and cooks amazing food. If we ever got hungry in the middle of the night, we'd just press the button on the intercom marked 'Daphne,' and she'd make us a buffalo chicken sandwich on a Kaiser roll. She'd complain about it the next day, but she'd do it. A town car took us to school every morning, and—"

"A town car. Aren't you fancy," Griffin murmurs.

"Be quiet, Griffin," Sierra says lightly.

"It didn't seem like a big deal," Casey goes on, "because lots of girls at private schools in the city are brought to school like that. And our dads continue on to the office after dropping us off. They're all masters of the universe. They run Wall Street. My dad likes to *win,* and for him that means taking over corporations and doing leveraged buy-outs. He's always been happier doing that than anything else. And he always loved the money he made, and loved spending it on us.

"We were mostly happy," says Casey. "That's the thing that people find hard to wrap their minds around. Nobody at Sedgefield—my rehabilitation hospital—really understood this. I tried to explain it to them, but they didn't get it. Even my mom's little problem didn't make us *un*happy."

Casey stops, and we all wait. "She drank," she says. "Not in the morning—never in the morning—but other times of day. I noticed it; we all did. It would put me on alert, make me feel kind of tense, like, 'Okay, there's Mom again, under the influence.' She'd go out to lunch with her friends, and she'd come home basically trashed. My sisters and I always felt worried when this happened. We had a code we used. We'd say, 'Mom took out the trash.' We'd even say it right in *front* of her, and she'd say, 'What do you girls mean? I didn't take out the trash; Daphne did.'

"She wasn't one of those mean drunks," Casey continues. "Drinking actually made her sweeter than she was, which was already very sweet. But she would sort of go a little bit *off*; it's hard to describe. The thing is, she's very charming. She's a redhead like me, and freckly. When my dad met her, he called her the Leprechaun. But even though she mostly *stayed* charming, and kept it together, I worried that when she had too much to drink she'd tip over into something kind of . . . embarrassing.

"And it did happen sometimes. Like, once, when Marissa Scherr came over, my mom was laughing too hard at everything we said, and Marissa noticed, and said, 'Your mom is weird. She laughs too much.' So I told her the dumbest thing. I said, 'Oh, she had laughing gas at the dentist today.' Which didn't even make any sense.

"But it was pretty rare for my mom to actually embarrass

us. I'd think to myself, *Please let this be okay,* when friends came over, or when she showed up for my school play. And usually it *was* okay. She was *appropriate.* I told myself that I could relax, that I didn't have to do that walking-on-eggshells thing.

"It was mostly in the summer that my sisters and I got worried. Because in the summer we moved out to our house in Southampton. You know, the Hamptons."

"Oh, give me a break," says Griffin.

"Our house was right on the ocean," Casey says, ignoring him, "and it even had a name: Treasure Tide. Every summer we swam all day, and made bonfires on the beach at night. My dad had to work during the week, so he could only come out on weekends. He didn't even mind. I knew he'd rather be in the office screaming on the phone to Hong Kong than lying on the sand under an umbrella. So in the summer, it was just Mom and me and my sisters, Emma and Rachel. And that was where things got sticky."

It almost seems as though that's the end of Casey's story and she's not going to tell us anything more than this.

"Explain," says Griffin.

"Mom did all the driving."

Now I see where this is heading.

"It was the summer before last, and we'd been at the beach at night," she says. "It was one of those August nights that are so suffocating the only place you can bear to be is by the water. We went to our friends', the Brennigans, who live only half a mile away. We'd built this bonfire, and we roasted wieners, and the little kids were going around saying the word *wiener* over and over, like it was hilarious. And afterward, all the parents headed back to the Brennigans' porch, while the teenagers stayed on the beach.

"Jacob Brennigan, the oldest, had been flirting with me since we were kids. And I always flirted back, but we were never really sure what to do with our relationship. Once, like a year earlier, we'd hooked up at a party. He was a very good kisser, and it was this really nice moment. That night on the beach he was chasing me along the shore, and I was running."

It's hard to picture Casey Cramer running, but of course, in this story, there's no wheelchair. In this story, nothing is wrong with her yet. The night in August that she's telling us about was the moment right before everything in her life changed. Her freckled legs took her across the sand, running away from Jacob Brennigan. Casey continues to tell her story of how she ran and ran, and how when she looked over her shoulder she saw that he'd given up and stopped chasing her. She was way too fast for him, and she stood down by the water, her hands on her hips, letting her heart slow.

"I remember thinking that I could outrun this boy I'd known forever," Casey says. "I liked him, but I didn't want him to catch me. I felt like an Olympic runner. And then my sisters started shouting that it was time to leave. So I jogged back to the Brennigans' under these amazing stars, and we said good night to everyone, including Jacob, who gave me this meaningful look.

"And then my sisters and my mom and I piled into the car. It was only a half-mile drive. It was nothing! I could feel the sand on my bare feet, and the bottoms of my jeans were all wet, and my mom was saying, 'Did you girls have a good time tonight? Because *I* did.'

"Emma was being a pain in the ass. She said, 'Mom, I don't think you should drive. You had a lot to drink; I can hear it in your voice. You should ask Mr. Brennigan to drive us home in their SUV, and we can come get the car tomorrow.'

"And my mom said, 'For God's sake, Emma, I'm *fine.*' My sister just kept saying it wasn't a good idea. And I thought she was being ridiculous too. 'All right, we'll put it to a vote,' my mom said.

Rachel said she didn't think it was a big deal if Mom drove. It was a split vote. So it was up to me to decide. 'You're the tie-breaker, Casey,' my mom said.

"And because my feet were all sandy and I was getting cold, I said, 'Let Mom drive.'

"And she said, 'Thank you, Casey girl.' That's what she called me a lot. I was sitting up front in the car, next to her. I was nervous, because Mom had that *way* about her. Everything was just a little too much, you know? And she started the engine and turned on the radio, and a Beatles' song came on. And right away she said, 'Ooh, I love this song! Just listen to the beautiful French horn solo in the middle.'

"She was too excited by it; I knew that. But I also knew how much she loves the Beatles, and here was this song on the radio, so why shouldn't she enjoy it? Those are the songs my mom loves the best, because they remind her of when she was young. And she would always tell us how much she loved being young. Staying out late, being kind of wild. She missed all that when she got older and got married and settled down.

"So my mom was singing along. And she was happy, and we were too, all of us except Emma, I guess—and suddenly there was this loud *thump*, and then the feeling of flying, but *bad* flying. And then I felt as if I'd been socked in the head, and I heard glass breaking, and someone shrieking. Someone who turned out to be me. And then I blacked out."

Casey stops there. None of us speaks or breathes.

"Okay, at ease," she says. "That's it. The story of how I became a cripple."

Sierra, Marc, Griffin, and I are all silent. There's not a thing we can say. I've never had friends with problems like these. The worst friend-problem I'd ever dealt with was a blowup between Hannah and Ryan about whether it was okay for Ryan to carry a condom in his pocket, "for when you change your mind." Hannah was insulted, and Jenna and I had to stay up all night with her while she cried and texted him every ten seconds. But I could handle that.

I'm in way over my head now.

"My mom had driven us into a stone wall," Casey goes on. "Everyone else in the car was fine. But I hadn't been wearing my seat belt—I mean, it was only a five-minute drive—and I'd slammed into the windshield. I severed my spinal cord and experienced trauma to my head."

There's that word *trauma* again. It's everywhere at The Wooden Barn.

"The airbag was faulty; it didn't go off," says Casey. "I was airlifted to the city, and I was in a coma for three days. Finally I woke up, and my parents were right over me in the bed, and they were both crying.

"I heard one of the nurses say, 'Well, at least it won't be manslaughter,' but I didn't know what she was talking about.

“As I recovered, I learned two things: One, I’d never walk again; and two, my mom’s blood alcohol level was way over the legal limit. She hadn’t been ‘tipsy’ when she drove us home. She’d been totally trashed.

“And then I remembered that I’d been the tiebreaker. Mom went to a court-ordered drug and alcohol rehab for a few months, and I went to a very different rehab. Sedgefield. It wasn’t that the doctors and nurses thought I’d walk again. They just wanted to teach me to get back my upper body strength, and use the wheelchair well.

“It was the grimmest place on earth. Pretty much everyone in my unit had had some kind of accident or disease. One lady was there because she’d gone to have the fat sucked out of her stomach so she could look good in a bikini when she went to Bermuda, and she woke up paralyzed. We were all so pathetic, sitting or lying in our bathrobes all day, drinking little containers of warm apple juice, making houses out of playing cards, and watching *Law & Order*. After I got out of Sedgefield, I didn’t stay in touch with any of those people. It was too depressing. They group e-mailed each other a lot, but I never joined in.

“And at home, my mom kept saying, ‘Casey girl, will you ever forgive me?’ She was totally sober now, and she was horrified at what she’d done. In her rehab they’d made her face everything. It was brutal. And here’s the thing: I forgave her right away. She’d just gotten so used to drinking all the time, and to people thinking she was this sweet, tipsy little leprechaun. I couldn’t be mad at her.

“I went back to school, but it was hard to focus. There was

a party one night, and some kids from the boys' school came. That was the first time I'd seen Jacob Brennigan since the accident. There he was, standing with his friends. He looked way uncomfortable seeing me in my wheelchair. One of his friends started whispering, and pushing him toward me. It was so awkward.

"He came over and said, 'Hey,' but he could barely look at me.

"I said, 'Hey, Jacob. What's up?'

"And he said, 'Not much. I'm glad you're out of the hospital. Well, I'd better go.'

"And that was it. The last time Jacob ever spoke to me. I'd been the cute girl he'd flirted with since we were kids, and now I was the crippled girl he couldn't deal with.

"Everyone felt sorry for me, and no one treated me normally. My friends had to wait for me to take the wheelchair lift to leave school at the end of the day, and sometimes it took forever to find the lady in the front office who had the key. I started doing reckless things, like once I positioned my chair at the top of the hill on Eighty-Ninth Street that was closed to traffic during the school day, and I just let 'er rip.

"That was when my parents decided to send me to The Wooden Barn. And I guess it's been sort of helpful so far. But then, the other night, I had one of those visions that Sierra described. Except what *I* saw, obviously, was different."

"Tell us," says Sierra.

"Okay," Casey begins. "Here's the situation. I'm at my desk, and I'm writing in my journal, and as I write, I feel like I might *hurl,* which—fun fact—is the thing that happens to me whenever I try to read or write in a car. And I look up and I see that I'm not at my desk anymore, but I'm actually *in a car.*"

She pauses, then says, "It's nighttime, and I'm in the passenger seat. I realize that something's happening to my brain. But then I know that I've been in this exact scene before, this exact moment. And I know when. I make a move to cross my legs, which are cold, my feet all dusted with sand, the bottom of my jeans damp. And my legs are *fine,* they move like normal. My mom and my sisters and I are singing along with the Beatles on the radio, and I think how lucky I am to be who I am. My family is great. Jacob and I are into each other. And the moment lasts. It doesn't end after half a mile with my drunk mom plowing into a wall.

"I touch my legs and I can *feel* them; there's total sensation there. They aren't paralyzed, nothing bad has happened, and we're just driving down the road. And I say to my mom, 'Things are going to be okay, right? They're going to be just the same as always?'

"She turns to me, and she doesn't have that silly, tipsy expression on her face, but instead she looks calm and serious, and she says, 'Let's not worry about the future, Casey girl. Let's just enjoy this moment.'

"So I don't say another thing, and we just keep driving, and the wind is in my hair, and the road seems to go on forever, and so does the Beatles song. At one point my mom stops the car and I get out and go running along the side of the road, and she starts the engine again and I keep pace with her. I'm so fast, and my legs are strong. Then I get back in the car and I can still feel my legs kind of pulsing with life, I guess you'd say.

"And that's it. It's this perfect, pure experience. The next thing I know, I'm back at my desk again, and back in my wheelchair. And when I look down I see that the pages of my journal have blown ahead. And all the papers on my desk have blown around too, like there's been a *wind* in the room, even though the window's completely shut. My roommate, Nina, comes in, and she says, 'What happened in here?'

"And I say something like 'I guess I got a little wrapped up in my homework.'

"'*I'll* say,' she says, and she just laughs. Nina's seen everything—she started stealing her dad's Oxycontin in sixth grade. But then, when I straighten up all my papers and stuff, I notice something: The pages that have blown ahead in the journal are covered with writing. With *my handwriting*. I don't even remember writing *any* of it, but there's five pages' worth. I must've written it when I was in my 'trance,' or whatever we're supposed to call it."

So not only are our journals the way into that world, but five is the automatic number of pages we each apparently write when we're there. Details like this are slowly becoming clear. But what isn't clear is why.

"Can I ask if anyone here has thought about the reason this is happening to us?" I ask.

"Oh, I guess it's because we're just so *special*," Casey says.

"Maybe," says Sierra, "it can't be explained."

"Only because we don't have all the information yet," says Marc. "But let's be logical about it. And the most logical question to ask is, Do we think Mrs. Q knows about it? Did she *plan* it?"

"She might have," says Sierra. "And maybe that's why we were chosen for the class. Because she thought we each needed it. The red-leather-journal cure."

"I'm not cured," says Casey. "My life still blows. Though I

guess for a little while when I was *there*, it didn't. I want to go back," she suddenly says. "I know you said not to, Marc, but I want to go back right now."

"Well, hold off," Marc says. "I think there are three possibilities concerning Mrs. Q. Possibility one: She has no idea what these journals do. And if we *tell* her, she'll report us. The journals would be taken away, and we'd never have our 'visions' again. We'd probably even have to leave school. Possibility two: She *does* know what the journals do, and maybe she made it happen. And she chose us on purpose because out of everyone at The Wooden Barn she thought we could benefit the most."

"Okay, fine," says Sierra. "But even if that's true and we ask her, she might still deny it."

"But there's also possibility three," says Marc. "Which is that she *does* know, and she's just waiting for us to bring it up with her. Now this seems to me really, really unlikely. My suggestion is that we act like nothing's going on at all. It's too risky to try and talk to her about the trance."

"I don't think of it as a trance, exactly," I say. "It's almost more of a *place*. I feel like I went to a place where people go when they can't take reality, because it's just too depressing."

"People who can relate to *The Bell Jar*," says Sierra.

"We should have a code name for it," Marc says. "Like Casey and her sisters did when their mom was trashed, remember? *Mom took out the trash*. In case other people are around when we need to mention it."

"Or even a name to call it when it's just us," says Casey.

"We could say 'I went to Bell Jar,'" offers Sierra.

"That's lame," Griffin says.

"Maybe we could do a riff on 'Bell Jar,'" I put in. "Something kind of exotic. Make it sound like . . . the name of a foreign country. Which it sort of is."

We all think for half a minute. "Trance-Land?" says Marc.

"Sounds like a crappy amusement park," says Griffin.

I feel like we're a group of grade-schoolers trying to name their crime-solving or bottle-recycling club. And yet naming it feels like it'll make it a little more manageable, and a little more real.

"Belzhar," I say.

"That's what I said before," Casey says.

"No, *Belzhar,*" I repeat. "Like the *zhuh* in *Jacques* in the middle. It would be spelled B-e-l-z-h-a-r."

"Belzhar," pronounces Sierra. "'I went to *Belzhar*.' It does sound exotic."

Griffin says, "I guess I could live with it." His "compliment"—a rare thing—pleases me.

"Okay, so we've got the name," Casey says. "Fine. But what about going back there? Is it okay to give in to a delusion? Because I really, really want to."

And so do I. Belzhar is the only way we can each have what we want. The only way to get back whatever it is we've lost.

"There have to be *rules,*" Marc says with a little anxiety.

"Why are *you* in charge?" asks Griffin.

"Fine, you be in charge. Go right ahead." Griffin doesn't reply. "I didn't think so," says Marc. "Look, someone has to steer this thing, and that's all I'm trying to do. I did it with student council. I'm just trying to make sure it doesn't take over our lives or make other people suspicious. Remember, the journals could be taken away from us. We could *lose* this thing for good."

Sierra takes out a pen and a few sheets of loose-leaf paper. Together we start to come up with a set of rules to live by.

CHAPTER 10

AND SO WE ALL DECIDE TO FOLLOW THE SAME simple guidelines: Visit Belzhar twice a week; and, just to be consistent, only on the days we've each chosen; gather every Sunday night at 10:00 p.m. in the dark classroom around the candle in order to discuss whatever might have come up during the week; and, finally and crucially, never tell a single outsider about any of this.

I've chosen Tuesdays and Fridays to go to Belzhar. This coming Friday is the next day that I'll write in my journal. I can't wait, though I'm also anxious to the point of feeling sick to my stomach when I think about it.

My journal sits in my desk drawer, practically throbbing like a little disembodied heart. Whenever I run into one of the other Special Topics people on campus, we behave kind of low-key and no-big-deal on purpose. "Hey," we say to one another. But truthfully we are all jumping inside, dying, impatiently waiting.

DJ is so smart; she seems to know something's up. Sometimes when we're both in our room she looks at me funny. "What?" I say one afternoon when she sits watching me, all owl eyed.

"You act like you've got a secret," DJ says.

"You're the one with the secret."

"True," DJ agrees. She and Rebecca Fairchild got

involved quickly, and the only two people in the world who know about it are me and Rebecca's roommate. The school discourages "intimate" relationships between students, and PDAs are forbidden. Although there's a rule that boys and girls can only be together in the common rooms of dorms and not in the dorm rooms, girls can be with girls everywhere, luckily for DJ and Rebecca.

And so, in the brief time since they've been seeing each other, they've been lying around both of their rooms together, sprawled on beds, painting each other's toenails, drawing *mehndi* patterns with a fine-line henna tattoo pen on the backs of each other's hands, and when no one else has been around, presumably kissing or going further.

I would've liked to go further with Reeve if we'd had more than forty-one days. I would've liked to let myself feel whatever feelings came up, and to follow them wherever they went. But I never had the chance.

Friday night at 8:00 p.m., a movie is shown in the gym, some totally idiotic comedy about identical twins who rob a bank. I've decided not to go. Instead, I'm going to wait for the dorm to clear out, and then, if it works the way it did the last time— and it just has to— I'll be able to be with Reeve again. *Leave,* I silently say as everyone takes forever to head off to the movie. *Leave. Just leave.*

Jane Ann seems concerned that I've chosen to stay behind in my room. "Don't you like movies, Jam?" she asks me.

"Yeah, but I'm just not in the mood."

"If you change your mind, come on over," she says. "Tonight we're handing out bags of *roasted soy nuts*!" she adds, as if this is an amazing detail that will definitely make me change my mind.

"Great," I say.

"I'll send someone to check on you in a while," she says, and after the slightest hesitation she leaves.

Finally the dorm is quiet. The only other people around are DJ and Rebecca, who are upstairs in Rebecca's room, and a girl named Jocelyn Strange, who, no surprise, is extremely strange. Casey and Sierra have gone to the movie; both of them are planning on returning to Belzhar much later, after lights-out.

In the silence of the empty room I go to my desk and slide my journal out of the drawer. I turn it over and over in my hands, feeling the cool skin of its leather. I pick up a pen and sit on the bed against the study buddy. When I open the journal, it makes that familiar, soothing cracking sound.

But what if going to Belzhar was a one-time thing? What if I write in the journal and nothing happens? It would be an enormous disappointment. Our rules would have proved pointless. All the anticipation would have been for nothing. Reeve would never appear again, which might actually be another trauma.

Quickly, anxiously, I find the first free page, and I begin to write:

By the time I left Dana Sapol's party, I knew that I loved this boy, and I started to think that he loved me too.

I have to wait only a fraction of a second. And then, just like last time, his arms are around me. It happens swiftly, almost naturally, and this time I'm shocked again, but not too shocked. Reeve holds me from the front, not the back, and I say into his neck, "I'm here."

"I know, I was waiting," he says. "It took so long."

I stand back and look at him. He's wearing the same brown sweater, and he's watching me as though I were the one whose presence here is a miracle. We look at each other for a long time, and then I lean my head against his chest, and there's that feeling again, that spill of happiness and relief.

"How have you been?" I ask when I can finally lift my head.

"Better now. Maybe I ought to know when you're planning to come next time. I hate not knowing. It gets me all agitated."

"Tuesdays and Fridays. It'll always be twice a week," I say, "probably at night, though the time can change depending on what else I have going on."

Reeve blinks at me with sleepy brown eyes. "Only twice a week," he says. "Why that schedule?" He pronounces it like *shed*-ule.

"Oh," I say, "it's what we decided."

He looks at me without understanding, and I explain how my whole class is involved, and I tell him about naming the place Belzhar. I also describe the other students, but I see that he's only half listening. The only person who seems to interest him at all is Griffin.

"The arrogant one, is he better looking than me?" he asks, and he turns his head in profile for me to admire. He's joking, but not totally. They couldn't be more different, Griffin so rude and blond and angry; Reeve lanky and witty and brown haired and kind.

"Griffin? Are you kidding?" I say.

We sit on the grass and lean together like two lovebirds on a branch, and Reeve suddenly says, "Oh! There's something here for you. At least, it ought to be here. Let's go have a look."

He takes my hand and leads me down a sloping hill toward a large object in the distance that I can't make out yet. It's a big blocky thing, but it's in the shadow of a tree, and only when we get near do I see that it's Courtney Sapol's amazing dollhouse, plopped down on the grass.

"Oh, how weird, the *dollhouse*," I say, puzzled, but kind of pleased. "What's it doing here?" We kneel down and take up our dolls. Within seconds, we're moving them around the house as if we're little kids, and then we settle them into bed, side by side.

Reeve turns his doll to face mine and moves it around so it seems like they're kissing. "Oh, Mama," he says in a deep voice, "you have a smoking hot bod."

At first we're laughing, but then we abandon the dolls in their little bed and start kissing for real. Very quickly it gets serious, and then we're not laughing. But because we're out in the open I worry about whether anyone can see us. And then I remember that there's no one here to see us at all.

I think of that night at Dana Sapol's party, how the kiss kept heating up, and Reeve's hand slipped under my shirt, moving slowly, as if to make sure it was okay with me. Then it slipped beneath my tank top, and I heard my breath catch. I put my hand under his shirt too, and felt his warm, hard chest, which shuddered and vibrated.

We didn't do much more than that kind of kissing and touching at the party, but it was a revelation. Once again, all alone but out here in the open in Belzhar, Reeve and I are kissing and touching, and I sit in his lap. Our mouths are together, and soon our hands are under each other's shirts, and all I can think is that this is the most exquisite feeling anyone could possibly ever feel.

But now I feel like I want more from him. I get the idea that I want him to see me without my shirt on and, even though it's not exactly the same thing, I want to see him without his shirt on too. I want us to look at each other as we sit entwined in Belzhar.

But when I try to reach down and pull off my shirt, my hand is frozen, paralyzed, unable to move.

I look down at my hand, opening and closing it. It seems to work fine. I snap my fingers. Again, no problem. But when I try to take off my shirt a second time, the hand still won't work.

And now I get it. All that Reeve and I can do in Belzhar is basically what we've already done in real life. We can't go further in any significant way. When I tried to talk to him about the new things in my life—specifically about Special Topics, and the kids in the class—he wasn't interested, and the conversation faded.

Belzhar lets you be with the person you've lost, or in Casey's case with the thing she's lost, but it keeps you where you were before the loss. So if you desperately want what you once had, you can write in your red leather journal and go to Belzhar and find it. But apparently you won't find anything new there. Time stops in Belzhar; it hangs suspended.

Reeve and I can play with a dollhouse, and we can do some of the other things we did during our forty-one days together, but nothing more. It's odd, though, that he doesn't seem to mind the limitations. "What's the matter?" he asks, as I think about how my hand won't allow me to take off my own shirt.

"Do you ever feel like you want to do something more with me?" I ask him.

"Like what?"

"You know," I say, embarrassed. "Like, see each other, *gasp*, unclothed from the waist up?"

Reeve tilts his head and looks at me in slight confusion. "What we do together is incredibly great," he says. "I love it."

"Okay, good," I say. "Just checking."

What I can have with Reeve now isn't newness. It's only old experiences, revisited. But I'll take them, of course. I'll take however much of him I can get. He and I lie down on the brown grass and whisper to each other, none of it new or deep, but all of it just what we need.

The sky starts to change color again, and it's like the intermission during a play, when the houselights blink, and you have to hurry back to your seat.

"Oh no," I say. "The light."

"*Shite*. It's too soon, Jam," Reeve says.

"I just want to stay here," I say. I know that I have to study for my math test tonight, even though I couldn't care less about math or school or much of anything in the real world.

This world, this other-world here with Reeve, which consists entirely of little pieces from the past, is enough for me. So what if we never do anything new together? If I were given the choice, I'd stay here with him forever, and never go back to The Wooden Barn. In fact, good riddance, Wooden Barn. Don't let the door hit you on the ass.

But the light has dimmed, and in a moment I'll be forced away from him. "Come back to me soon," Reeve says. "Please, Jam. *Please.*"

His voice has gotten different in the middle of a sentence; it sounds like a girl's. I look up sharply, and Sierra is standing over my bed in my dorm room, saying, "Please, Jam. *Please.* Come on, wake up."

I blink several times. "What are you doing here?" I ask.

"Jane Ann sent me to check on you during the movie. I knocked, but you didn't answer. And when I came in, you were writing in your journal, but you were making these little noises. It was weird, Jam. You've got to be more discreet. What if Jane Ann had found you? Or someone else from the dorm?"

Looking down, and flipping quickly through the journal, I see that once again I've filled in five whole pages. I've somehow managed to write about what we were doing while we were doing it. Yet I have no memory of writing more than the first line.

Sierra sits down beside me and we're both quiet, and then she says, "Are you okay? It seemed like it was such a big moment, whatever was happening to you there."

"I can't even describe it."

"You don't have to."

She doesn't want anything from me. She's just looking out for me. I certainly never had a moment with Hannah as strong and personal as the one I'm having with Sierra. Not even close. Best friends: That's what we're becoming.

"And look at this," she says, flipping lightly through the pages of my journal, making a point of not reading any of it. "If you keep going twice a week, it's going to fill up fast."

We're both silent, and I expect we're wondering the same thing, which stupidly hasn't occurred to me before. What happens to Belzhar when our journal are finished?

CHAPTER 11

Dear Jam,

Dad and I think about you all the time and hope things are settling down for you. I bet that by the time you read this, you're totally involved with your schoolwork, or a new friend. Or both. You sounded so much better when I called the other evening, and I was glad to hear that. It seems as if that panicky episode—when you called me, wanting to come home—is behind you now. Good for you, babe.

Jam, there's something I wanted to write to you about. As you've heard, Leo has come out of his shell lately because of a boy at school named Connor Bunch. At first Dad and I were thrilled. You know your brother hasn't had many friends, and that he's been teased. But Connor is a bit of a "wise guy," and some of that seems to have rubbed off on Leo. I can't put my finger on it exactly, but I'm not thrilled. I wish you were here, Jam, to tell us, "Oh, lighten up, you guys. Twelve-year-old boys are total jerks, don't worry about it."

So I thought maybe you could write to Leo,

reminding him that he can always talk to you about what's on his mind. It would be terrific if you let him know you're there for him, even though you're away in Vermont. And I think it would be great for YOU to have something like Leo to focus on—something outside your own problems.

Well, that's all I wanted to say. Bye for now. We love you lots.

xoxo

Mom

I fold the letter back into its envelope. My family feels so far away from me, and I can barely even picture the way our house looks. What color exactly is the rug in the den? I try to see it in my mind, but I can't quite do it. I hope Leo's okay. I will definitely write to him tonight.

I'm so caught up with my own life, but not in the way my mom thinks. Though I've only been to Belzhar twice so far, I'm already obsessed with my new fear of finishing the journal eventually and what that will mean. I try to remind myself that there are plenty of pages left, and many more visits before I have to think about what happens when the last line is filled in.

I've already done the math. Because each trip takes five pages, we'll get through the semester, and at the very end the journal will be completely done.

And then what? How will I be with Reeve?

Don't obsess about this, I tell myself. Remember that you've got Reeve back for now. *Enjoy* him.

And each time I go to Belzhar on a Tuesday or Friday, I do enjoy him. But after a while the light gets dim, and I'm thrust back into the world of boarding school and homework and increasingly cold weather. And now, as of this week, into the world of a cappella singing. Against my will, I've been forced to join the girls' a cappella group, the Barntones.

"Every student needs a club," Jane Ann tells me one evening. "And this one had a slot to fill, so it's the club for you."

"That's not in The Wooden Barn handbook," I complain.

"We'll be sure to put it in the next edition."

I have to say that I am no fan of a cappella. Some people can't get enough of voices singing without any instruments behind them, but I am not one of those people. Reeve wasn't one either. We both disliked how all a cappella groups sing the same unoriginal set of songs. "'Moondance'?" he'd exclaimed after a concert at the high school in Crampton. "'Good Vibrations'? Are they pensioners?"

"I don't know what that means," I said.

"Old people."

"Yeah, it's like listening to one of the XM oldies stations in the car. And they just *smile* so much."

But despite the way I feel about a cappella singing, I'm given no choice about joining the Barntones. The first practice is Monday afternoon in the music building. I'm just okay as a singer, not great, and I resent that I have to be in this group, so I enter the practice room in a particularly unfriendly, closed-off mood—even more so than usual. The leader of the Barntones, a girl named Adelaide, blows on a little pitch pipe and gathers us together to start rehearsing our first song.

To my surprise, it isn't some cheesy golden oldie, but instead it's a Gregorian chant from the tenth century. "And we're going to do it with a speeded-up tempo," says Adelaide.

This seems peculiar to me, and when we take our places and start to learn the music and the words, which are in *Latin*, it does sound kind of terrible. I wish I could just slip out the door. I'm sure no one would even notice I was gone.

I don't belong in the Barntones. The only place I belong at school is in Special Topics. But it's a strange kind of belonging, because I don't really understand why I'm there. What Mrs. Quenell saw in me. Why she chose *me*, out of all the people at The Wooden Barn.

Everyone in my class has theories about why we were chosen, but truthfully we have no idea. And we also don't know what Mrs. Quenell does or doesn't know about the journals. We've dropped hints all over the place, saying things like, "This is turning into the most intense class ever, Mrs. Q," or even, "We've all been having big experiences when we write in the journals."

When we drop these hints, Mrs. Quenell asks if anything is "too much" for us.

"Does anyone here find the experience of writing in the journal overwhelming?" she wants to know. "Please tell me right now." She searches our faces.

The question can be taken on two different levels. Is she talking about the journals the way *we're* talking about them? Or does she think the journals have a power over us because of the intensity of what we're writing about?

We still don't know. And the more we've gotten used to going to Belzhar, the more it doesn't matter.

I was such a mess after I lost Reeve. And now, twice a week, he and I are together again.

I don't even hate eating all my meals in the dining hall that much anymore. Or not being able to text people or go online, which, at least in the beginning for me and everyone else here, was really hard. And I don't even hate not being able to live in the same house as my parents and Leo.

Leo. Oh, no, I realize that I never wrote to him, like my mom wanted me to. Once again, I vow to write to him tonight.

I don't even hate singing with the Barntones, I suddenly realize as the rehearsal comes to a close. Finally, at the very end, the singing starts to sound better. I hear my own voice poking through, and it's loud and clear and surprisingly decent.

On the following Sunday night our class meets once again in the classroom at 10:00 p.m. Everyone is on time. Casey has brought a box of miniature peanut butter cups with her, and we all eat. Soon there are little brown wrappers scattered all over the floor, and then Griffin pulls a big orange can of Four Loko from under his coat. At first no one says anything.

"Where'd you get that?" Marc finally asks.

"A trip to town. I have my cousin's ID."

The penalty for drinking at The Wooden Barn is getting expelled. There are kids here who have substance-abuse issues, and the school has a zero-tolerance policy, even if you're found with some gross, sweet, alcoholic energy drink. "This is a bad idea, Griffin," Marc says. "And that stuff's disgusting, and people drink it till they get smashed."

"Oh, calm down," says Griffin. "Getting a little smashed isn't going to lower your grades."

"It's not that," Marc says.

"Then what?"

Softly and uneasily Marc says, "Casey."

"*Shit.* Sorry, Casey," Griffin says.

"Don't sweat it," she says lightly. "It's not like I'm never going to be around people drinking to get drunk. Just not yet."

Griffin stows the can, and I'm sure that alcohol will never again make an appearance at one of our late-night meetings. Casey looks over at Marc and nods, and he nods back. They've become close in this one instant; it's amazing how that can happen. It happened to Sierra and me too. A single shared moment.

"Okay," Sierra says. "Time is limited, so no offense but I really want to change the subject." Everyone turns their attention to her. "This has been on my mind. Jam and I were talking one day, and we wondered what happens when you fill the journal up. We got kind of worried that it means you can't go to Belzhar again."

"I've been worried about that too," says Casey. "Because we can't even control how much we write. It's five pages a pop."

"Which is why," I say, "we should definitely stick to the twice a week rule. The journals will last us through the semester, and that's it."

"I know," says Marc. "I did the math too."

"Of course you did," says Griffin.

The remaining journal pages, and the remaining weeks left in the semester, still work out perfectly and unexplainably, the way some things do in life.

Suddenly I remember one of the only things that stayed with me from Dumb Math: Fibonacci numbers. They go like this: 0, 1, 1, 2, 3, 5, 8, 13, 21, 34, 55, 89, 144. To get a number, you add up the previous two numbers. So 0 plus 1 equals 1, and 1 plus 1 equals 2, and 1 plus 2 equals 3, and so on and so on.

Our teacher told us that for reasons no one has ever been able to explain, Fibonacci numbers can be found throughout nature. They're in the leaves on a stem, in the flowering of an artichoke, in the way a pinecone is arranged. A *pinecone*! How random is that? It makes no sense that you can find evidence of Fibonacci numbers everywhere, but it's true.

Thinking about this makes it seem less improbable to me that there could be a bunch of journals that take the people who write in them back to the place where they need to be. Some things just can't be explained, *ever*, and your brain could burst if you think about them too hard.

Thank you, Mr. Mancardi, I think, remembering my cute Dumb Math teacher, who I'll probably never see again, now that I'm living so far away in Vermont. Dumb Math seems like it took place hundreds of years ago. And Reeve—he too is from the past, and yet because of Belzhar I'm able to keep him with me in the present.

Marc says, "I don't know about any of you, but I can't handle the idea of not going to Belzhar when the semester ends."

Casey asks, "What's the deal for you there, Marc? You haven't said yet. No pressure or anything, of course."

"You really want to know? Now?"

"Sure. If you want to say."

"All right," he says. "I have to give you a few facts first, or it won't make sense."

As Marc starts to talk, he seems to be telling his story to Casey alone, and the rest of us are basically eavesdropping.

"Whenever we had to write those essays in grade school answering the question 'Who Is Your Hero?'" Marc says, "my answer was always 'Jonathan Sonnenfeld.' My dad was so smart. He knew everything! He was a lawyer, and late at night he'd be in his study, on the computer."

Marc takes a long gulping breath, as if he were a swimmer

who's just surfaced. And then he says, "It was last April. A school night. I'd said good night to my parents—my mom was already upstairs, and my dad was working late down in the study. I'd gone up to bed, but I couldn't sleep. I had all these plans for the next student council meeting, and I wanted to ask my dad's advice. He was once student council president too.

"So I went down to his study, and the door was half open. He wasn't in there. I could hear him in the kitchen getting himself a snack. But his computer was on, and it was tilted toward me. And this is the part I can't deal with."

Marc stops, his mouth drawn tight. "There was porn on the computer," he finally says. "A sex tape. A woman was *doing* a guy. And I was like, wow, my dad watches porn. And then I thought, okay, big deal, I've seen my share of it too. My friends and I used to search the web at Harrison Sklar's house, when our moms thought we were making flashcards. So what if my dad watches porn? That's none of my business.

"But then I realized . . . I can't believe I have to say this out loud . . . the guy in the sex tape, getting stuff done to him? He *was* my dad. And the woman definitely wasn't my mom."

Everybody is silent. "Shit," says Griffin.

"My dad came back into the den carrying a plate of crackers and cheese and a bottle of beer, and he saw me looking at the screen. He lunged forward and shut it off. It was just the worst moment. And then he said that horrible thing that people in TV shows always say. Want to guess what it was?"

He looks around at our faces. I don't want to guess. But Casey says, "Your dad said, 'I can explain.'"

Very subtly, Marc smiles at her, nodding. "That's right. And I told him, 'I really doubt it, Dad.'

"And then my dad—my *hero*—said, 'Well, your mom and I have been having some problems.'

"And I said, 'So, wait, in order to solve these problems—which I bet Mom knows nothing about—you decide to go to some woman who's probably a *hooker*, and have sex while filming yourself?'

"And he said to me, 'This whole thing has got to be between us. Please. I'm begging you.'

"'Don't fucking *beg* me, Dad,' I told him. 'You're just this middle-aged loser. You're not my hero. Not anymore. And not ever again.' I started yelling, and I grabbed my dad's beer and threw it at his computer. The screen shattered, and my mom came rushing downstairs in her robe.

"She said something like 'What in the world is going on here?' My dad and I had never once had a fight in our lives.

"And I shouted, 'Dad and some woman made a sex tape!'

"And she said, 'No.'

"And I said, '*Ask him.*'

"So Mom looked at him, and in this little voice, she said, 'Jonathan?'

"I don't even remember the rest of the night. There was a lot of yelling and crying. My sister got into it too. And finally my mom kicked my dad out. He moved into the Marriott, and I haven't seen him since. He's called and begged me to see him, but I said no. So why am *I* at The Wooden Barn, when my dad is the one with the problems? Because I stopped sleeping and couldn't concentrate on school or anything. My mom was crying all the time; my dad kept calling me. And the psychiatrist they sent me to suggested I get out of the 'toxic family environment.' She recommended this place, which she thought would be 'gentle.' Not to mention far away."

"I'm glad she did," Casey says.

"I broke up my family in one night," says Marc. "If I hadn't come downstairs, my parents would still be married. My family would be together. My dad would be my hero."

We're all quiet, taking this in. "Tell us about Belzhar," I say. "What happens to you there?"

"I'm saying good night to my parents," says Marc. "I have no idea that within half an hour my family is going to be ruined, and that I'm the one who's going to ruin it.

"The first time I went there, I stayed on the stairs, just hanging out, and my mom was up in bed calling good night to me, and my dad was downstairs calling good night. I know that sounds really feeble for a fantasy, right? It's like . . . the opposite of porn. Standing on a staircase hearing your parents say good night to you. But the fact that nothing bad had happened, and nothing bad was *going* to happen, *ever* . . . it was huge.

"The second time I went there, I realized I could walk around more," Marc continues. "I talked to my parents, and my sister, and I called a couple of friends, and played a video game. The whole house was mine to roam around in. I had no worries. Which will never be the case again in real life.

"Because in real life my mom's depressed, and so is my dad. She put the house on the market; she doesn't want us to live there anymore, because the memories are too painful. She even had a yard sale, and people went in and out, *buying* things that belonged to us. One family bought our *Ping-Pong table*, just carried it away. We used to play doubles, Dad and me against Mom and my sister. That'll never happen again.

"The worst part is that even though my dad won't say it, I know he's really pissed at me. Because he begged me not to tell my mom, and I refused, and then the whole family exploded. My sister has checked out emotionally. She was so relieved to go off to Princeton. I always thought I'd follow her there eventually, except after this happened I started getting Cs in school, so there goes Princeton. Me—Cs! I was the biggest grind you ever saw. Anyway, that's all over. So here I am at The Wooden Barn. Like everybody else here, I'm damaged goods. And the only time I get to feel okay now is when I go to Belzhar."

Marc leans back against the wall, worn out. Beside him, Casey touches his hand, a quick gesture, and then her own hand darts away like a little bird. All of us say sympathetic things; we tell him we're glad he told us about this, and that we admire his honesty.

"I don't think you're damaged goods," Casey says.

"Thanks."

"I mean it. You shouldn't be so hard on yourself," she tells him.

"What happened to me," says Marc, "I know it isn't in the same league as you and Sierra. It's not a car crash or a brother getting abducted. Or," he says, directly to me, "a death." I look down at my hands; I can't bear to look anywhere else.

"Maybe not," says Casey. "But it's the worst thing that's ever happened to *you.*"

The only ones who haven't really told our own stories are Griffin and me. When Sierra asks if anyone else wants to talk now, both of us stay silent.

CHAPTER 12

"OH, I WANTED TO TELL YOU THAT THE BARNTONES performed at morning assembly," I tell Reeve one day in November, as we lie together on the unchanging grass of Belzhar. "And despite the fact that it's a cappella, I don't think the group is a total embarrassment to our species. I know you'll probably find that hard to believe, considering that we share the same views about a cappella singing."

"The Barntones," he says without recognition.

"I told you about them. How I was forced to join?"

"Right."

But he doesn't ask any questions, and I wonder if he was paying attention when I told him about the group in the first place. It's not that I *like* being a Barntone, I say to him, but I've gotten used to it. And the musical selections that Adelaide picks are usually pretty good. Gregorian chants, Elizabethan songs, a couple of recent indie numbers. It's hard to ignore how little interest Reeve seems to have in anything that goes on in my current life. If I mention something from The Wooden Barn, he gets that glazed look. I know it's not his fault; Belzhar just seems to be set up this way.

"I have a surprise for you," he suddenly says. Then he reaches out a hand. We walk together across the flat, hard fields toward a point in the distance where two soccer goals have been set up. "A quick match?" he asks, and though I'm not in the mood, I agree to play a little.

He pulls off his sweater, revealing his red Manchester United T-shirt underneath. Then he takes a soccer ball from where it's been lying in the grass, and we kick it around, the same way we did once back at school. Though he's so much better at this than I am—"football," he calls soccer, in that British way—I actually make a goal, and I do a two-second happy dance.

"Manchester's going to sign you," he says, pleased.

"I'm not so sure," I say. "I think Arsenal has their eye on me."

Standing on the makeshift soccer field with Reeve, both of us a little windblown, I wish I could hurry home to my house on Gooseberry Lane in Crampton and take a quick shower, then get dressed up and go to dinner with him at the Canterbury House, the one really good restaurant in our town.

I'd always had a fantasy of taking Reeve there as a surprise. People say that you're given your own little hot loaf of bread on a slab of wood, and a silver cup of whipped honey butter. Maybe we'd go for our two-month anniversary, I'd thought. I was going to try and scrounge up the money to pay for it.

But dinner at the Canterbury House never got to happen in real life, so of course it can't happen here in Belzhar.

Reeve is oblivious to the limitations. He drops the soccer ball back into the grass and we walk together through the damp, cool afternoon, our hands linked. He tells me about the first time he saw me in gym class. "You were adorable," he says.

"No, you were."

"You were."

"You."

"'They had to agree to disagree about their mutual

adorableness,'" he says, as if quoting from a famous book about our relationship.

We come together and kiss, and it gets serious and deep, our mouths together and then pressed against each other's face and neck, breathing unsteadily and harder. Once in a while we pull back to look, then come forward again.

But then the sky dims, and Reeve says, "Bloody hell," and I say, "Oh shit," and I'm thrust out of Belzhar without even saying good-bye.

Back in my room, it's late at night. DJ's deeply asleep, breathing loudly. Some instinct causes me to go pick up the hand mirror lying on my dresser. I take it over to the window, and in the moonlight I have a look at myself. On my neck is a small purple hickey. I reach a hand toward it, startled, but it starts to fade, and within seconds it's completely disappeared.

Whatever happens in Belzhar leaves no trace in the real world. No shadow, no residue at all. I let my hand stay on my neck and I just want to cry.

The next morning Sierra pops into my room to exchange phone numbers so we can stay in touch over break. It's the week of Thanksgiving vacation, and everyone will be leaving in the next couple of days. I'll miss her even during that short period of time. "Hey," she'll sometimes say when we've been hanging around together and she can see that something's made me suddenly shut down. "You're thinking about Reeve, right?" And I'll nod, and then we'll just stay in silence for a while, neither of us needing to say anything more.

Other times I'll sit in the dance studio watching her rehearse, and I always admire her grace and her force. She has these amazing, tough dancer's feet. And we've gotten into the habit of walking back from the library together during the time of day when the shadows get long and you can drop hard into a gloomy mood if you don't have a friend with you.

I tell her I'll definitely call her when I'm home. But some people at school are getting a little worried that they won't make it home for Thanksgiving at all. A big snowstorm is blowing in from Canada, and will arrive just in time to maybe screw up travel. Some girls are asking permission from the administration to get out early. Me, I'm not concerned, and truthfully I'm in no hurry to leave. While I miss my family sometimes, I still haven't gotten over how my mom wouldn't let me leave school when I'd called and begged her.

Also, I'm a little worried about what it will be like at home. It'll feel strange sitting at Thanksgiving dinner keeping my enormous secret and pretending that I still fit in there, when I don't.

I just want to stay at The Wooden Barn, and in Belzhar with Reeve, but my parents know none of that. They think I had an "episode" the day I called home, and that somehow it passed.

They think I'm recovering from the "trauma" of Reeve. That I've begun to accept that he's gone. They have no idea of what's happened to me, and where I go twice a week, even if it's just inside my mind.

I'm also a little worried about running into my old friends at home. It would be so awkward to see Jenna, Hannah, and Ryan at the mall. "Hi, Jam . . . ," they'd say, tilting their heads to one side and making identical "concerned" faces. The kind of faces they might have learned from a pamphlet called "How to Talk to the Emotionally Troubled Teen." They all feel sorry for me, but I know they've moved past me too. When they see me, a memory will lick at their brains, but then they'll go back to thinking only about themselves.

I actually haven't thought of any of *them* too much either since I've been here. Now I wonder whether Hannah and Ryan have had sex yet, or whether he'll be carrying around that ancient "reservoir tip" condom ("*Ugh!*" we'd shrieked when Hannah told us) for the rest of his life. And if they *have* had sex, whether it was as meaningful as Hannah had wanted it to be, or whether it was awkward, like a trying-too-hard a cappella concert. It's sad that I know almost nothing about Hannah anymore, even though for a long time she was my best friend.

The only thing that will make the trip home okay is knowing that I'll have my journal with me. Once we've gotten through the big Thanksgiving dinner, and I've helped load the dishwasher and scrubbed the crust from a couple of pans, I'll be able to go to bed. And the next morning, when Friday arrives, I'll join Reeve again in Belzhar.

"You missed Thanksgiving!" I'll say to him when we're face-to-face.

"I'm British, Jam, did you forget? Thanksgiving is as meaningless to me as . . . Boxing Day is to you."

"Boxing Day? That's not a real holiday. You made it up."

"Did not."

"Did so."

"Ooh, our second fight."

By Tuesday at The Wooden Barn, the snow is coming down hard, and many people have already left. My parents call and beg me to get on a bus "ASAP," but I don't want to spend an extra day at home if I can help it.

The bus I have a ticket for doesn't leave until Wednesday afternoon. But on early Wednesday morning, with more than half the school gone including DJ, who flew home to Florida the night before, I'm starting to pack my bag when there's a knock at my door. Jane Ann is gathering everyone who's still left for a meeting in the common room.

"Bad news, chickadees," she tells us. "The highway has just been closed. Everything's a sheet of ice."

"What?" someone says, not getting it, but the rest of us understand that no one in this room is going home for Thanksgiving.

"But stay positive," says Jane Ann. "We'll have a lot of fun here. We'll have our own Thanksgiving. I make a mean cranberry sauce. And *lentils,*" she adds. "Mean, mean lentils."

All of sudden, though I'd been nervous about going home, I feel like I might cry. I slip away from the common room, put on my coat, and push through the front door. The snow is really packing the sky, and I can barely see anything, but with my head ducked down I plunge right into it, wanting to be alone and feel sorry for myself.

I am stuck here, a holiday prisoner. I won't be going home at all. As I trudge along the path in the snow, someone standing in the distance waves to me, but I can't make him out. He steps closer; it's Griffin. He stands with his hands in his pockets, his boots planted in the snow.

"Wait, why didn't you go home?" I ask. "I heard that everyone else in Special Topics got out."

"I live right nearby," Griffin says. "My dad's coming to get me with the snowplow. He'll be here any minute. Why are *you* still here?"

"I didn't take an early enough bus, and now I'm trapped," I tell him. And then, idiotically, I start to tear up for real. The tears ice up my eyelashes almost immediately.

"You're crying," he says, confused. The idea of being faced with a crying girl in the middle of a snowstorm just doesn't compute. He won't know what to say or do. Except, after a few seconds, he does. "Come home with me," he says.

"What?"

"You can fit into the cab of the plow if we squeeze you in. You're small."

I look at Griffin through the snow. He's never said anything particularly kind to me before. But I guess the sight of me looking so pathetic, freeze-crying in a snowstorm and stranded on a major holiday, has made him remember that Mrs. Q wanted us to look out for one another.

My parents, naturally, are crushed that I won't be coming home. But on the phone they say at least they're glad I'll have a family to go to on Thanksgiving, even if it isn't them. I'm sent up to my room to quickly finish packing. I do, and then by the time I hurry downstairs, the snowplow has arrived. It's a big, quivering orange monster with an extremely loud motor. Griffin's already inside, and he reaches down and pulls me up.

Suddenly I'm sitting high up in the plow, but with horror I realize that I'm sitting on Griffin Foley's lap. There's nowhere else. His dad's at the wheel, a thicker, bigger, shorter-haired version of Griffin, still good-looking. He shouts something I can't hear, then guns the engine and we're off, shoving snow out of the way with the big curved silver plate of the plow for the entire mile and a half.

I don't move or speak until we pull up at the gate. FOLEY FARMS, I can barely read on the hanging wooden sign. HAND-CRAFTED ARTISANAL GOAT CHEESES.

In the big main room that's crisscrossed with wooden beams, a fire pops and claps in the hearth, and Griffin's mom, a pretty, delicate woman, comes to greet us.

She shows me to my bedroom. It's small, neat, and a little bit on the freezing side, but there's a thick patchwork comforter folded at the foot of the bed. I unpack quickly, taking out my clothes, my toothbrush, and my subject notebooks.

I stop.

My journal's not here.

I paw around inside my weekend bag, but there's nothing else in it. In my hurry to go to Griffin's, I left my red leather journal in the desk drawer in my dorm room, and now I won't be able to go to Belzhar this Friday. This is disastrous, not only for me, but also for Reeve, who'll be waiting, and starting to lose it when I don't show up. Twice a week isn't enough for either of us, but we've both come to accept the schedule. It's still only Wednesday now, and this means I won't have my journal in hand until Sunday afternoon. An eternity.

I turn around to see Griffin in the doorway. "What's the matter?" he asks.

"I forgot my journal."

"Oh," he says. "Well," he adds, not very convincingly, "it'll be okay."

"No it won't. I'm sure you're going to write in your journal while you're here, right?" I ask him. "You wouldn't want to go too many days without doing that."

"Yeah," he admits. "I go on Friday."

"I was supposed to go then too."

"No one would believe how much I write in that thing," he says. "I always had to go to the learning specialist in grade school. I hated to write. One sentence would take me half an hour." He shifts from leg to leg uneasily, and finally he says, "I know you're upset. I don't know what to say."

"There's nothing."

"Sorry." He pauses. "Want me to show you around or something?"

"Sure."

The snow has let up a little, and as we walk around the grounds, I see flashes of well-kept white wooden buildings partially poking up from beneath the snow. The barn looks much newer than all the other buildings on the property.

"Is that where the goats are kept?" I ask, and Griffin nods. "Can we go in?"

"What for?"

"I don't know, just to see them."

Griffin shrugs and says, "Whatever," and we go inside. Goats are everywhere, milling around in clusters or alone. I'm overcome by the sharp, strong smell, which, after a second, I realize I actually sort of like.

"Look at this place," I say. "It's like a goat cocktail party. Can I pet them?"

"If you want."

I pet a few heads, and I think how easy it would be to go through life as a goat. You don't have any problems. You don't fall in love, so you don't get crushed by loss. You just have your simple, farm-animal life, which I envy now.

I go over to a small goat and kneel down, stroking its narrow head. The goat regards me with inexpressive eyes, but doesn't move away. Nearby, a lumpy-looking goat is kept separate from the others in a stall. "What's with that one?" I ask.

"Oh, Myrtle," Griffin says. "She's in the kidding stall."

"You're kidding," I say. It's the kind of dumb line that Reeve and I would've said to each other.

But Griffin just says, "Do you even know what a kidding stall is?"

"Is it . . . when you tell a joke, but you take your time with it? Get it? *Kidding? Stall?*" This, too, is the kind of dumb line Reeve and I would've said to each other.

Griffin just says, "It's where a pregnant doe is sent to give birth. That's what the females are called: does. And the babies are called kids. She's probably going to go into labor this week. My dad's overseeing the whole thing." I look at the face of the poor, isolated doe. I may be reading into things, but she looks fearful, and I don't blame her.

"Is she okay?" I ask.

"She's fine. Let's go," Griffin says, and he leads us back outside. For him it's time to go. End of story. No emotion. He's one of those boys who can get away with being like this. Moody. Silent. There have been boys like that since the beginning of time, and there's nothing to do but try not to let them get to you.

Late that night, fast asleep and actually warm beneath the comforter in my cold little room, I'm awakened by loud talking.

"I'm asking you—no, *telling* you—to get dressed and come help me," says a man's voice.

"I already told you—" says another voice. Griffin's.

I quickly pull on my robe and head out into the main room. Mr. Foley is standing fully dressed and facing Griffin, who looks sleep-stunned in drawstring pajama bottoms and no top. "I'm not trying to give you a hard time," Griffin is saying.

"Then just *do it.*"

"Hi. What's going on?" I ask.

"Sorry we woke you. Our doe is laboring, and she's got a problem," says Mr. Foley. "I need someone to come out there with me. My wife has arthritis in her hands and that rules her out, but Griffin refuses to help."

"Dad, I told you, I'd only fuck it up."

"Watch your mouth, sir. And you have no way of knowing that. You've never done this before."

"Exactly. I *can't,*" says Griffin. "Why won't you get that through your head, Dad?"

"That's all you have to say?" says Mr. Foley. "What is *wrong* with you?"

They look like they're going to take a swing at each other, so I step up and say, "I'll help."

Both of them look at me as if they've already forgotten I'm there. And then, when they remember, they seem to think it's stupid that I've inserted myself into this. How could *I* possibly help? I'm small, and not very strong, and I don't have any useful skills whatsoever. I spent most of a year lying in bed at home until I was shipped off to a misfits' boarding school. But I keep picturing the frightened eyes of the doe in the birthing stall.

"Thanks, but you can't help," says Griffin's father.

"No, I can," I say. "I'll get dressed. Wait, I'll just be a sec."

In our coats, with the snow still coming down, the two of us head out into the cold with Mr. Foley's industrial flashlight. Griffin stays in the house, and as we pick our way through the snow, I turn around and see him framed in the lit window, looking out unhappily. He sees me and steps away.

At night, the barn is a very different place from the day. The doe is moaning, and we crunch quickly across the straw in the dim light to reach her.

"This is Myrtle," Mr. Foley says, though I already know. "Griffin's mother named her." It's as if he wants to assure me that he doesn't believe in anything as sentimental as cute names for goats.

We get right down to business. The problem is that the doe has started to deliver the baby goat—the kid—but the legs are coming out, not the head. "This is a very dangerous presentation," says Mr. Foley, showing me the alarming sight of two baby goat feet sticking out of the mother. "She's a young doe," he says. "A yearling, very small. Hasn't been used for milking yet. I tried to get in there and position the kid's head, but it turns out my hand's too big."

He looks at me in expectation, and I realize he needs me to reach my hand inside the mother goat and straighten out the kid's head. I look at the doe, who's quietly moaning, and even though this is way outside my experience and my comfort zone and way above my disgust level, of course I'm going to do it. Or anyway I'm going to try.

I was wrong earlier when I thought about how easy it was to be a goat. That isn't always true. This goat is in pain, and her eyes are so sad and desperate. I think about how everyone suffers: animals, people, *everyone.* I almost know what she feels, and I have to do what I can.

While Mr. Foley rummages around for a box of rubber gloves that will fit my hand, I go over to Myrtle and stroke her head, saying, "It's okay, it's okay," even though it's not. And then I whisper into her pinkish, hair-prickled ear the first thought that occurs to me, which is a ridiculous one.

"Do you like poetry?" I ask the goat, absurdly. "Sylvia Plath wrote a poem about being pregnant. I think the end goes 'I've eaten a bag of green apples / Boarded the train there's no getting off.'"

All she does is moan further. "Oh, you *don't* like poetry?" I say. "That's okay, you don't have to." Mr. Foley appears with the box of rubber gloves, and I pull one out as if it's a Kleenex. My heart is pounding as I struggle to snap it onto my hand, and it takes two tries.

Now, without thinking, I gently poke around inside the goat. That is what I'm doing, and that is where my hand is: *inside a goat.* How bizarre is that? If somebody back at The Wooden Barn had said to me: "Guess where your hand will be over Thanksgiving vacation?" it would have taken me the rest of my life to come up with the correct answer.

I want to explode with embarrassed laughter now. But then I hear Myrtle moan again, and I forget about the strangeness. Mr. Foley coaches me, and when I locate the head, I try to grasp it but it's slippery, and I have no idea what I'm doing. I make a couple of feeble tries, but I can't get a grip. I'm no good at this. I'm the worst person for this job, totally useless.

Myrtle has boarded a train and there's no getting off; and by agreeing to help her I've boarded a different kind of train. I have to see this through to the end.

"Okay, easy now, Jam," says Mr. Foley. "Take a deep breath. You can do it; I know you can."

And then, suddenly, I get hold of the whole head, feeling the contours, understanding what I need to do. Turning it is like turning a dial, and almost immediately I feel the baby goat shift into a better position, and the nose points down and out.

"There you go," says Mr. Foley.

I pull out my glistening, gloved hand and we watch as Myrtle immediately starts pushing out her kid. How does she know how to do this? She never even attended a single childbirth class. "A single *goatbirth* class," Reeve would have said. "La-m-a-a-a-aze," he might have added, making a sound like a goat.

After a number of pushes, the kid comes out in a glistening heap behind its mother. Mr. Foley goes to look, and announces that it's male—a buck. The umbilical cord ruptures on its own and doesn't need to be cut, like it would with a human baby's. Almost immediately Myrtle, who's no longer moaning, turns around to investigate. She begins to lick her kid to clean off the mucousy stuff that's all over it like glaze. All I hear now is the steady sound of licking, and the occasional nighttime goat noises from all around the barn.

This has to be one of the most thrilling things I've ever done. I wish Griffin had been able to see it. I wish he'd seen me in veterinary-obstetrical-girl-action-hero mode.

"Why don't you go on back to the house and get cleaned up, Jam," Mr. Foley says. "I'll stay here with them."

"Oh, I thought I'd just let Myrtle clean me up," I say. Then, seriously, I ask, "Why didn't Griffin want to be here for this?"

"Well, you know, the fire," he says. And when he sees my blank expression he continues, surprised, "He didn't tell you?"

"No. We're not actually good friends. He was just being nice when he invited me here."

"I see. Well, he doesn't like to talk about it. If I were him, I wouldn't want to talk about it either." He waits a moment, as if trying to decide what else he can tell me. Then he adds, "I'll just say that there was a barn fire here last year and every goat was killed."

"That's *horrible,*" I say, thinking of the goats, and Griffin.

When I get back to the house, Griffin is curled in the window seat of the main room, wrapped in a blanket and asleep. I guess he's been waiting here the whole time. And now I know why. I go stand over him, watching as he sleeps.

"Griffin," I say. "It's a boy."

CHAPTER 13

AT THANKSGIVING DINNER, OVER AN ENORMOUS turkey and various kinds of goat cheese, Griffin's dad raises a glass to me. "There's one person in particular who I'm thankful for. Our guest, Jam," he says. "She was heroic."

"It was nothing, I do it all the time," I joke.

Griffin knocks his glass against the others, but he doesn't smile. After the meal, his mom insists she has the kitchen covered and sends us off. I want to go see Myrtle and her kid, who Mrs. Foley has named Frankie. Reluctantly, Griffin comes with me. In the barn, I crouch down to pet the now cleaned-up buck, who, astonishingly, can already stand and walk, while Griffin stays to the side.

I assume his aloofness is because of the fire. But you'd think he'd be cheered up even a little by seeing the baby goat doing so well. Finally he asks me, "Are you done?" and we leave the barn.

By the next morning, the snow has stopped, and after Griffin takes care of some jobs around the farm, he suggests we go cross-country skiing. I've never done it before, but it turns out not to be as hard as I'd thought. He leads the way across broad white spaces and a frozen lake. Together our skis move back and forth, making identical quiet sounds out here in the open. It seems as if no one is around for miles. Being outside in the wildly white, silent day with Griffin, even after having barely slept the night before, is somehow *bracing*—I think that's the word. When the grounds narrow and he moves ahead of me, I see how graceful he is on these skis.

Then, back at the house, he prepares some cocoa in a little copper pan with a cinnamon stick thrown in. "Mexican style," he calls it, and we take our mugs over to the fire and play a round of the card game Bullshit. His parents are off in the barn, and we have the place to ourselves for a while. Our faces are warm and flushed as we slap down cards on a small, scuffed table.

Without thinking I say, "Your dad told me about the fire."

He looks up from his hand of cards. "Nice going, Dad," he says.

"Well, I'm glad he told me. It's this huge, awful thing that happened to you."

"Not everything should be talked about."

"If you do want to talk about it," I say, "I'd like to hear."

"Why, so you can get all the gory details and discuss it with Sierra back at school?" says Griffin.

"Hardly."

"What happened was my friend Alby came over early that night," he says, his tone flat. "And we got high in the barn, and I guess at the end he must've tossed the joint. Did my dad tell you *that*?"

I try not to react to this. "No," I say. "I didn't know."

"Well, now you do." He slaps down a card. "And in the middle of the night I heard my parents shouting, and I ran outside to the barn. By the time the firemen got there, all the goats had died from smoke inhalation." He sounds entirely unemotional; it's as if he's telling me a story about something much more ordinary. Like about how goat cheese is made.

"That must have been the worst thing in the world," I say.

"It was," he says. "But it's over now."

"That's it?" I say. "'It's over now'?"

"What do you want from me, Jam? There's nothing I can do about it, so I try not to think about it. I try to stay away from the barn, and all the new goats. Don't you ever want to forget what happened to you?"

"Of course. But it doesn't work that way."

Then I realize how little I've thought about Reeve since I've been at the farm, except when I first realized I'd forgotten to bring my journal. I was so upset about not going to Belzhar this weekend, and yet look how well I've adjusted.

Griffin says, "So, what about you? You want to tell me more about that guy? Your boyfriend? Reeve, right?"

I'm surprised he's remembered his name. "What do you want to know?"

"Whatever you want to say."

I dip my head down, looking away. I do want to tell him things, and I think I might actually be able to, a little. I take my time with it, and he doesn't hurry me along. I say, "It was just so *intense*. It kind of took up my entire inner life."

"Go on."

"I woke up every school day and thought about how I'd be with him soon. Our relationship was like one of those YouTube videos of a flower growing in speeded-up motion. All of a sudden we were in love."

"Sounds amazing."

"It is," I say. Present tense.

"You want to say anything more?" he asks. "Like how he . . . Like what happened?" A wave of bad feeling crosses me, and I shake my head. Griffin quickly says, "Sorry, I shouldn't have asked that."

"It's okay," I tell him, but he's right; maybe he shouldn't have asked, for now the subject of losing Reeve is changing the atmosphere, the room temperature. It's amazing how that can happen all of a sudden.

"I didn't mean to upset you," he says.

"I just miss him," I say. "I started to think I was okay about not going to Belzhar this weekend, but I guess I'm not."

"You could write in *mine,*" he suddenly says, and when I look at him, not understanding, he explains, "My journal. Maybe you could get to Belzhar that way."

"*Your* journal? But you'd lose five pages. One whole visit there. You'd do that?"

"Sure," he says, shrugging.

"Well, thank you," I say.

Neither of us has any idea if it will even work, but we go upstairs, and Griffin pulls down a folding ladder from a hatch in the ceiling. Following him, I climb up into the attic bedroom where he tells me he's lived since he was little. It's darker here than everywhere else in the house, because the windows are small and narrow, and the walls are painted blue, like a man cave. The ceiling is sloped, and old posters of grunge bands are tacked up and curling at the edges. The room smells like the inside of a cedar chest. Griffin goes to the desk and opens the top drawer, taking out his journal and solemnly handing it to me.

"Sit here," he says.

I sit down at the little school desk. Carved into the surface in a crude handwriting, it says, MRS. COTLER SUCKS and SCHOOL'S OUT 4 EVER. And in smaller, slightly anxious letters, FUCK IT ALL.

I lay the journal down on the worn surface and open it. "You're sure about this?" I ask him, and he nods. Shuffling through the pages, I try not to read anything, but a couple of phrases pop out: "she was a tease," and "so peaceful it was awsome."

Finally I find the first blank page, and I smooth it down with my hand, and then I smooth it down again. Then I just sit there.

"Go ahead," he says. "I'm serious."

"And you're just going to stay here?" I ask nervously.

"If it's all right with you," he says.

"Okay then," I say. "See you later." And I pick up the pen and write a single sentence:

It's been so hard to be without him.

Right away I'm there. This is the first time I haven't been leaning against the study buddy, and now there are no arms circling me. The light's even gloomier than usual in Belzhar, and it smells strange. A kind of spoiled-milk and fur smell. Goaty, I think, now that I know what a goat smells like.

I'm standing in the middle of an empty space, straw scattered under my feet. This isn't the Belzhar I know, and I'm not on the playing fields; I'm somewhere else.

It's the Foleys' barn, I think. At least kind of, except there aren't any goats here, just their lingering smell. And though I liked the smell before, it's sort of disgusting now.

In the distance comes the peculiar *maa*-ing of a goat, as if the animal is trapped behind the barn wall. I worry that it's Frankie.

Over in the corner of the barn I notice a shape, and I go to see what it is. There, bizarrely, is Courtney Sapol's dollhouse. Kneeling in front of it, I look around for the mother and father dolls, but they're not here now. From somewhere deep inside the dollhouse, a tiny male voice calls, "Jam! Jam!"

"Reeve!" I shout, putting my head at eye level with the house. "Where are you?" I peer into the rooms, but every one is empty.

"I'm here! Where are you?"

"I'm right here. Wait, I'm coming!" I call, but of course I can't get to him. We're in different worlds that overlap a little, but not enough.

Now I thrust my face deep into the living room of the dollhouse and peer out the windows on the other side. A pasture is visible, and in the distance is a single, solitary figure. I can't make him out, but he's tiny, doll-size, and as he comes toward the windows I'm so relieved to see that it's Reeve.

But then he trots closer to the house, and finally he's up against the windows, and, yes, he's Reeve, but he's got the body of a goat, with hooves and white fur with pinkish skin beneath.

Reeve and the goat have been hideously fused together, and the freakish creature they've become opens its mouth, draws back its upper lip, and cries out, "Ja-a-a-a-a-a-a-a-am!" The syllable sounds half human, half goat—the agonized cry of a creature that isn't one thing or another, and can't bear it.

"Jam, come back!" I hear. "Come out of Belzhar!"

The words snap me sharply to attention like a phrase spoken by a hypnotist. With a violent pull, I'm suddenly thrust upward and out of that fucked-up, hybrid version of Belzhar.

And now I'm facing Griffin, who just stares at me, while I stare right back. We sit together for a minute, not saying a word. I realize my heart's been beating very fast, and I put a hand to my chest, calming myself down and trying to get back to normal as best I can.

"What was that? You seemed frantic," Griffin says quietly. "And you're shaking."

I hadn't realized, but it's true.

"Put this on," he says, and he takes off his maroon hoodie, one of his rotation of several hoodies. It's huge on me, of course, but it somehow makes me feel better. I actually stop shaking.

"I was half in my Belzhar and half in yours," I explain. "And Reeve was there, but he was part goat. It was like a nightmare. Writing in another person's journal, I guess, creates a mash-up of two totally different Belzhars."

"Amazing."

I think about how the goat was bleating, and Reeve was calling my name, and I was shouting from my place in the empty barn that lies on the boundaries of those separate worlds.

"And you know, the way you were writing was pretty strange," says Griffin. "It was like an in-class essay and you had a lot to say. So then I looked down at what you'd written."

"But that's private."

"Sorry. My eye just went there, and I—" He cuts himself off in the middle of a sentence.

"What?" I ask.

"Have a look."

He hands me his journal, and this is what I see:

> *It's been so hard to be without him.*
>
> *AFykapoufdaba"jdqcsdgyjepayriq;'a*

"What *is* this? After the first line, it's just *nonsense,*" I say. "And I kept writing on top of my own writing. *That's* what I was doing?"

"Yeah."

"At least I barely took up any of your space," I say. "I don't think you'll have to give up a whole trip after all." Then I ask him, "Why were you so generous to me, letting me do this?"

Griffin shrugs and looks uncomfortable. "I don't know your situation, exactly," he says. "But being in love, and having your boyfriend die suddenly? That's so unfair. I know you didn't tell us the specifics, but I'm thinking maybe it was violent or something." I don't reply. "You don't have to answer me, Jam," he adds. "You never do. I just wanted to say that."

It's up to me to say something back, but I can't. Think about what happened, Dr. Margolis always said, and the way you describe it.

But it's so hard to talk about, and my thoughts get all chopped-up. It's a lot easier now to talk about anything other than myself. "Your journal," I suddenly say. "Can I read it?"

"First you complain about me looking at the nonsense *you* wrote," says Griffin. "And now you want to read what *I* wrote?"

"I don't really know much about you."

"As I told Mrs. Q," he says, "I suck ass as a writer."

"I don't think you used those exact words."

"Maybe not."

So Griffin agrees to let me sit on his bed and read his journal while he waits at his desk. The writing and the spelling are awkward and immature in places, but it's definitely him. It's not only that I don't want to talk about myself anymore. I'm also very curious about him. I start with the first page:

> *My name is Griffin Jared Foley and I am sixteen years old and live on Foley Farms where my family makes goat cheese. I have always been different from the rest of my family. They are*

country people in all ways. They love it here and don't see the need to go anywhere else. It is very beautifull here in Vermont I agree. But I guess I am restless. Ever since I was little I was that way. In school when I was a kid I hated sitting still, and I always jumped up and talked too loud and got in trouble with Mrs. Cotler, who looked like she would have a conipshion.

I was sort of wild, I can totally see that now. I liked to go sledding, and not just on sleds but on anything I could find. Pieces of cardboard, cafateria trays, etc. Once when I was ten I and two freinds took our sleds out to Hickory Hill in the middle of the night. Like at three AM. It was awsome. We got grounded for days but we didn't care. We would always have that sled ride to remember.

"You can skip ahead, you know," Griffin says from across the room, his voice kind of strained and self-conscious. "The first part is just me as a dopey kid. You can go to a later part if you want."

So I skip far ahead in the journal:

I don't like to write very much about that night. There's no point. Obviously it was horrible. My parents say I owe them a big apology. But what good would that do? Nothing can help. It's best to just try and move on. To say, what happened was really bad. And it was.

I was at a party at Lee Jessup's a mile away that night. It was just a bunch of local kids getting wasted. So what else is new. I had gotten bored with this to be honest. It was all we'd been doing since ninth grade. There would be junk food like Ho-Hos and Pringles. And weed. Mountains of weed. Alby Stenzel grew it in his bedroom with special lights. Somehow his parents had never noticed. I stayed late at the party, mostly because of Alby's sister Grace. I was flirting with her even though everyone said she was a tease. Also I don't think she's too intelligent. I know I am a sucky student, but that is different from not being intelligent. At least in my humbul opinion.

Finally Alby and me (Alby and I?) left. Standing in the road it was so peaceful it was awsome. Alby didn't want to go home yet, and I said he could hang at my place for a while. So we rode his dirt bike to my farm, and we lay in the straw in the barn with the goats. Man I loved those goats, but especially Ginger, who'd recently been born, and who kind of thought she was a dog. She had such a dog face, it was so cute.

I was petting her, and Alby lit a joint like he always did, and we lay around talking about how we'd be the prisoners of our parents for only a few more years, and then we'd be liberated. I said, "But what if being on our own is too hard? My mom makes all my meals. I don't even know how to do anything like that. I only know outdoor stuff. But I still want freedom."

He said, "We should learn to cook, man."

And I said "Yeah." We made a plan that we would get together and teach ourselfs to cook 3 things: eggs benedict, pan-fried steak, and chicken any style. We talked like this until really late. And then he left, and I went to bed. And the next thing I knew my mom and dad were screaming, "The barn's on fire!"

We couldn't get inside, it was too late, and the fire trucks took a while to come, so the goats died of smoke inhalation. Every single one of them. When the flames were out I went into the barn and saw them laying there, and it was just the worst thing I've ever seen. It's been imprinted on me forever. I see it all the time. Poor Ginger was in the corner, and her eyes were open. She was staring at me.

My parents were yelling, "How did this happen?" And then one of the firemen said, "Come look at this," and he showed us the joint end. And I felt a chill go across my whole body. Without thinking, I said, "Fuck."

"It was you?" my mom said. "You killed the goats, Griffin?"

"Yeah, I'm a goat murderer, Mom," I said. "That's exactly what I am."

"How could you do this?" my dad shouted. "Smoking your stupid pot like that. You know how we feel about it. Get out of my sight. Tomorrow I will deal with you."

I was freaking out. They were blaming me, not knowing the facts. Not knowing that Alby was the one with the weed. The one who must have thrown the joint out, and it smoldered. Plus, no matter what they said, blaming me wasn't going to change anything. The goats couldn't be brought back to life.

I felt like I couldn't breathe, and I couldn't see. Later, when the firemen and the police were gone and my parents had finally gone to bed, the animals still lay all around because nothing could be done with them until morning. Ginger would be out there staring at nothing all night long. Nobody had even closed her eyelids like they do with dead bodies in movies.

I lay in my own bed, staring at nothing too. My eyes were dry though. I couldn't cry. They were dry and wide open.

So the next day my dad would "deal with me." Oooooooo, I thought, I'm shaking. Big angry Dad.

But I wasn't going to stick around for that. I snuck out of the house with the keys to my Dad's pick-up truck at 4 AM. I had a learner's permit, but no plan. I just knew I had to get away. I drove on the highway heading north, up to Maine, blasting a heavy metal station the whole way. Finally I was so wiped that I pulled over at a rest stop. I closed my eyes and fell asleep with my head on the steering wheel.

Suddenly two cops were banging on the window. I rolled it down, and they said "your under arrest for possessing a stolen vehicle."

WTF?

My parents had called the cops on me and reported their truck as stolen, in order to teach me a "lesson." I was brought back to Vermont in cuffs, which is very painful, and I spent a few hours in a special cell with other "minors." There was a crazy violent kid in there who looked like a teenaged meth head. He literally had black teeth, and he called me Blondie and punched me in the nose because he said I was looking at him funny.

Yeah well, buddy, I thought, maybe you should try not having black teeth, and then no one will look at you funny.

Finally my parents came to pick me up, and they were shocked to see my bloody nose. My mom started crying. I was, like, what did you think was going to happen? We were all screaming at each other again, and I couldn't stand it.

So over the next few months I stayed quiet. I just did not engage. And then there was a court date about the stolen truck, and the judge said my family had "a lot of anger," and that I had to go attend school at The Wooden Barn.

So here I am. Lucky, lucky me. Griffin Foley, professional goat killer and truck stealer, unloved by his mother and father both.

That's where the last entry ends. I close the journal and tell him I'm done, then he gets up from the desk and comes over to me. "You want to start yelling at me too?" he asks. "Tell me how I fucked everything up?"

"Stop it. You sound like—"

"Such a dick?"

"I wasn't going to say that."

"But you thought it. It's only when I'm in Belzhar that I feel okay."

"Well, me too, Griffin. It's the same for all of us. I know you haven't talked about it—"

"It's not easy for me."

"I know," I say. "And no one's going to make you." But it occurs to me that maybe, now, he wants to tell me. "What happens to you when you go there?" I ask. "Can you say?"

"I'm in the barn again," he says. "Me and Alby. The old barn, not the new one, and we're talking about life, and I'm stroking Ginger's head, and everything's cool. The goats are safe. The original goats, not the replacements. And no one's blaming me for everything. I'm not this *monster*. I feel good."

I wish he could have that good feeling all the time, not just when he's in Belzhar. I want to feel good, too; when I'm here, not just when I'm there. And I suddenly have the idea that it's possible. Without stopping and trying to think it through, I stand up and kiss Griffin on the mouth, hard.

"Whoa," he says, backing up. Then he touches his own mouth and laughs. I've shocked him; I've shocked myself. But then he comes forward and we kiss again. I know that he is a big, inexpressive, withholding boy and that I am in love with Reeve and should not be doing anything like this. But I am.

We sit on his bed together, looking and looking at each other. I remember the way Griffin had angrily said to me at the social, "What are you looking at?" Now I'm allowed to look, and I take my time. We touch each other's face and hair and hands, and then he unbuttons his shirt and shrugs out of it. Both of us just want to feel good again, that's all we want. I take off his hoodie that I'm wearing, and then with a shaky hand I remove my own shirt, and then even my tank top.

I never got to do this with Reeve, and because of the rules of Belzhar, I never can.

But in this attic room with Griffin, I can do what I want. My hand is free to move wherever my brain instructs it to. Griffin and I lie down together, our arms around each other, and I feel his warm skin, his cold belt buckle. When we kiss again, it lasts. For a few minutes in this place and time, we're both actually so happy.

In the distance, then, we hear voices. "Griffin? Jam? Are you up there?"

"*Oh, fuck,*" says Griffin, leaping away, climbing over me to grab his shirt. His face looks guilty, and I'm sure mine does too, as I grab my own shirt. He's got his parents to worry about, but I've got Reeve, which is worse.

There's no way to make what's just happened be okay. I can't do this with Griffin when I'm still in love with Reeve. It will never happen again.

I quickly glance into the mirror over the dresser, and that's when I see the very small hickey that Griffin has left on my neck. Boys can't seem to help but leave marks; they scatter them as carelessly as pebbles in a pond. I run my hand across it, expecting it to fade instantly like the one Reeve gave me in Belzhar. But this one stays, because it's real.

CHAPTER 14

"WHERE HAVE YOU BEEN?" REEVE SAYS WHEN I finally get back to Belzhar. "I thought you'd be here *days* ago."

"I'm sorry," I say, which is a totally inadequate reply. He doesn't make a move toward me, but stands in the field with his arms crossed. "See, what *happened*," I say, "is that I accidentally left the journal at school. It was a disaster."

Reeve just keeps standing there, looking at me, trying to decide whether or not to forgive me. And when, after thirty seconds he does forgive me, I know it's not as if he even had a choice. He's been here agitated and waiting, while I've been out in the world. He doesn't ask a single question about the journal, or where I was when I wasn't with him. He's never showed much interest in how I travel to and from Belzhar. Or even that I *call* it that. He just knows that somehow I always get here, and that's what counts.

It's Sunday afternoon, not a day that I ever go see him, but I've just returned from the long weekend at Griffin's farm, and I didn't want to wait any longer. Girls have been trickling into the dorm with their suitcases. DJ isn't due back for at least an hour, so I have time to write in the journal I left behind and make the trip uninterrupted, instead of having to wait until late at night when she would be asleep.

So here in Belzhar, after Reeve forgives me, we walk together through the brown fields and gray day arm in arm, but he's still distant. "You don't *seem* like you forgive me," I finally say.

"It was a bit much," he admits. "Give me a little time." We walk farther, and then he says, "I wondered if you were ever going to come back."

"You really thought I might not?"

"Sort of."

"I wouldn't do that to you," I tell him.

But our lives are so different. I've got people around me all the time, and school. Mrs. Quenell's class has picked up speed. We're deep into analyzing Sylvia Plath's poetry, and line after line is so tricky and surprising. Plath uses words that you'd never expect; they just seem to come out of nowhere, and when I'm reading her I often think, *How the hell did you come up with that, Sylvia Plath?*

Even when I can't relate on a personal level, she makes me know what *she* feels, and that's really something. To find out what another human being feels, a person who isn't you; to get a look under the hood, so to speak. A deep look inside. That's what writing is supposed to do.

Then there's Mrs. Quenell herself. I wasn't sure of what to make of her at first, but I've come to see that she's an interesting person and a great teacher. I think everyone in the class would agree by now. I know that Sierra does; she and I talk about Mrs. Q fairly often, and about how involved we are in Special Topics.

Casey's been arriving on time every day too. Somehow she's figured out a way. We all show up and throw ourselves into the discussion, even Griffin. We might have an argument about a line of poetry from Plath's collection, *Ariel,* but sometimes I know in those moments that we're really arguing about something much bigger and harder to describe.

Everyone seems like an exaggeration of themselves during Special Topics. Marc gets ultralogical, Sierra sees the sad beauty in everything we read, and Casey always defends Plath's "edginess," as she calls it, while Griffin is really big on anything he considers "blunt."

And me, whenever there's something on the page that's about love, I'm there right away, practically in tears.

We still don't know why Mrs. Q chose us, what she saw in us, or if she has a clue about the journals. But we do know that the journals are saving us, and the class discussions are making us better too.

We all have a lot to occupy our thoughts, and Reeve has very little. I feel the difference, and maybe I'm guilty about it because now, in Belzhar, when he's obsessing about his fear of being abandoned by me, I remind him, "Being with you is what I want," and I make sure my voice sounds forceful and true.

"There was one point when you were gone this weekend," Reeve says, "when I thought I heard your *voice*. But it couldn't have been you, because you were a *giant*. It was very frustrating." He pronounces "frustrating" with the accent on the second syllable. Frus*tra*ting. Reeve and his British-speak.

"That *was* me," I say. "We were stuck in different worlds."

"I didn't know what to do," Reeve says, sounding vulnerable and uncertain. Which is appropriate, considering. I've betrayed him with Griffin, and he didn't do anything to deserve it. "I'm sort of beat," he goes on. "Mind if we take it easy today?"

"Sure."

"I thought we could watch something," he says, and in the

distance I see a couple of folding chairs set up on the grass, and a flat-screen TV. A telly, as Reeve would say. I sit down beside him, relieved that now we won't have to talk. He presses the remote control and the show starts. It's the dead parrot sketch from *Monty Python* that he and I have already seen together. He'd wanted to show it to me early on in our relationship because it was something that was important to him.

On-screen, the comedian John Cleese enters a pet shop and says, "'Ello, I wish to register a complaint." And there's some back-and-forth conversation, and he says, "I wish to complain about this parrot what I purchased not half an hour ago from this very boutique."

The pet shop owner asks him what's wrong with the parrot. And John Cleese says, "It's dead, that's what's wrong with it!"

And the owner says, "No, no, it's resting, look!"

But I'm a little bored watching it again now; I know everything that's going to happen in the sketch, just as I know everything that can possibly happen in Belzhar. Or at least I know the rough outlines of what can happen. When the sketch ends, Reeve says, "Come here, you," and pulls me down onto the grass. We stay like that, lying on our backs and looking up at the sky.

There isn't all that much to talk about today. What's he supposed to say to me? "Let me tell you some stories you've already heard a few times? And you can laugh and murmur and respond to them as if they're new?"

And what am I supposed to say to him? "Let me tell *you* what happened between me and Griffin?"

Instead I say, "Hey, news flash from my life. Guess what I did over my Thanksgiving vacation?"

"No idea."

"Had my hand in a goat's vagina. But then again, who *didn't*?"

Reeve raises an eyebrow, but doesn't ask me what the hell I'm talking about.

"You're not even curious about what I mean by that?" I ask. "A goat's vagina?"

"Of course I'm curious," he says, and I launch into the story about helping to deliver the kid. But of course he isn't really interested. The goat exists outside the world of our past, the world of him and me.

But it's right inside the world of Griffin and me. I look down at the swirl of Reeve's hair, his sweater, his eyes, and his nose and mouth. His philtrum. Then, for lack of anything more to say, I start to touch his face, running my hand along the curling lips, the chin, hoping we can get over the strangeness between us.

When we kiss, it seems a little off, because I'm distracted. No matter what angle I approach him from, it doesn't feel right.

"Something's different about you," he says after a moment.

"No, nothing."

But I remember the kiss between Griffin and me, and how it felt, and how we took off our shirts, and looked and looked at each other. The way our chests touched like two hands meeting in prayer.

Two hands meeting in *prayer*? That's like the crappiest line of poetry that Sylvia Plath might've written when she was twelve years old and then immediately thrown in the garbage. What happened between me and Griffin wasn't poetic; it was unthinkable. Yet it's also something I keep thinking about.

Reeve says, "Promise me everything's sorted between us."

And at that moment the light does its predictable big fade, so luckily I don't have to promise.

Back on my bed at The Wooden Barn, I've barely had time to recover, when I hear a loud *thump* out in the hall. The door swings open and DJ appears, lugging in her giant suitcase. She's a little sunburned from her trip home to Florida, and a sunburn looks out of place on a girl who mostly dresses in black, with the occasional flash of startling color.

"DJ, you're here! And you're early. I'm so glad to see you." It's true. All I want is for her to talk to me about her vacation and tell me funny, snarky stories and cheer me up. But DJ starts to cry.

"Oh, Jam," she says. "Everything's destroyed."

"What do you mean?"

"Between me and Rebecca."

"What happened?" I sit her down on her bed and hand her a box of tissues.

DJ blows her nose emphatically and then says, "She went home to Connecticut, and we were texting each other like crazy, right? Getting my phone back was *dope*. It was like . . . discovering penicillin all over again."

"Yes, I remember when you discovered penicillin the first time."

"You know what I mean. Technology, remember that?" she says through her tears. "I've been *starved* for it. Anyway, we sent each other a ton of sexy texts."

"Okay," I say, waiting, afraid that I know what's coming.

"We weren't *sexting*—that's gross—but we'd write 'u r hot in your Dora the Explorer T-shirt.' Or, 'sneak into my bed when u get back and say it wuz 1 on 1 tutoring.' Well, her mom read the texts and did a big freak-out. And she told Rebecca that she can't come back to The Wooden Barn, because it's turned her into 'a female homosexual'! That's how she put it! Like someone might think she'd turned into 'a *male* homosexual!'"

"She's making Rebecca leave school?" I say. "In the middle of the year?"

DJ nods and wipes her hand across her face, smearing her mascara in a big black wave like a calligraphy brushstroke. "I'll die if I can't be with her."

"I understand."

"No offense, but I doubt it," she says. And then without warning DJ strides over to her bed, flips up the mattress and goes rooting around under it. She grabs an armful of hidden loot: granola bars, Fruit by the Foot, and packets of those bright orange cheesy peanut butter crackers. Then she goes to her desk and pulls out a bag of shortbread cookies and a bag of M&M'S and even the squeeze bottle of Hind's ketchup.

"What are you doing?" I ask. She doesn't answer. "DJ, *stop*," I say, but she keeps going around the room, hunting and gathering. She yanks open my top dresser drawer and roughs up all the underwear inside, searching.

"*Look!*" she says, brandishing the treasure she's found: the jar of jam Reeve gave me.

"STAY THE FUCK AWAY FROM MY TIPTREE LITTLE SCARLET STRAWBERRY!" I scream in a voice I never knew I possessed. DJ and I look at each other, equally shocked. In a much more sane and controlled voice, I add, "It's just that it's kind of a *memento*, this jar. I don't want anyone opening it, okay?"

I take a deep breath, then take the jar from her, burying it deeper in the drawer. When I turn around, DJ has already gone back to plundering the room for food.

Finally she seems to have enough. She flips down her mattress, plants herself on her bed cross-legged with her bounty in front of her, and begins to make her way through the pile, crying while she does. I've never seen someone cry and eat at the same time.

"Come on, stop," I say, but she ignores me, and just chows down cookies and crackers, methodically pushing them into her mouth without any pleasure. "Please, DJ," I say. "You'll just get sick and puke like a frat boy."

I grab some of the food from her, but I can't manage to get all of it, and she eats what she can. Appalled, I watch as she pops open the ketchup, tilts back her head, and squeezes. The bottle makes a loud farting sound, and she lets a long, slow red stream of ketchup descend into her open mouth.

The door bursts open then, and we both look up. DJ's girlfriend, Rebecca, stands there in her white winter coat and long violet-colored scarf, her face bright with cold. DJ leaps up. "You're back?" she cries. "No shit?"

"No shit."

"But what about your mom?"

"I told her if she didn't let me come back to school to be with my girlfriend, she'd regret it. I said I'd send e-mails to every member of the Connecticut Moms for Traditional Values Club, telling them I was a proud member of the LGBTQ community. But course she was like, L-G-*what?* So I had to explain what LGBTQ *meant* in order to get her flipped out enough to let me come back to you."

"But you did come back," says DJ.

"I did."

She and Rebecca embrace, but then after a few seconds Rebecca pulls away and looks at her and asks, "What's that red junk on your face?" DJ says it's nothing, she'll tell her later. Finally Rebecca notices me and says vaguely, "Oh, hey, Jam," and then she and DJ walk out of the room together and go off to draw on each other's hands with henna tattoo pens or make beautiful love or whatever.

I plan on giving DJ a lecture later about how she can't use a crutch—in her case junk food—to calm herself down every time there's a bump in the road. But as a student of Mrs. Quenell's, I'm embarrassed by those clichés and mixed metaphors—"crutch"; "bump in the road." And anyway, I'm hardly one to talk. I used Griffin to feel better about not getting to see Reeve over Thanksgiving vacation.

Isn't that what I did? Just used him for his looks and how aloof he is? When someone's withholding, it makes you want them more. I'm just not sure of anything now. I wish I could binge out on food like DJ did, going over to the pile on her bed and taking comfort from some tasteless old granola bars and a long drink of ketchup. But I know that none of it would help at all.

CHAPTER 15

IN SPECIAL TOPICS THE NEXT MORNING, ON OUR first school day after break, it's obvious that so much has changed since we were all together last. I barely look over at Griffin, afraid that if I do, someone might notice what's happened between us. As we all sit at the oval table waiting for class to begin, Griffin is no longer slouched down, his head in his hoodie. Instead, the hoodie is off and he looks over at me, his eyes alert and questioning. But I keep my expression neutral and turn toward the window. I don't want anyone to know what's happened.

But it isn't just us. Casey enters pushed by Marc, and both of them distinctly seem to have a secret. Even Sierra seems different. Though we'd hung out when she got back from break, she seemed quiet. And now she keeps to herself before class begins, busying herself with her papers, shuffling them a lot more than necessary.

When Mrs. Quenell comes in, she sits down, looks around at us with a slow smile, and then says, "Together at last."

"How was your break, Mrs. Q?" Casey asks.

"Oh, fine, Casey, thank you for asking. I got a head start on packing, because as you know I'm moving out of my house right after classes end. Right now I'm still swimming in a sea of bubble wrap. How about the rest of you?"

Everyone says vague, positive things about Thanksgiving.

"You all seem a little . . . heightened," Mrs. Quenell says, and that's an accurate word. But nobody's willing to say specifically what's going on with them.

The odd energy in the classroom carries over into our discussion about Plath, who we return to as if she were an old friend. Today we're talking about an early poem called "Mad Girl's Love Song." She wrote it in college, and Mrs. Quenell asks Casey if she would read the first three stanzas aloud. Casey takes a breath and starts to read:

"'I shut my eyes and all the world drops dead;
I lift my lids and all is born again.
(I think I made you up inside my head.)

The stars go waltzing out in blue and red,
And arbitrary blackness gallops in:
I shut my eyes and all the world drops dead.

I dreamed that you bewitched me into bed
And sung me moon-struck, kissed me quite
insane.
(I think I made you up inside my head.)'"

During the short but intense reading, I can barely move or think. I feel my heart knocking inside me. Sylvia Plath understands everything about love. What it does to you. What it did to me.

She knows me.

For a little while after the poem gets read, I sit very still, trying to calm the knocking. I see that Mrs. Quenell is looking at me, and I feel sure she knows something. Just like Plath, she seems to know everything.

I remember some meditation trick that Dr. Margolis taught me—how if I start to feel overwhelmed, I should just focus on my breathing. "Breath goes in, breath goes out," he'd said in a slow, hypnotic voice. "Breath goes in, breath goes out."

I keep breathing rhythmically now and try not to think of anything at all. At first it seems to work, and my thoughts of Reeve start to disappear. But then a new batch of thoughts arrive. Thoughts about Griffin, who's sitting only two seats away from me. I didn't want to sit right next to him today, because it would have been too much.

Belzhar can't be explained, but what went on between Griffin and me can't really be explained either.

I think I made you up inside my head, I think, and the line refers to Reeve and Griffin equally.

After class, Griffin stops me in the hall and says, "You left something at the farm." It's the first time we've talked since we've been back at school. He reaches into his backpack and pulls out the maroon hoodie he'd lent me.

"No, that's yours."

"You take it. I have others. Like, five hundred of them."

"I noticed." He presses the hoodie into my arms. "Listen, Griffin," I say. "The thing that happened when we were at the farm? It can't happen again."

He looks hard at me. "Oh," he says. "Okay." Then he pauses and adds, "Are you sure?"

"Yes. I'm sorry," I tell him, and then I turn away before he can say anything else. I'm still carrying his hoodie in my arms, and I don't have the heart to give it back.

But late that afternoon, alone in the dying light of my dorm room, trying to make sense of my French homework, I put on his hoodie again. It's much too big, but it keeps me warm, and it smells human, physical, as if another person's arms and chest have been inside it day after day. A specific person. Him. I like knowing that. Wearing the hoodie makes me feel as if he's nearby.

Which is somehow what I want, despite having told him that what we did can never happen again.

That night the five of us gather in the dark classroom, a special Monday night meeting because Marc got back late the night before. The meeting feels as urgent as our very first one, back when we were all trying to make sense of what was happening to us.

Marc helps Casey out of her chair, then positions her beside him. "Well, we have an announcement," he says.

"*We?*" says Griffin.

"Marc and me. We kind of got together," Casey says shyly. "But it's more than that. It's become something big."

"That's excellent," says Sierra. "How did it happen?"

"Oh, we started texting over break," Marc says. "And I asked if I could take the shuttle down and see her in New York. It was too depressing in my house. We went to the Museum of Natural History to look at the dinosaurs, and out for Chinese dumplings. We had a great time."

"So it's serious?" I ask.

"Oh yeah," says Casey. As if to demonstrate, she leans her

head against Marc, and they look like the most serene, long-term couple in the world.

Sierra lifts a paper cup of green Gatorade in their honor, and says, "This is the best news." Then, when Casey and Marc have said everything they want to say, Sierra says, "Now I have to tell you all something too."

Has she fallen for someone? Have love and sex swept over our entire class the way Belzhar did? But when she leans forward I can tell this isn't about hooking up or falling in love. This is something else, but I don't know what.

"I think I might know who took my brother," she says.

"*What?*" I say.

"I went to Belzhar over Thanksgiving, of course," Sierra says in a rush, "and I was sitting on the bus with André, like always. When he fell asleep, I started looking around at other people. I've been to Belzhar a lot, of course, but I've only really focused on my brother. I can't believe it took me so long. And I noticed this one guy in his fifties—white, scrawny, gray hair. He was just sitting there kind of watching André like it was the most interesting sight in the world.

"I said to him, 'Excuse me, can I help you?' He just turned away from me. So I spent the rest of the ride thinking about where I'd seen him before, because I knew I had.

"And then I remembered. He'd been to one of our dance concerts. They're open to the public, and tickets are free. But I remembered that he'd been to both performances, the early one and the late one, and that he'd sat up front. And when I noticed him on the bus, looking at André, something clicked.

"So over Thanksgiving, after I went to Belzhar, I called

Detective Sorrentino again and described this guy to him. And he said something like, 'So I'm supposed to believe that after *three years*, you suddenly remember a particular person on the bus that day?' And I said yes. And he said, 'So what is it, a recovered memory?' I said I didn't know what that meant, and I begged him to try and track down this guy. But when I called back on Sunday, he admitted that he hadn't done anything, like interview the staff of the dance academy again, or talk to people who said they'd been to those shows back then. 'I decided it isn't a high-value lead' is what he said."

"But you *saw* the guy," says Casey. "What could be higher value than that?"

"I saw him in Belzhar," Sierra reminds her. "What am I supposed to tell Sorrentino?"

"But it's infuriating," I say. "It could be a real lead. Can't you get your parents involved?"

Sierra shakes her head. "No, not anymore. Every time I think I have a lead and then it turns out to be nothing, it's so hard for them. I can't involve them again. They're worn out, they're barely functioning. Just because this guy was looking at André on the bus in Belzhar doesn't prove anything. But I have to get Sorrentino to follow up. I'm going to keep calling all the time from the pay phone. But I don't have a lot of faith in the system, to put it mildly."

She stops talking and we're all silent, and she looks over at Griffin, and then at me. Then she does it again. Sierra is a perceptive person, and since we've gotten so close, she knows me. "Wait, what's the deal?" she asks.

"What do you mean?" Griffin says.

"Come on," says Marc. "I saw something in class today too. You and Jam. What's going on?"

I can't imagine what to say, but I don't have to say anything, because Griffin does. "Something happened between us," he says, and I'm shocked.

"Griffin, that was private," I say. "And besides, I told you it can't happen again."

Everyone is totally fascinated by our little soap opera, and they just keep looking back and forth between us.

"I'm sick of keeping everything in, okay, Jam?" he says. "Walking around *feeling* things, and then they can't be talked about. I'm just sick of it."

"But you still didn't have to announce it," I say.

We stare at each other. "It can really never happen again?" he asks.

I can't believe we're talking about this in front of everyone. "I don't know," I finally say, which is the same as saying, Yes, Griffin, it can happen again. And if you want to know the truth, I want it to happen again.

The others are still watching us, and I realize I'm not mad at him anymore. It's done now; it's out. I take his hand. It's past time for us to go back to the dorms, but no one wants to get up. We all sit for a little while longer in this close and glowing circle.

CHAPTER 16

SNOW FALLS ON VERMONT, BUT NOT ON BELZHAR. Griffin and I walk along wet, white paths together in our down jackets and boots. Only when we're deep in the woods do we hold hands or stop to touch or kiss, and our hair and eyelashes become dotted with snow. We barely talk, because he knows what I'm thinking, and there's nothing we can say that will make me feel okay about my double life.

In Belzhar, the air is cool but not cold, and the grass remains brown, without a single flake of snow. Each time I go there, Reeve is tensely waiting. He has no idea about Griffin, and though I've explained to him how the journals work, he doesn't understand what all of us in Special Topics fear: that a rapidly filling journal is like a ticking clock.

Back and forth between worlds I go, like a demented, hallucinating bigamist.

One afternoon during mail call, I receive a letter from my mom that upsets me further:

Dear Jam,

We were so sorry to miss you over Thanksgiving, but Christmas will be here before you know it, and we're all THRILLED that you'll be home for two and a half whole weeks. First, a little news. I ran into Hannah's mom at the mall, and she told me that Hannah and Ryan broke up. Naturally, that was a surprise, and I thought maybe you'd want to drop Hannah a line. I'm sure she'd love to hear from you.

Now, on to what I really wanted to discuss. As I told you, Dad and I have been concerned about Leo since he's been hanging around with that Connor Bunch. Then this week something shocking happened. I'm just going to go ahead and write it: Leo was arrested for shoplifting at Price Cruncher. Yes, that's right, LEO.

Introverted, nerdy, twelve-year-old Leo, *arrested*? She's right; I'm shocked too. Far more shocked than I am about Hannah and Ryan, which is also pretty shocking. After I read my mom's news about Leo, I have to put down the letter for a full ten seconds before continuing:

He stole a can of orange spray paint, can you believe it? He shoved it down his shirt, and Connor did the same thing, and they were caught on video. Store security hauled them into a special room in the back for shoplifters that's like a little jail cell with bars, and they actually called the cops. Because they're both so young, the store was persuaded not to press charges, but you can imagine how Dad and I feel.

Jam, what I want to say up front is that I really can't wait for you to be back in Leo's life.

Lately I wonder if we did the right thing, sending you to The Wooden Barn. Maybe you won't feel the need to go back up there for spring semester. Maybe you've been able to deal with what happened last year a little better by now.

After a rough start this fall, it sounds like things have gotten easier. You even sounded chipper on the phone this week. Dr. Margolis thinks it's great that you're so involved with your a cappella group and your Special Topics in English class. We told you it was important to try living there. But maybe, because you're doing so well now, you've gotten all you can get out of it. We'll have to have a sit-down and discuss this in person.

I thought that over Christmas break, you could make sure to spend extra time with Leo. He's still struggling with how to be a social person in the world, which he never really had to deal with before. But now that he is more in the world, and less in his fantasy world with all those wizards and driftlords (is that the right word?), he needs guidance.

Darling, you're someone who's been through tough times. Like a driftlord you've "drifted," but like a wizard you now seem "wise." So maybe when you're home you could give your little brother a hand. Dad and I would be grateful.

xoxo

Mom

I put the letter back in its envelope, feeling terrible as I remember how, earlier in the semester, she'd asked me to write to Leo, and I never had. Later in the afternoon, I take my calling card down to the pay phone and call home. It's not the end of the workday yet, so I know my mom and dad will both still be in the office at Gallahue and Gallahue LLP. But Leo should be home by now.

After half a dozen rings he says hello in his slightly nasal voice.

"It's your sister," I say. "Remember me?"

"Maybe," Leo says. "Long brown hair?"

"Yep. How was Thanksgiving?"

"It was all right. Aunt Paula and Uncle Donald came from Teaneck. They brought kale."

"Sorry I missed that."

"The relatives or the kale?"

"Both," I say.

There's a pause and I can hear crunching. Leo's eating an after-school snack, probably cool-ranch-flavored chips. In the background I hear the TV, or maybe the computer, and then a boy's voice saying, "Where'd you go, Gallahue?"

"I'll be right in!" Leo calls.

"Who's that?" I ask innocently.

"A friend."

"You don't have friends," I say. "Not the kind who come over after school." I know this sounds mean, but it's true. "Maybe you have forty-year-old online friends who live with their parents," I go on. "And who play *Magic Driftlord*."

"*Dream Wanderers,*" he corrects me. "Driftlords are *characters* in *Dream Wanderers.* And I do have a real friend. Connor Bunch."

"So I've heard. Do Mom and Dad know he's over?"

"Why, are you going to tell them?" Leo asks in a nasty voice.

"Whoa, little bro, who *are* you these days?" I say. "By the way, I know about the shoplifting."

There's a silence. "It wasn't supposed to go down that way," Leo bursts out. "Connor said there weren't any security cameras in that part of the—"

"*Leo,*" I interrupt. "You don't just go from being an unconscious little dweeb to being a *criminal.* Look," I say in a softer voice, "I know it's good to have a friend and everything. But use your head! You can't go along with whatever Connor Bunch says just because you're glad he wants to hang out with you."

"I *don't* go along with whatever he says. You should hear some of the things I say no to!" Leo lowers his voice and says, "But he's the only one who's *nice* to me, Jam."

"What were you going to do with the spray paint? Vandalize the school?"

"Connor had an idea. He just hadn't told me yet. We didn't get that far because we got caught."

"Well, I'm sure it was something incredibly idiotic," I tell him. "And I'm glad you got caught, Leo. Otherwise, you might've done it a second time."

There's a long, long pause, and Leo confesses, "Actually, this *was* the second time. The first time, we didn't get caught. But we hardly *took* anything then. Just a couple of Snickers bars. Connor says that stores don't even *care* about the little stuff, that they factor it in—"

"Are you nuts, Leo? It's *stealing.* You're cheating hardworking people out of the money they earned. Just think about Mom and Dad."

"What about them?" he says glumly.

"What if a guy came to Gallahue and Gallahue LLP, wanting them to be his accountants? And after Mom and Dad did a little work for him—a little hard work that they went to school to learn how to do—he ran out of the building without paying. And our parents had done this work so they could afford our food and clothes and our orthodontia. And so maybe we could all take a vacation once in a while. But the guy decided, 'Screw the Gallahues, I won't pay.' Would *that* be right?"

"No," Leo says with a tiny, choking sob.

"Exactly," I say.

I realize that I sound a little like my mom or dad now, but not in a bad way. I listen for a second or two while Leo struggles to contain his emotions. I don't want to make him feel *too* bad, so I say, "Listen, I'm coming home for Christmas. I'm not going to get snowed in this time. And you and I are going to hang out, okay? We can sit in my room—I'll let you come in more, I won't say 'Go away' through the door—and we can have life conversations and stuff."

"Really?"

"Yep."

"Will you play me some indie rock?"

"Indie rock? Is that what you want me to do?" I'm completely surprised by this. I had no idea that Leo even knew music existed.

"Yes," he says, snuffling. "I think it's time."

"Okay, then," I say. "I will."

When our class meets again in the darkened classroom around the candle, our main topic of conversation is the end of the journals. We've each got an average of three more visits left before the last line gets covered with writing.

"And then what?" says Marc. He's so agitated about this that he can't sit still, but keeps drumming his fingers on the floor like a hyperactive kid.

"And then we find a way to keep going back," says Sierra. "We have to. I'm not going to leave André there."

"No one says you have to," says Casey.

"But no one's told us how to keep going."

"No one's told us *anything,*" Griffin says.

As the end of the journals seems to be closing in, none of us knows what to do, and we're all getting increasingly anxious.

"Maybe, on the last day of class, Mrs. Q will give us a *second* journal," says Casey. "And we can take it with us when we go home for Christmas."

"A blue leather journal," says Marc.

"Nah, that's not going to happen," says Sierra. "And you know it."

I feel a pressure building up in my chest, and my throat gets thick. "Oh, Jam," my mom used to say in the first weeks and months after I lost Reeve, "where did you go?" I was empty then, I was barely a person. But because of Belzhar, I've been coming around, returning to my "old self," as my parents would probably say if they could see me now. To lose Reeve a second time would empty me out all over again.

"I don't think I could live without seeing André," Sierra says. She isn't being melodramatic. She's stating a fact.

Everyone's quiet and worried, and finally someone says it's getting late. Griffin leans over to blow out the candle—he's always the one who makes sure it's out, and since the trip to the farm I know why—when we hear tires on snow, and see a spinning red light pour through the windows.

"Oh, come *on,* this can't be happening," says Casey, and Marc helps her into her chair as car doors slam, and then campus security barges first into the building, and then the classroom. We're busted.

A little while later the headmaster, Dr. Gant, meets us for an "emergency meeting" in his office. He's been called away from the boys' dorm, where he also serves as houseparent, and where he was probably just starting to get everyone settled down for the night. We all take seats around his woody, dimly-lit room, a place I've only seen once, the first day I arrived here. I was in such a state that afternoon, monosyllabic and furious.

How long ago that day seems. I remember how my mom stood in my dorm room punching the edges of my orange study buddy to distribute the filling evenly. And how DJ stared at me from her bed, and I was positive that she and I would always dislike each other.

All I could think about, that day, was how much I missed Reeve.

Everything's different now.

"People," says Dr. Gant. He's a mild, middle-aged man who looks as if he'd be very sorry to have to discipline anybody. "What were you thinking? You can't go off unsupervised like that. And you know that candles are a forbidden item here, in a school full of old wooden buildings."

"I was *on* it," says Griffin defensively, his chin up. "I would never have let anything happen." Me, of all people, he means.

"But there are *rules*, Griffin," says Dr. Gant. "Have you met there at night before?" No one wants to answer. "Security says they found older wax drippings on the floor, so I'm guessing the answer is yes."

"All right," Casey says. "Yes, we have."

"But why?" he asks. "Is it really just to 'hang out,' like you told security? Is that it?"

"Sort of," says Marc. I can see how hard it is for him to lie to an authority figure, or even be vague.

"It sounds a little more complicated than that," says Dr. Gant. He pauses. "We've had a couple of issues with the Special Topics in English people in previous years. They tend to be a very close group. One year they all wandered off into the woods for an hour, and no one knew where they were. Another year they seemed to . . . invent their own language. But I don't want to talk about students from the past. I want to talk about what's going on with all of *you* right *now.*"

Of course, it's interesting to get this information about previous classes, but none of us can ask any more questions about it. And what are we supposed to say about ourselves: All right, Dr. Gant, here's the deal: Twice a week we write in our journals, which take us to a place where our wrecked lives have been restored. Except now we're just about out of *room* in the journals, so we need to figure out how to extend our time in that place we go to, because we can't bear to stop going there.

So, please, Dr. Gant, can you just pretend we *weren't* busted, and let us keep meeting once a week in the classroom late at night?

But we reveal nothing to him, and finally he removes his rimless eyeglasses and rubs his eyes, then puts the glasses back on, looping the wires carefully over his ears.

"I'm very sorry," he says, looking at each of us one by one. "But for the rest of the semester, with the exception of classes and meals and rehearsals, consider yourselves members of another class. Let's call it Special Topics in Being Grounded."

CHAPTER 17

EVERYTHING'S CRACKING APART NOW, AND WE know it. Kept separate from one another all week, we can't talk openly about what to do about the rapidly arriving end of the journals. We only get together in class and at meals, but we never have extended privacy. And finally we're each down to having five pages left. One single trip remains, and then no one knows what will happen. Or maybe we do know, and it isn't good.

At breakfast, speaking as cryptically as possible, we all agree to postpone our next visits. None of us will go back to Belzhar until we have some kind of plan in place.

"*Belzhar*?" asks DJ from two seats down the table, her mouth full of egg. "What's that?"

"Nothing," I say. "It's just, you know, a thing in a book." This seems to satisfy her. Or at least bore her enough so that she immediately loses interest.

Maybe, I think, once the last line of a journal is filled in, that person's Belzhar ceases to *exist.* Maybe it shuts down for good, like a business whose owners have left town overnight. Or maybe it explodes like something deep in space, unseen and unheard by anyone, gone for good.

What would it be like to leave Belzhar behind? I have to ask myself this, because we're all wondering. When I think about letting go of that world, I picture myself off in the *real* world—maybe back in New Jersey, living my life again, a new version of it.

What would that life look like? I guess I'd just be myself. Someone in high school with some kind of future. Maybe I'd join the a cappella group there. I could even try and convince Hannah to join too; she has a good voice. I might have things to look forward to again, things I can't even imagine yet.

On Friday night I'm in my dorm room watching DJ get ready to go out to the social. "Being grounded is so unfair," I say, sitting on my bed in Griffin's hoodie. "I feel like a prisoner."

"I don't get it," she says. "You hate socials as much as I do. What do you care if you can't go?"

Of course, DJ has no idea about Belzhar, so she wouldn't understand why I need to be with everyone in my class now. And, also, why I need to be with Griffin. "I do hate socials," is all I say, "but it would be better than being grounded."

"I'll come back and tell you all the highlights," DJ promises, and then she's gone.

So I sit and try to do my homework while the whole school except the Special Topics people stands around under the disco ball in the gym. I resist going to Belzhar now, though it would be the easiest thing in the world to simply write in my journal and be with Reeve one more time, in that place where everything's familiar and predictable and easy and good. I'd worry later about how to get back there even after the journal is filled.

But, like we agreed, I keep myself from making that visit. Instead I throw myself into math, which is pretty hilarious, given my subnormal math skills. And what's even more hilarious is that I actually understand all the concepts for once, and I have a feeling I'm going to ace the homework, and the upcoming test. I've actually been doing well in most of my classes since I started going to Belzhar. This, like so many other things that have happened, is totally unexpected.

In the morning I sit at breakfast with Sierra; Griffin hasn't shown up yet, and I keep looking toward the door to see if he's coming in. Then Casey enters and comes right over to our table. She parks her chair in front of us as if she has an announcement to make. "What is it?" I ask nervously. "What's the matter?"

"Nothing's the matter," Casey says. "But I have to tell you both something." She looks around to see who else might be listening. It seems safe, and she pauses for several seconds, then quietly says, "I went to Belzhar last night."

"You *did*?" I say. "I thought we weren't going to do that yet."

"I know. But Marc and I were kind of talking in code at dinner last night. And we both basically decided, enough already. We hated the stress of not knowing what was going to happen when the journals finally ended. And we decided to find out. To take the plunge, despite what we all agreed. So we both went back. Yes, even Marc, who never breaks rules."

"And?" Sierra says, staring at Casey, and I realize that I'm staring at her too.

"What exactly do you want to know?" Casey asks.

"Well, *everything*," says Sierra.

"Like, when it was over and you looked at your journal," I say, "was it definitely filled in all the way to the end?" Casey nods. "So did you figure out a way to get back there next time?" I ask. I know we really shouldn't be talking like this out in the open, but there's no other choice.

Casey shakes her head no. She looks at us as if she feels

sorry for us; we're ignorant about all of this, and she's knowledgeable. "There's no way back," she says gently.

We're both silent. "Are you sure?" Sierra asks.

"Yes. I'm sorry," she adds, as if we might think it's her fault.

So: Once you're done, you're *done*? This means that Casey will never have a place to go where she can walk, and run.

And after I make my final visit, I can never see Reeve again. I won't touch him, or talk to him. I'll never hear his voice again. I want to shut out what Casey's just told me, and make it not be true.

"So we actually lose Belzhar, and everything that comes with it?" Sierra asks in a dull, low voice.

"Right," Casey says.

If Sierra were to go back, at the end of the visit she would lose her brother all over again, but this time it would be forever.

"But what's it actually *like* going there for the last time?" Sierra asks. "Is it different from all the other times?"

"Oh yeah," says Casey.

"How?" I press.

Casey takes a moment. "It's traumatic," she says.

This is not what either of us wants to hear.

"I can't really put it any other way," Casey continues. "I don't want to scare you, but I have to tell you what I know. The thing that happened to you in real life, on your worst day? You have to live it again. At least, I had to."

"Oh," I say, my voice coming out so small. I don't think I could live through that last day with Reeve again.

"For me, it started out like every other trip to Belzhar," Casey tells us. "But soon it was different. I was in the car, and my mom was driving, but this time it was clear that she was drunk and that *no way* should she be behind the wheel. I could finally, totally see through all the charming leprechaun bullshit. Her judgment was *off.* The car was weaving. It skidded off the road and slammed into that stone wall. And it was like a building fell on me."

Casey is suddenly crying, and Sierra and I both lean forward and try to comfort her. Other kids look at us from their tables again, and one girl, a friend of Casey's from the dorm, gets up and starts to come over, but Sierra waves her off.

"I felt *everything,*" Casey says in a quiet, fierce voice. "I didn't black out as soon as I thought I had. My mom was leaning over me when the ambulance came, and she was saying, 'Oh God, it's all my fault. I'm drunk, Casey, and I did this to you. I did this to my little girl.' I never remembered that before. And you know what, it *was* her fault, and I *can't* totally forgive her, at least not now. It's so hard, but at least now I remember what's what. At least now it's real."

Sierra and I both nod, not saying anything.

"Then they put me in the ambulance, and I was slid forward, and the light dimmed and it got really quiet. I was, like, where are the EMT guys? They were here just a second ago. But I was alone. And I sat up and looked around, and I was back in my bed in my dorm room here at school, with my journal next to me. It was all filled in; there wasn't a single line left to write on.

"And I knew that that was that. I'd relived the worst thing I'd ever been through, and then I came out the other side. So for me, that's the end of Belzhar.

"I was just sort of sitting there in a daze. I looked over and saw my wheelchair folded and leaning against the wall. I saw the gray rubber handgrips, the silver wheels. It made me want to cry. But I was also relieved that I was back. That I'm here. At school, with my friends, and with Marc. He doesn't take the place of being able to walk. Nothing can. And I'll always miss that so badly. Walking, running. But I'll never forget what it felt like. Oh wait—" she says, looking up.

Marc comes toward our table, and Casey backs up and wheels herself over to him. They meet in the middle of the room, and Sierra and I watch as he bends down and says something to her.

"Could you actually do that?" I ask Sierra. "Go there for the last time and go through the whole thing all over again? And then come back here and be like, 'Okay, now it's time for me to get on with the rest of my life.'"

"No, I couldn't," Sierra says.

"So what are we supposed to do?" I ask her. "Mrs. Q is going to collect the journals. One way or another we're going to have to do something."

"It's a hopeless situation," Sierra says. "I can't go to Belzhar, and I can't not go. You know, I snuck downstairs yesterday to call Detective Sorrentino. I left him another voice mail saying the same thing I already said to him over Thanksgiving: 'Please, please try to track down that scrawny guy who came to the show at the dance academy.'"

Griffin appears at the table now, near the end of breakfast. He's in his hoodie again, and right away I can see that he looks closed up and miserable. Not being able to meet in the classroom at night has been a strain for all of us. "Hey," he says, sitting down.

"Bad night?" asks Sierra.

Griffin nods. "Yeah, but keep talking, I don't want to interrupt."

"I was just telling Jam about calling the detective in DC again. He's not interested in what I have to say. I don't know what else to do."

"You've got to keep pushing him," I tell her.

"But I've gotten nowhere. Going to Belzhar is basically the only thing I have. I can't pull a Casey and Marc."

"What does that mean?" Griffin asks.

We explain that Casey and Marc each went to Belzhar the night before, and that it was the last time for them both, and that, no, there's no way to ever go back. And we tell him how they each had to live through their traumas and end up with the journals all filled in, and the rest of life—that imperfect thing—waiting.

"It sounds rough," Griffin says.

"I just can't imagine seeing André walk off that bus," Sierra says. "Just letting him go, knowing something was going to happen to him."

"So don't, this semester," says Griffin. "Keep trying with the detective, but don't write another word in your journal. Why would you put yourself through that, Sierra?"

"Well, she has to," I say. "Because Mrs. Q is going to take back everybody's journal on the last day of class."

"She'll have to rip it away from me," Sierra says, and abruptly she stands and carries her tray off, not even saying good-bye.

When she's gone, Griffin says to me, "I just made a decision. I'm never going back to Belzhar. I'm going to hand in the journal to Mrs. Q with the last five pages empty, and say sayonara. I can't go through the fire again, Jam. And that whole fucking night. My parents always want to make me talk about it, but I am *done.*"

"I think what your parents want," I say, "is for you to see the whole thing."

"Yeah, right."

"They do." I don't know how I know what I know, but I keep talking. "They aren't bad people. I met them. They're not trying to torture you."

"Then why do they keep bringing it up?"

"Maybe they need you to admit you made a big mistake."

"It wasn't me, it was Alby," he says with self-righteousness.

I don't say anything. I just keep looking at him, and he gets uncomfortable. He knows he can't dump all this on his friend Alby, and he knows that I know he can't. Griffin was there too, he smoked that joint in a barn full of straw and living goats. It was his barn, his goats; he was in charge of himself and his friend.

He looks more uncertain, and he says hoarsely, "I wouldn't know how to apologize."

"Yes you would."

"I'd probably break down crying or something. That would be pathetic." And he probably *would* cry. He'd have to see the devastation, and feel his part in it, even though it wasn't on purpose, and even though he's not *bad*. It was just a stupid, careless teenaged thing. An accident.

He'd have to feel everything all over again and not shut down the way he did after it happened. He'd have to get high with Alby once more, then go to sleep for the night and wake up smelling smoke, and seeing all the goats lying dead, including Ginger, his favorite. And he'd have to feel the rage of his parents, and hold himself accountable.

"Go back there," I tell him. "Just do it. And then come out

and call your parents and say what you have to say. And then maybe you can love the goats again. The ones that died, and the new ones. Frankie, the new kid."

For the first time in this conversation, Griffin smiles very slightly. "The kid that you delivered," he says. "My girlfriend, the goat obstetrician."

My girlfriend. The words are startling. I can't be his girlfriend; I love someone else. Someone very different. But whenever I'm alone in my room, I wrap myself tightly in Griffin's hoodie.

Griffin agrees to go back to Belzhar early that evening, before the winter concert begins; I'll be performing with the Barntones. "When you see me after the concert," he says, "it'll be done."

He doesn't want to have to wait until much later when his roommate, Jack, is asleep, the way he usually does. Instead, without being seen, Griffin is going to close himself in the closet in his room, among the gym shoes and damp boots and fleeces and crumpled hoodies. And under the dim light of the bulb he's going to write in his journal and disappear into another world one more time.

I tell him I'm so glad he's decided to do this. That I think it's a very good idea.

"If it's so good," he says, "then you do it too."

"Not yet" is all I say.

At night the auditorium is all decorated for the winter concert, with little lights scattered around, and tinsel in the aisles. I wait backstage with the other Barntones during the jazz band's performance and then the acoustic guitar duet. Everyone in the a cappella group is dressed in a white shirt, black skirt, and heels. Glancing at myself in the mirror before we're about to go on, I realize I look slightly older than when I came here. My hair is longer than it's ever been in my life—halfway down my back—and it shines a little, and my face seems more angular.

Sierra comes out onstage in a black leotard and black silk dance skirt. The program lists her as a soloist for *A Dance for André,* which I've seen her practice several times. Now, as the music teacher accompanies her on piano, Sierra performs the ballet again, sometimes dragging around like a person who's half dead from grief, other times propelled by manic hope. She does a few hip-hop moves too, in a nod to her brother's dance style. At the end, when she takes a bow, the applause goes on for a long time. Sierra hurries into the wings, where I'm standing. We collide and hug, and her body is boiling from exertion.

"You killed!" I say. "You're such a big talent." I know that Sierra will go really far in her life.

Finally, it's the Barntones' turn to perform, and though I have no illusions about how talented *we* are (average to above-average), we walk single file onto the stage and into the white spotlight. After all my complaints about the Barntones, I'm actually excited, and though I can't see anything past the stage, I know Griffin's out there somewhere.

Later, he'll tell me all about his final visit to Belzhar, and I'll praise him for what he's done. But now he'll have a chance to hear me sing, and maybe he'll be a little bit impressed. I wish Reeve could hear me too. But he can't ever hear me, and in fact he'll never really know all that much about me.

Adelaide leads us in our three songs, ending in the fast-paced, raplike Gregorian chant. In the audience, several of the youngest boys at the school start to make those howling and woofing sounds, and a whole foot-stomping thing gets started. This room contains two hundred of the most extremely fragile, highly intelligent people around, and we've all been cooped up away from our normal lives and our families and technology and civilization for so long that we're starting to burst out of ourselves. The foot stomping gets louder and louder, shuddering the floor of the auditorium, as if trying to send it crashing down around us.

CHAPTER 18

MUCH LATER, AFTER PUNCH AND COOKIES AT THE reception, and after Griffin tells me he went to Belzhar for the last time and that it was a hard thing but he thinks he's all right now, and after he and I stand with our arms wrapped around each other in the cold night until a teacher pries us apart, I'm sleeping a sleep so deep that I've left a little circle of spit on the pillow.

Everything has accelerated in speed and intensity, and I need to be unconscious. No Griffin, no Reeve, no Belzhar, no end of journal, no thoughts about reliving the terrible day back in Crampton. Just sleep. Sleep, and a pool of saliva on the pillow, when voices suddenly break through and wake me up.

"Someone call the nurse. I'll stay with her!" I hear Jane Ann yell, and I spring up from bed and hurry out of my room to see what's going on.

"It's Sierra," says Maddy from across the hall. She's standing in a pack of worried, excited girls.

"Same as last time?" I ask.

"No, not a nightmare," she says. "I heard she's sick. Like a *seizure* or something."

I take the stairs two at a time. Several girls are milling around outside Sierra's door, and I push through even as a bossy senior says, "You can't go in there, Jam—"

But I'm already in. The room is dim, and Jane Ann and Jenny Vaz, Sierra's roommate, are standing over Sierra's bed. Sierra is sitting up with her eyes open, staring straight ahead. One hand is in the air, moving jerkily back and forth.

"Sierra!" I say sharply. There's no reply. "Sierra, it's *Jam,*" I say right into her face. Again, no reply, so I turn to Jane Ann frantically and say, "What's wrong with her?"

"We don't know yet."

"Sierra!" I try again, but she doesn't respond at all. "Oh, come on, Sierra," I say in a softer voice. "Please don't do this. Whatever's going on with you, snap out of it, okay?"

Then I think, *What if this somehow has to do with Belzhar?* I pat the bed around her, lift up the blanket, checking for the journal, but it isn't there. "Sierra, I need you here," I tell her. "Come *on.*" I realize that I've started to cry a little, and then I can't stop.

Jane Ann has to come over and put an arm around me and pull me away. "Honey, it's going to be all right," she tells me.

"But why can't she hear me?" I ask, as Sierra remains in her twitchy fog, her face blank, her hand restlessly moving.

"I don't know. I'm sure the doctors will figure it out."

"But what if they *can't*?"

Jane Ann says, a little stiffly, "There's no reason to believe that's going to happen."

But we both understand that what's wrong with Sierra is obviously very serious. My tears go on and on, and I start to talk obsessively. I tell Jane Ann, "I was much closer to her than even to Hannah Petroski. *Much* closer. It was a really deep friendship. We shared things. Our real feelings. I've never had that before at this level."

And Jane Ann says, "I know," even though she's obviously never heard of Hannah Petroski and has no idea of what I'm talking about. I let her pat my back and say kind mom-like words to me. Soon the nurse hurries in, and I quickly move out of the way.

I watch as she removes a few items from her black bag, then crouches down beside Sierra. First she shines a little light in her eyes, then she wraps a blood-pressure cuff around Sierra's arm and squeezes that bulb thing, and then she takes her temperature with an ear thermometer.

"Sierra, have you taken a drug?" the nurse asks in a very loud voice. "And if so, which one? Ecstasy? Ketamine? PCP?"

"She doesn't take drugs," I say, cutting her off. "She *hates* drugs."

When the nurse is done, she shakes her head and frowns, then murmurs something to Jane Ann that I can't hear, and finally she says, "I'm calling an ambulance."

Jane Ann lets me stay with Sierra until the ambulance arrives to take her to the local hospital. "I know you really love her," she says as I stand helplessly patting Sierra's shoulder, or occasionally taking her hand in mine—the hand that's not moving.

"I do," I say, but already I'm thinking, *I did.*

I've never seen anyone just disappear so deeply into herself the way Sierra has. When the EMTs arrive, they lower her onto a gurney and fasten the straps with authoritative clicks. Sierra doesn't resist, and barely seems to notice that she's being taken away. Her arms are strapped to her sides, and from beneath the blanket I see a tiny bit of motion, and realize that it's Sierra's hand, still subtly twitching under there.

Jane Ann says I'm not allowed to go in the ambulance, and that I have to go back to bed now. "I promise to let you know as soon as I hear anything," she tells me.

But she still looks very upset as she heads out to send the other girls off to bed too. Sierra's roommate is out in the hall, so I stand alone in the room for an extra few seconds, looking around, and then I go to Sierra's bed and peer down into the space between the mattress and the wall. It's narrow and dark, and I can't see a thing. I plunge my arm in; it barely fits, and my fingertips graze the dusty wooden floor. Suddenly I brush against something.

It's smooth and cold, and even before I pull it up I know it's the journal.

I still think it's possible she was writing in it just before the seizure. Did something go badly wrong in Belzhar, and that's what this is about? I'm dying to look at the journal right now, but I know I should get out of here. I slip it under my arm, then head quickly back downstairs to my own room.

DJ has miraculously slept though the commotion. So in the darkness, leaning against my study buddy and with my book light switched on, I speed-read through the pages of Sierra's journal. Her handwriting is so different from mine; it seems much more mature, the words leaping across the page.

Forgive me for invading your privacy, Sierra, I think. But this is an emergency.

I read and read until I find the last entry, which of course begins five pages from the end. The entry is dated tonight. Like Casey and Marc and then Griffin, Sierra made the decision to go back to Belzhar for the last time, even without an actual "plan" in place.

And while she was in Belzhar tonight, she wrote and wrote like she always did, and her last entry describes what happened. She had to relive the night that André went missing, which she'd said she couldn't bear to do. But who could? Did the experience of losing him all over again send her into shock? Into a permanent seizure?

I see that she filled in the journal to the last line at the bottom, and that there's no room left.

Her journal is done. This is exactly what she said she didn't want to do, and yet she's done it. I squint into the darkness, and read the last paragraph:

> *Suddenly he stands up and tries to get off the bus, just like when it really happened. And this time, instead of saying, okay, get that cookie dough, I say to him, nah, we'll make chocolate chip cookies another time. And the light gets dim in the way it always does here, but I hold onto his arm and don't let go. I have to see if this will work; it's the only thing I can come up with. In dance class we do improvisations, and this is like one of them. I'm still holding on now, and we'll see what hap*

And there it ends, right in the middle of a sentence. Right in the middle of a word.

Is *that* what happened? When her journal ran out, Sierra held on to André, and was able to stay in Belzhar?

Of course. She's still there now. Her hand isn't moving because of some seizure. It's moving because she's still somehow writing in her journal, or at least writing in the air.

Sierra tried a frantic experiment in Belzhar; when the light dimmed, she refused to let go of André's hand. She didn't even let go when she felt that sharp suck of pressure pulling her away from Belzhar and back toward this world. And she managed to keep her grip on André with one hand. The other hand is the one that's still writing in an imaginary journal, writing and writing long after the real journal got all filled up.

And maybe, as long as she keeps doing this, she can stay there with him and protect him. He never has to get off that bus, and neither does she.

She doesn't have to go through her own trauma again, the way Casey and Marc and Griffin went through theirs. But she also has to stay there with André forever.

Sierra's in Belzhar for good, having given up the chance to get older and dance and have experiences and explore all the possibilities of the world. This world, not the other one.

I'm agitated for the rest of the night, turning in my bed, flipping the pillow, not knowing what to do. At dawn I finally get an idea, and I become so excited that I hurry downstairs to the pay phone, calling the hospital, asking to speak to someone about Sierra Stokes, who was admitted last night.

The nurse who gets on the line is really nice and doesn't even question whether this is a legitimate call. To my surprise she agrees with my peculiar and very specific request. "Sure, honey," she says. "It's worth a try. We really don't know what's going on with this gal."

So she puts down the phone at the nursing station, and a lot of time passes. Finally she gets back on the line and tells me that she did what I asked, but it didn't work. She had gone to Sierra's room, stood over her bed, and followed my instructions, shouting, "Sierra, come out of Belzhar!"

I'd had the idea to try this because I remembered that when I got trapped in that horrible *goat* version of Belzhar after writing in Griffin's journal, he'd shouted something to me like "Come out of Belzhar!" And it *had* worked.

But the nurse got no response from her. No sudden spike in alertness. Nothing registered on the monitor. "Sorry, sweetheart," she tells me over the phone. "No luck."

I'm all out of ideas.

In the morning the campus is somber, with everyone whispering at breakfast about the terrible thing that happened to Sierra Stokes in the night. There's a rumor floating around that Sierra OD'd on Xanax, and had to have her stomach pumped.

Then another rumor starts going around that Sierra had a "major seizure" and is permanently brain damaged. On the oatmeal line, people are talking about what a loss it is. Sierra was such a talented, smart girl, they say, using the past tense. Such an amazing dancer. So intelligent. A real winner.

I just want to scream in their faces, "Shut up, you don't know what you're talking about!"

A few girls are crying and embracing, even though most of them know Sierra only superficially, because she keeps pretty much to herself with everyone but us. In the dining hall I look for Marc and Casey and Griffin, and I go over to each of them individually and whisper exactly what I've figured out.

"She stayed there," I say. "She held on to André. She's there right now." I explain the whole thing, and, like me, their first reaction is shock. But they also understand why she did this.

After breakfast Dr. Gant calls a special assembly for the entire student body. He and the nurse and a couple of teachers get up and give us a talk about relying on one another for companionship and strength when something difficult happens. They remind us that they're here for us too. By the time the fairly useless assembly is over, we're running so late that Dr. Gant cancels all first-period classes.

Now that there's no Special Topics today, the rest of the free period gives the four of us who've been grounded a chance to huddle outside in a patch of cold sun and talk a little.

"I don't blame her for doing it," Marc says right away. "It makes sense."

"I don't blame her either," says Griffin. "Going back that last time is hard for anyone. It was hard for me."

"Mysterious you," says Casey. And I'm reminded that Griffin hasn't told anyone but me what happened to him in the past. No one else knows about the fire, or what his version of Belzhar is like. And they only know slightly more about me and *my* past. Griffin and I have both remained pretty opaque, and the others have allowed it. I'm grateful to them.

But Sierra told us the whole story. "I think she did the right thing," Griffin says.

"I just can't imagine her not being here anymore," I say. My voice starts to crack apart a little. We're talking about Sierra as if she's dead, and has taken her own life.

Griffin puts an arm around me, and I think about how, unlike Sierra, he's here with me, and he's not going anywhere. I know it, but I can't quite believe it. Sometimes you think people will be around forever, and then you lose them with no warning at all.

In the evening, after a day in which none of us is able to concentrate, our class is driven downtown in a van to attend Mrs. Quenell's retirement party, which is held in the restaurant of a big old hotel called the Green Mountain Arms. Sierra had really been looking forward to the party; she'd said she was glad to have the opportunity to dress up, and to walk around the room like a normal person at a normal party.

I'd been looking forward to the food; I am beyond sick of meals at The Wooden Barn. It's basically all quinoa, all the time. And I'd liked the idea of celebrating Mrs. Quenell. We've all been granted special permission to leave our rooms for the evening, despite being grounded. Now, of course, none of us is in a party mood at all. Yet here we are.

The hotel is stately and grand. Our teacher looks grand too as she receives guests at the entrance of the glittering restaurant. She wears a red silk blouse and an emerald necklace. Christmas colors. "My wonderful students," she says, lightly hugging each of us. Behind her I can see glittering silver and candles. Waiters circulate with trays of hors d'oeuvres, and though I'm wearing my best clothes—among the only good clothes I have with me—I feel awkward and unhappy to be here at this party, which is basically a roomful of dressed-up teachers.

"Come in, don't be shy," Mrs. Quenell says to us. "Stuff yourselves with canapés. Take some back to the dorms for your poor deprived roommates." But we hesitate at the door, and she quietly says, "*I know.*"

A pause. *What* does she know? Obviously, she knows that

Sierra has fallen ill, but does she know any more than that?

She looks at us. "I know how hard it is for all of you, attending a party when Sierra is sick. I'm thinking about her tonight too. Please know that."

But she doesn't know what we know—at least I don't think she does. Sierra made her own decision, and though, yes, we're all upset, we understand it and respect it. All we can do now is thank Mrs. Quenell, and then head inside. Griffin hits up a waiter for a couple of puff pastries. The serving staff has been instructed not to let us drink any alcohol whatsoever, so all we get offered is "sparkling water."

"When did seltzer become sparkling water?" Griffin asks.

"Oh, around the time that *impact* became a verb," says Mrs. Quenell with a smile, then she walks off to greet some newly arriving guests.

I pop a canapé into my mouth whole. I don't even know what it is—maybe a scallop? And is that cream cheese in it?—but it may be the best thing I've ever eaten. I haven't realized how much I miss "real" food. I think about my dad's excellent cooking. And the dumb "Chef Dad" apron he wears, and how when Leo was little, Dad always let him drop a fistful of spaghetti into the boiling water.

Leo. My dad. My mom. I picture my whole family in the kitchen at home in a life I used to be part of and no longer am.

"I want to talk to you," Griffin says, pulling me so suddenly toward the side of the room that my sparkling water sloshes over the side of the glass. When we sit down on a sofa he says, "Everyone's journal is done except yours."

"I know." My voice is soft and ashamed.

"We're leaving for break, Jam."

"I know."

"Go there and say good-bye to him," Griffin says. "Get it done already."

There's a horrible silence. I just can't speak.

"Don't you want to be with me?" Griffin asks.

Of course I do. Griffin and his soft, worn hoodies. The way he feels so much, and feels so much for me. I nod, but I can't tell him that I also still want the funny and ironic English boy in the brown sweater who I am certain is waiting frantically in Belzhar, having no idea of what's taking me so long, or if I'll ever be back.

Griffin just wants me to go there and get it over with. Go there and end it.

But what if I go there to end it and realize I can't? We all know now that there's a way to stay. Sierra held on to André and didn't let go as the light dimmed. They were like two people making a human chain during a hurricane, bracing themselves against being uprooted and torn apart.

I could go back there and do the same thing.

The idea starts to form for real as I sit on the fancy sofa at the fancy party with a crumpled cocktail napkin in my fist. I wish I could grab one of the pale pink cocktails the waiters are passing to the teachers, who as far as I can tell are starting to get a little buzzed, their voices growing louder. I hear the usually mousy Latin teacher start to *shriek*. The drinks are cosmopolitans—pretty ironic since we're in rural Vermont, which is not exactly the most cosmopolitan place in the world. If I had one I would just guzzle it down, and maybe even a second one, and then I'd feel more certain about whether I should go back to Belzhar and stay.

"So you're going to end it?" Griffin pushes. I nod weakly. "You promise, Jam?" And I nod again.

"*There* you are," says Mrs. Quenell, appearing above us. "Come say hello to Dr. Gant." Griffin and I reluctantly get up, and all the Special Topics people stand together uncomfortably with our teacher and the headmaster.

Mrs. Quenell says, "John, you should know that this is perhaps the most gifted group of students I've ever taught."

"That's saying a lot, Veronica," he says. He looks at us and says drily, "I hope you're enjoying being 'sprung' for the night." We tell him we are. "Well," he goes on, "when you come back from Christmas break in January, it will be time for a clean start."

By January, of course, Special Topics will have been over for weeks. Whatever is going to happen to me will have already happened.

Someone calls everyone to attention now, and the guests gather; several toasts are given. A few teachers tell inside jokes about Mrs. Quenell and quote lines from books that she loves.

An old lady who works in the kitchen gets up and says how polite Mrs. Quenell has always been to the kitchen staff. "She always separates her plates and silverware," she says, "unlike *some* people."

Yes, Mrs. Quenell is good. She's good and kind and she expects the most of us. But above all, she's still a mystery.

What does she really know? Will we ever be told? Soon our class will end, and winter break will begin, and when we return in January, Mrs. Quenell will be gone. Some new family with little kids will move into her house, and they'll probably put up a swing set in the yard.

Suddenly Casey bangs on a glass with a spoon, and everyone looks over at the small girl in the wheelchair, surprised. She unfolds a little square of paper in her lap. "I just want to say," she says, reading aloud, "that being in Special Topics in English has meant everything to me."

She stops, then looks up from the paper and says, "We had a real shock with what happened to Sierra. But we're a tight group, Mrs. Q, and that's because of you. Remember at the beginning of the year, that thing you said? How we should look out for each other?"

I glance over at Mrs. Quenell, who nods. She's absolutely focused on Casey, the way she's always absolutely focused on each of us when we talk in class around the oval oak table. Like we are the only people in the world for her. Something surges in me, makes me feel that I might cry.

"I think we've done that, Mrs. Q," Casey continues. "And that included looking out for Sierra. But I guess, you know, there are some places a person can go where no one else can follow them. And sometimes you just have to trust that they know what they're doing."

None of this is actually written on Casey's piece of paper. She's just improvising, trying to tell Mrs. Quenell something without saying it out loud: If you do know about the journals, then you should also know that Sierra went there and *stayed*. She did it on purpose. And maybe it's not the worst thing in the world, because she's with her brother now.

"Mrs. Q," Casey goes on, looking back down at the page, "you're an awesome teacher. At first I thought you were too strict. But I'm really glad you were. Because I got a lot out of it. And I also got a lot out of all the class discussions, which could be *fierce*. And, of course, out of the journals."

She mentions the journals lightly, waiting to see whether this gets a reaction from Mrs. Quenell. But it doesn't. Not even a glimmer.

"I know that I'm speaking for the whole class when I say that you made a difference," Casey says, and then she's done.

"Hear, hear," calls the Latin teacher, and then all the teachers raise their glasses and drink to Mrs. Quenell, though I'm sure that none of them has a clue as to what Casey was really trying to say.

CHAPTER 19

OVER THE NEXT FEW DAYS I CARRY MY JOURNAL with me everywhere, as if I'm afraid someone will steal it, or I'll lose it, and I'll never be able to see Reeve again. Despite what I promised Griffin, I'm still not ready to go to Belzhar for the last time. I'm the holdout, because I'm split.

One half of me wants to go there, make the break, leave Reeve for good, and come back to Griffin. The other half thinks, fuck it, I'm going to stay with Reeve. Just the two of us in our neutral territory, standing in a field embracing. The brown wool sweater. The curling mouth. The way we joke around, and then get serious and lie down together, turning toward each other. Reeve's long arms, and his whole body, slender, familiar, magnetized to mine. We can have this forever. No stress, no change, no problems, and nobody else to complicate our simple life.

I don't know which half of me will get its way, and I won't know until I go there. But I do have to go there, one way or another. If I hand in the journal with the last five pages empty, then I'll be leaving Reeve in a permanent waiting state, which would be torture for him, and for me.

Whenever I see Griffin walking alone across campus, his shoulders hunched, his long blond hair blowing, his boots leaving deep impressions in the snow, I wave and hurry over to him in relief. No one else in my class was as paralyzed as I am about the decision to make a final trip to Belzhar; everyone just finally went there and did what they had to do.

I'm different.

"*Go* already," Griffin says when we stand together one day in the bluish late afternoon, under a tree hung with icicles. When I don't say anything, he says, "You're not actually thinking of doing what Sierra did, are you? You'd better not."

I think of Reeve in Belzhar now, a place where there are no icicles and no snow. I picture him sitting next to me that day in art class, and how I drew him. And then how we kissed at the party over the dollhouse. And how he showed me the Monty Python sketch. How he gave me a jar of jam because of my name. How we fit together.

I'll go to Belzhar after lights-out, I suddenly decide. I don't have any idea whether I'll ever return to The Wooden Barn again.

It's suddenly much too cold out here under the frozen trees, and I need to get back inside. "I'll go there tonight," I promise Griffin.

At dinner, sitting at a loud, chattering table, I barely eat the mound of bow-tie pasta on my plate, and I keep to myself. Griffin somehow knows to give me a little distance. He's sitting with a few guys at a table across the way, and he slowly raises a hand to wave to me, and I raise mine back. We don't take our eyes off each other, and I nod to him, as if to say, don't worry, I'm going to do what I said I would.

And then, finally, the end of the long day comes, and DJ and I are lying in our beds before going to sleep when she says to me, “The thing about adulthood that I keep thinking about is that there’s never lights-out. At least, not a *mandatory* lights-out. That sounds really great, doesn’t it?”

“Yeah, it does,” I say.

“You make your own decisions. I’ll be totally ready for that,” she adds, and yawns a big, unselfconscious DJ yawn.

I’m not ready to make my own decision about Reeve, but I have to.

“Can you believe the semester’s about to end?” she goes on. “People say ‘Time flies,’ and I’m, like, ‘No shit.’”

“I know,” I say. “It’s pretty unreal how fast it went.”

We adjust ourselves in our beds in the dark, and I suddenly say to her, “You’ve been a really good roommate, DJ.”

“Thanks, Jam. You haven’t been an axe murderer either. But we’re not done. We still have next semester.”

“I know that,” I say, but I think, I may never see you again. And if I don’t, good luck in life. I hope you and Rebecca stay together for a long time, or forever, if that’s what you want. I hope you continue to get over all your food issues. I hope you do enjoy the fact that adulthood has no lights-out. I hope you get the chance to do everything you want to do, because you deserve it all.

I wait for her to drift off, and I listen to her breathing get regular and loud in that way of hers. Then, feeling afraid and alone but steadying myself as well as I can, I sit up and lean against the study buddy and place my journal in my lap, switching on the little book light.

By now, Reeve has been waiting so long for me; I wonder what he thinks has happened.

I can feel the cool leather cover of the journal against my

knees. There are five pages left blank, and at the top of the first one I carefully write:

I'm off to be with him again, finally.

And then I'm there. But this time his arms aren't around me. I'm not holding him, and he's not holding me. Instead, I feel only the wind, which is blowing more strongly than usual. I remember that there was a strong wind on the last day I was with Reeve in New Jersey. As I left the house that morning for the school bus, my mom had called out, "Take a hat!" But I'd ignored her, because I hate hat hair. All that static electricity hangs around your head with a crackle. I'd gone sprinting out into the cold, hatless and excited, not knowing that everything was going to change that day.

That I would lose him.

Now the playing fields in Belzhar are empty and silent. I call his name tentatively. "Reeve?" I try, but he's nowhere. Something's not right, and I start walking more rapidly along the field. Then I remember Casey said that when she went back to Belzhar for the very last time, it was just like the time that the bad thing had happened to her. She'd had to relive it fully.

That's right. This is just like my last day with Reeve. It's beginning again automatically, now that there are only five pages left in my journal. I didn't even have to do anything other than show up; it's all starting on its own.

I'm not ready for this. Why did I think I was? All I can do is walk along the grass in an inevitable march toward something bad, the way I did that last day in New Jersey. I walk and walk, heading toward the conclusion to my own story, and there's nothing to see up ahead, until suddenly there is.

Someone stands in the distance. As I get closer, I see that it's actually *two* people, wrapped up in each other. A girl and a boy, her hair flowing around them both. His head is buried in her neck, and her head is thrown back. He's laughing as he kisses her.

I feel my jaw lock, my fingers stiffen with tension. I wish I could crack my knuckles, each one as loud as a warning gunshot. I keep walking toward them. I know why the girl is here, though I really don't want to know at all.

"Sometimes it's easier to tell ourselves a story," Dr. Margolis had said to me in a kind voice that made me want to hit him, the day my parents brought me to his office. I did not want to listen to a word he said.

The girl on the field sees me now, and she says something to the boy, who turns around.

It's Reeve. Reeve Maxfield has been kissing Dana Sapol, the girl who has hated me ever since I was the only one who knew she'd forgotten to wear underpants that day in second grade. I mean, what kind of sick person holds a grudge like that? And at this point, it's obviously no longer about the underpants. She was never once nice to me until she found out Reeve liked me. And then she invited me to her party, where I kissed him above her sister Courtney's dollhouse. The party where he gave me the jar of jam.

Though I feel like my head might crack apart along the sides of the skull from seeing Reeve and Dana together, I'm still steady enough to keep walking toward them. And instead of looking guilty or shocked or saying something like, "I can explain," the way Marc's dad did when he was caught with that porn tape of himself, Reeve just hangs on to Dana, and she hangs on to him, stretching the sleeve of his brown sweater.

They stand and look at me, and with a smirk Dana says, "Well, well, look who we have here."

"Be nice," says Reeve.

I didn't know what to do when this happened that day in New Jersey, out in the real world. I just did not know what to do. The boy I loved had been hooking up with this dreadful, mean girl, which made no sense at all.

"Reeve," I say to him now, exactly as I said to him that day. "What are you doing?"

"Come on, Jam," he says softly.

"But I thought . . ." I let my voice fade out.

"You thought what?" His accent is as British as ever, but he sounds exasperated, as if he wishes I'd just say it and get it over with. And then he can say what he has to say too, and then we'll be done.

"I thought we were together," I say miserably.

Dana Sapol hoots. She lets out a sound like one of the exotic birds at Pets 'n' More Pets at the mall. Reeve grips her arm tighter, as if to quiet her.

"Jam," he finally says. "We're not together. You know that, right?"

"But what about what we had?" I say. "Starting with that night at her house. At her sister's dollhouse."

"You know what really happened that night," says Reeve. He doesn't seem like he's being cruel, or trying to humiliate me.

I shake my head no.

"Do I have to remind you?" he asks. "You can't recall?"

I close my eyes in the wind, not looking at the beautiful face of Reeve, and the pointy, unkind face of Dana. *Can* I recall that night at the Sapols' house?

At first I can't. I can only see it exactly the way I've always seen it, all the details lined up as neatly as a row of polished stones. Arriving at the party. Seeing Reeve in his wrinkled shirt standing with those other guys. Going down the hall with him, where he gives me the jam. Kissing him and feeling so much. Letting him touch me under my tank top. Groaning in the dim light of that little girl's bedroom, as blissful as I've ever felt.

What I've been doing is telling myself a "story," as Dr. Margolis said.

Telling yourself a story is always easier, he continued.

Yes, it's definitely easier for me. Because when I let go of the story I've been telling myself, and just try to think about what's objectively *true,* I can barely get a grip. But even so, I go way, way back in my mind to much earlier than that night at Dana Sapol's house. I go back in my mind to the first day I ever met Reeve.

I was in gym class playing badminton that day, and there he was, the exchange student from London in the long shorts and the Manchester United T-shirt, ducking as the birdies whizzed by his head. And at the end of class I said to him, "Good strategy."

He looked at me with a squint. "And what strategy was that?"

"Avoidance."

He nodded in agreement. "Yeah, it's basically how I've gotten through life so far."

We half smiled at each other, and that was the end of it. I

saw him around school during the week, and I made excuses to talk to him, and he made excuses to talk to me. That was exactly the way it happened. I thought about him so much, and whenever I did I felt light and excited and hyperalert.

And one day in the cafeteria, Reeve was sitting with a bunch of people, and instead of sitting with Hannah and Ryan and Jenna like I always did, I slipped in at the other end of the bench where he was. None of those kids even noticed me; I just sat there with my tuna fish sandwich—the quietest food ever invented—eating and listening as he talked. Reeve was the center of attention at the table, because he was new and cute-looking and funny and had an accent. Dana Sapol was at the table too. I think she was sitting right next to him; it's hard for me to remember the details, after everything that's happened.

"My host family, the Kesmans," he said to everyone, "enjoy singing rounds. Do you know what rounds are?"

"Rounds?" I suddenly said, trying to make my voice heard in the loud cafeteria. "Oh, like 'Row, Row, Row Your Boat.'"

But I was all the way at the other end of the table, and my voice didn't carry that far. No one seemed to notice I'd even said a word, so I just went back to softly chewing my sandwich, trying to make it last a really long time. I listened to Reeve talk in that accent, that *scrape*, feeling as if he and I were having our own private conversation, and that no one else was there.

"It's excruciating. After dinner," Reeve went on, "we all have to stay at the table, and we sing rounds for *hours*. Or maybe it only seems like hours. This is the most wholesome family I've ever met. Are all American families as bad as that?"

"No," I said, in a louder voice. "Mine isn't."

This time he heard me, and looked down the table. "Lucky girl," said Reeve.

Dana Sapol said, "Yeah, Jam Gallahue is so lucky. That's how everyone thinks of her."

There was a momentary murmur of surprise and embarrassment, which always happened when Dana took a little jab at me. Everyone knew that, for some unexplained reason, Dana hated me. Over the years she'd take any opportunity to say something casually nasty. So each time it happened, there would be this weird, uncomfortable pause.

No one understood why she did this. I wasn't a loser. I wasn't like Ramona Schecht, who'd been sitting alone at lunch ever since the day in seventh grade when she'd been found picking a crisp scab off her elbow and eating it like a kettle chip.

Reeve was new, and had never seen Dana make fun of me before. It was awkward, but then the moment passed. A couple of kids leaned in to talk to Reeve, and my view of him was blocked. Then finally, when they leaned back, I saw that Reeve had already left the cafeteria. It was such a little thing, him not saying good-bye to me, but it just made me feel so forgotten.

I went to the garbage pail to throw out my crusts, and the tears in my eyes blurred the entire room. Blurry Hannah saw me and said, "Why weren't you sitting with us today, Jam?" I couldn't even answer. "What's the matter?" she said. "Jam, are you *crying*?"

There was no way to explain it to her. I felt so much for this boy, but even after he'd been so nice to me that first day in badminton, and every day since then, he was suddenly indifferent now. Didn't he like me? It was urgent that he did.

And then there was that day in art class, when we were drawing landscapes, and Reeve came and sat next to me. Well, okay, he actually sat next to me only because Ms. Panucci, the art teacher with the dangly earrings, said, "Reeve Maxfield, I want you separated from Dana Sapol." So Reeve stood up with his pad and pencil, and Ms. Panucci pointed to me and said, "Go sit there."

Reeve flopped down hard beside me, and Ms. Panucci said to the class, "No talking. I am serious, people!"

He turned to me with a sly smile. What we had was special and subtle. We sat in stillness, not talking, not touching, though I wanted him to touch me more than anything. I wanted his shoulder against mine. I could easily imagine kissing him, feeling the chocolate-brown sweater wool, his bright face, his neck, his mouth.

I stopped drawing the hills in the distance like I was supposed to. They were just too boring, and didn't deserve to be immortalized. Instead, my hand that was holding the charcoal began moving across the pad like it was a Ouija board.

I barely knew I was drawing, until someone said, "Yo, Reeve, you've got an admirer."

The drawing wasn't even that good. I accidentally forgot to give him a shirt. Instead I just drew his face and his bare shoulders. His clavicle, which is the real name for the collarbone. I made him look kind of buff, even though he's pretty skinny. Suddenly there was all this laughter around me, and Ms. Panucci came over, took the pad from me, and said, quietly, "Jam, what's going on? It's not like you to act out. To deliberately do what you're not supposed to."

I couldn't explain. I couldn't tell her I hadn't even *known* I was drawing Reeve, because it wouldn't have made sense to her. Everyone was laughing and looking at the half-naked drawing of Reeve Maxfield, the British exchange student.

He didn't say anything to me, but just got up and walked off. I had displeased him, which made me want to gouge out my eyes. But maybe, beneath his displeasure, he was also flattered and excited. He just had to be.

Please God, make this be okay, I thought, even though I've gone back and forth between believing in God and being an atheist ever since I was nine and my friend Marie Bunning's dad had a heart attack and died. If there really was a God, I sometimes thought, He would never have taken Mr. Bunning, who used to actually make paper dolls for Marie, with little ski outfits and everything. Why wouldn't God have left Mr. Bunning on earth, with the people who loved him?

At home that night after art class I didn't want to eat dinner, and my dad, who likes to cook dishes with one weird ingredient ("You catch the undertone in this stew?" he'll say proudly. "I poured in a can of Dr Pepper!"), was concerned. "What's going on?" he and my mom wanted to know, but I couldn't tell them that I had dropped into a deep, dense cloud of feeling, and that I was still in free fall.

Later, in bed, I pretended that Reeve was beside me. I felt his arms, and his long torso. In the morning, getting dressed, it was almost as if he whispered to me, "Wear the black jeans. I like those."

The next time I saw him at school he didn't seem mad at me at all, and I was so happy I could have danced down the hall. Maybe I did dance a little, because Ryan Brown said to me, "What's with *you*? You look all hyper. Are you ADHD?"

And later on, in the few minutes of freedom between history and Conversational French, when Reeve glanced across the hallway, I was sure he was looking at me. But maybe he wasn't. It's like when you're at a concert and you think the singer is singing directly to you, and all the thousands of other teenaged girls don't even exist. I was inside that cloud of feeling and I couldn't see or feel anything else.

I suppose Dr. Margolis was right, and it *was* easier to tell myself this story, because what was true was just not acceptable to me. Like that day at the lockers, when Dana Sapol looked up and said, "My parents and Courtney the brat are going to our grandparents' this Saturday, so it's par-tay time. You should come."

All right, so maybe she wasn't only talking to *me.*

Or maybe she wasn't talking to me at all.

Maybe thinking that she was talking to me was just part of the "story."

Dana generally never talked to me except to say something mean, but I tried to make myself think we'd turned a corner because she saw that Reeve and I obviously had something between us. Finally, I thought, I was no longer hated by Dana. My locker was five lockers down from hers. Jackie Chertoff, who was a less powerful version of Dana, was two lockers down.

"Excellent," Jackie said about the party, and she pumped her fist in the air.

I started to think about what it would be like if I could go to that party. Maybe Dana really was including me in the conversation; her eyes always did kind of look into the distance when she talked, like she couldn't really commit to one person. Maybe she was telling *everyone* at the lockers about her party, not just Jackie Chertoff. It wasn't clear to me at the time which it was. I thought about how maybe I'd been invited, and I pretended that being invited was no big deal. Though of course it was huge.

And then Dana added, meaningfully, "The hottie exchange student will be there."

And this *had* to have been directed at me, because clearly I was very into Reeve, and everyone knew it since art class. All morning I'd been drawing his name over and over on the cover of my history notebook, in different styles: bubble letters, Olde English calligraphy, and even the Greek alphabet, which I looked up online. This is how his name looks in Greek:

Ρεεϝε Μαχφιελδ

Everyone knew I was into him, and to most people this made sense, because even though I wasn't in the most popular group, I was a nice, cute girl who had a close group of friends. In no way was I like Ramona Schecht, Devourer of Scabs. So I told myself a story that I'd been personally invited to Dana Sapol's party. I could even picture an invitation, engraved with my name on the front, just like the bar and bat mitzvah invitations I'd received in seventh grade, which came in the mail and always weighed a ton. In my mind the invitation said:

The presence of your company is requested
At the home of Dana Helene Sapol
Saturday night at half past the hour of eight o'clock
Dress: casual but sort of slutty, because Reeve
will be on the premises
No gifts, please, since Dana Helene Sapol owns
everything already. Also, this isn't a birthday, it's
just a teens-getting-wasted party
Be prepared for something momentous to happen

I stood at my locker feeling so excited that I couldn't even speak. I just closed the shaky metal door quietly and gave the dial a spin, so no one could break in and steal—what? My clarinet? My rain poncho? Nothing in that locker would interest anyone, least of all me. All I could think about was being with Reeve at that party, and what would happen there. Something *momentous.*

I turned down the usual offer to hang out with Hannah and Jenna on Saturday night. No doubt all we would've done was click on a bunch of different websites, some where you had to press a button certifying you were at least eighteen. And then we'd go on Facebook and laugh at people's dumb posts. And we'd watch TV and order stuffed crust pizza and individual molten lava cakes, and finally fall asleep at 1:00 a.m. in sleeping bags on the rug in the Petroskis' den, beneath the framed poster of the sad-looking diner by the artist Edward Hopper, where we'd slept a thousand times.

"What are you doing instead?" asked Jenna when I told her and Hannah that I wasn't free. "Something with your family?"

"I'm going to Dana Sapol's party."

They were shocked. "No offense, but you couldn't have been invited to that," Jenna said. "Dana Sapol has never hidden her feelings about you, even if they are twisted."

"Well, I *was* invited," I said.

"But anyway, why would you go?" asked Hannah, to which I could only look at her in amazement.

Why would I go? Didn't she know *anything*?

"Oh," said Jenna coldly. "Because of your crush."

"He's not a crush," I said, equally coldly.

"Get over it already, Jam," said Hannah. "And I say this as your best friend who cares about you."

I looked at these two girls I'd been through everything with since the beginning of time. We'd had so many sleepovers, so many hours of flat-ironing our hair and doing dance moves, and so many sleepy Saturday afternoons at the mall, waiting for someone's mom or dad to come pick us up in the rain. But now it all seemed far behind me. They couldn't understand where I was in my life. They couldn't know the connection I had with Reeve, and how I had to see it through.

"See you," I said, turning away, and I could already hear them start to talk about me.

CHAPTER 20

THE NIGHT OF THE PARTY, MY PARENTS AND LEO dropped me off and continued on to their lame-ass evening of a movie at the mall, and I slipped into the Sapols' enormous house. Several kids said hi, a little surprised to see me at Dana's house. There were lots of people there, and the smell of weed, and the undersmell of puke, and it was only eight thirty. I looked for Reeve but didn't see him right away, so I acted really casual, even though my heart was beating hard. Without thinking, I wove my way through a cluster of people and headed deeper into the party.

Among the drone of American voices, I easily picked out Reeve's English voice. His accent was special, like him, and it pierced the air of Dana Sapol's long, gaudy living room and led me right to him. There he was, standing with some guys, holding a beer in one hand and a brown paper bag in the other. They were all talking and joking, and Alex Mowphry called Reeve a douchebag, and then Danny Geller saw me and said, "There's the artist who drew your portrait, Maxfield."

"Screw you," Reeve said in a friendly way.

"Nice picture, Picasso," Danny said to me.

I knew that if I acted embarrassed and upset, he'd tease me even more. So I had to act like I was in on the joke. "Thanks," I said. "The Museum of Modern Art called to see my portfolio."

Danny turned to Reeve and said, "You better go off with this girl and pose for another one. Full frontal this time, bro. I dare you."

"Oh, you dare me?" said Reeve. He turned to me. "Want to go somewhere and talk?" he asked.

"*Talk,*" said Danny. "Right."

I nodded, and Reeve and I walked down the hall together, past the people leaning against walls drinking and smoking and talking. We opened a couple of doors and found people playing strip poker, or in the process of hooking up.

Finally we opened the door to Courtney's room, with the over-the-top dollhouse inside. No one was there, and Reeve and I went in, and he put down the bag he'd been carrying. English groceries, he explained when I asked. He'd brought them to the party as a kind of joke, because everyone at school had been asking him what he ate back in London. He was planning on taking all the different foods out later, when everyone had the munchies.

I pawed around inside the bag and saw scones, and a can of something called, disgustingly, "spotted dick." Everyone would have a good laugh over that.

Then I saw the jam, and right away I got the pun.

"Jam!" I said, thrilled. "So can I have it?" I held the jar up and pointed to myself.

"Sure," he said lightly. "It's good stuff."

Then we started ironically playing with the dolls at the dollhouse, and he leaned forward and kissed me. He smelled beery, weedy, kind of fermented, which made me realize, *Oh, he's not 100 percent lucid.* But then it didn't matter, because kissing him made me feel sort of high too.

I leaned into the kiss almost too hard, and let the sensations pour over me. We both felt equally excited, and what was happening was so clearly *inevitable*, and had been building up since that very first day in gym class. It had been building and building, and everyone knew it, and now here we were.

By the end of the kiss, I was positive we were falling in love.

But then the door opened with a loud thud. "Reeve," said Dana Sapol.

He looked up at her, wiping his mouth, which glittered with traces of my lip gloss—frosted plum, with "patented extra stay-long" moisture.

"I'll be right out," he said.

"Take your time hooking up with your pathetic groupie girl."

"Lay off, Dana, okay?"

Dana shot me a death-ray look. "First you crash my party, Jam," she said. "And then you basically throw yourself at Reeve, not even caring that he's shit-faced. I actually feel sorry for you. You have no idea of what's normal behavior."

"That's harsh, Dane," said Reeve, and he looked over at me for half a second, but didn't say anything. His lips were still glittering.

Wordless, she pulled him from the room.

Instead of going to the front door and standing outside in the cold, crying a little and texting my mom a line like "I know u r at the movie, but can u come get me?" I followed Reeve and Dana in the darkness. They slipped down the hall and went outside to stand by the covered pool. I pushed open the sliding glass doors a crack so I could hear them.

"Oh no? So what were you doing?" Dana asked.

"I was *plastered*. And she's really into me."

"God, Reeve, you're such a man-whore."

"I guess I am." And he smiled at her.

I closed my eyes. Reeve had to be intimidated by Dana, like a lot of people in the grade, and was just telling her what she wanted to hear. Yes, he was kind of high and kind of drunk, but our kiss had still had clarity. It was filled with feeling, and we couldn't turn back from it. We were falling in love. I was confused by what he was saying to Dana, but I reminded myself that it wasn't the truth. He was lying to throw her off.

I slipped out of the party but I still didn't text my parents to pick me up. Instead I walked all the way home in the darkness on the shoulder of Route 18. The cars were so close that when they roared past me my hair was lifted in a big wave. It took me an hour to get home, and by the time I let myself into the house, I was even more excited about Reeve than I'd been all week.

On Monday at school he was a little distant toward me at first, but I knew it was only because Dana was around. She had an unrequited thing for him, I now understood, and he didn't want to upset her because she could be such a bitch, and she'd never let him hear the end of it. He walked past me without saying anything, but I knew why, and I knew it was temporary. I waited and waited for Reeve to make contact with me when we were alone.

And later in the day, when I saw him at the doors of the school library, he tilted his head at me, and I followed him inside, and then into the stacks. We were in the 920s, and we didn't turn on the light with its little timer, but instead stood together in the shadowy, unlit space.

"You didn't even talk to me today," I whispered.

"What we have is private," he whispered back. "And it's fun to sneak around. Me and my little groupie," he said, knocking his shoulder lightly against mine.

"I get it," I said. "This is just between us."

"Right." He pulled me toward him.

"Here?" I said.

"No one's nearby. Christ, no one in this country even reads."

So we began to kiss in the library stacks, leaning back against the metal shelves and the spines of books. Distantly, timers ticked, but otherwise it was quiet, and the books were the only witnesses to what we were doing. He scooped a hand up under my shirt, and I felt myself shudder. When we heard footsteps he pulled back so suddenly that I gasped, almost as if I were in pain.

"See you" was all he said, and then he backed off, leaving me stunned and dizzy in the dark, with the crumbling forest scent of old books all around me.

Over the following days we met in the library two more times, and once beneath the exit sign in the hall, and another time behind the school, against the rough brick wall, where he put his tongue in my mouth and made me laugh afterward with a joke about how there's no sunlight in England, and even the queen is lacking vitamin D.

We goofed around on the soccer field once when it was empty, but only for like a minute, because he reminded me that everything we did had to be private. I was fine with that, though sometimes I felt like I might explode.

At night I lay in bed with my eyes wide open, my thoughts churning at a rapid rate, cycling through images of Reeve seen from different angles.

"You have dark circles under your eyes, babe," my mom remarked at breakfast one morning. I quickly ran to the bathroom and patted on some liquid foundation. Even if I didn't sleep much at night, I wanted to look rested and good.

In school I frequently looked over at Reeve and was positive we were sharing a smile, a signal, even though it turned out he was often just smiling generally, in the middle of a group of people. I was always on the edge of the group, following, except when Dana came along, at which point I made myself invisible, like one of those camouflage animals that can freakily blend in with their background.

I was there in the background when Reeve showed the Monty Python dead parrot sketch to everyone on a TV monitor in a classroom during break. I slipped into the room and sat on a chair in the back. No one saw me.

"'Ello, I'd like to register a complaint," the customer in the pet shop said, and Reeve thought the sketch was hilarious, and he kept rewinding it and showing the whole thing over and over. Other kids laughed, though mostly the boys and me. Dana Sapol looked bored to death.

"I don't get why this is supposed to be funny," she kept saying in a whiny voice.

But I loved it. Reeve and I had the same sense of humor. I heard him explain that he wanted to go to "university" at Oxford or Cambridge, like the members of Monty Python, who had met when they were in college. I knew he would have a great life ahead of him, and I imagined myself being part of it. I saw us at a comedy club in England, where he and his troupe were performing. I'd be in school over there too, maybe spending my junior year abroad.

I pictured us having high tea in London, though I don't even know what high tea really is. I saw myself on the back of a lime-green Vespa as he drove us around lamplit streets. If I thought about it hard enough, I could picture a whole life with him.

We were in love, and finally I had to tell Hannah and Jenna, though I knew Reeve wouldn't approve. I told them one morning in the parking lot outside school, and they were all, like, "What evidence do you have that he's in love with you, Jam?"

I told them I didn't need "evidence," that this wasn't a courtroom, but they only shook their heads.

Hannah came up to me in the cafeteria later, when I was standing near Reeve and Danny Geller, and she said in a nervous, quiet voice, "Would you come sit down already?" But I just ignored her and stood listening to Reeve talk about Manchester United's most recent game being entirely "brill." As in, brilliant.

During classes, I couldn't think about much else. My teachers seemed to be saying nonsense words, and everyone obediently wrote them down in their notebooks. Life went on in this way, and it was trippy but exciting. Apparently this was what love felt like. Reeve and I had to lie low, making sure we didn't piss off Dana Sapol, who still held on to the idea that Reeve was really into her, which he wasn't.

But then one morning when I got to school I smiled at him and he didn't even smile back, but kept walking. The coast was clear, too; he could've *easily* smiled at me. It would've been safe. No one would have seen.

Later, I loitered outside the library when I thought he might be there, but he never came. Something was wrong; maybe he was having trouble at the Kesmans. Singing rounds could have been driving him crazy. Or maybe something was wrong in his family back in London. His "mum" was sick, maybe. Didn't he know he could talk to me about it? That's the kind of thing that people in love do.

When I saw Reeve with Danny, I said to him, "Can I talk to you?"

Danny looked annoyed when Reeve turned to me. "Jam," Reeve said, "it's not a good time."

"Well, when *is* a good time?" I asked.

"I'll let you know."

So I waited.

Finally, on a Friday after school let out, forty-one days after we first met, when I hadn't slept in a while because sleep was boring, and I'd barely eaten anything because food didn't offer nearly the same nutritional value as love, I found myself walking along the field behind the school, where sometimes Reeve would hang out with his friends. Maybe I would find him there.

I planned to go up to him and quietly say, "Is this a good time?"

And I hoped he'd say yes, and that we would go beneath the bleachers, and we'd kiss, and he'd tell me he was stressed out about his homework, which was why he'd been kind of distant. I'd reassure him and make him feel calm, and our love could resume as planned. And then we'd kiss some more.

But it was that day, that afternoon, when I saw the figure in the distance and walked toward it.

As I got closer, I saw that it was two people, arms around each other, kissing. Reeve and Dana.

My heart was going so hard inside me; it struck me with force, and I put both hands to my chest to calm it down.

Then Dana said that thing "Well, well, look who we have here."

And they just kept talking at me while I stood in the wind. Tears started to come down my face, and my hair was blowing everywhere, and Dana's hair was blowing too. Reeve stood there in his brown sweater and skinny jeans, asking me if I could remember what really happened that night at Dana's house.

Asking me to own up to what was true and what was not. I felt myself shatter inside. He was a boy, he was just a boy. I was in love with him, but here he was with Dana now. "For *realz*," as Hannah would've said.

"You're with *her*?" I asked, nodding toward Dana.

A long, long pause, and a look between the two of them.

"Yeah," he finally said.

"You're not with me?"

"Of course he's not with *you*," said Dana, but Reeve stopped her from saying anything more.

"I can handle this myself, Dane," he said sharply. Then he came over to me and looked me in the eye. His gaze was too much for me, like the brightness after you go to the eye doctor and he gives you drops, and then you have to go outside into the world, and you feel so unprepared for all that light.

But I couldn't turn away, even though I was crying. "Look," he said in a quiet voice, "you don't want to keep doing this. It doesn't make you look good, all right? I'm not an arsehole, Jam. Don't make me out to be one. I'm just here for a term, having a few laughs. Yeah, I sort of have a thing going with Dana. It might be getting serious. But you and me, we were just having fun. You know that."

"I can't believe you're saying this" was all I could tell him. And then, even more desperately, I asked, "You don't love me?"

"What is it you don't understand about what he's been saying?" said Dana, practically shrieking. "He's not in love with you!"

"You're not?" I asked him.

"No," said Reeve.

"You've never been in love with me? Not even that night at the party?"

"Christ, it was a *hookup.* I was tight." Drunk, that means, in England.

"But . . . the jar of jam," I persisted.

"What jar of jam?"

"That you brought. The Tiptree Little Scarlet Strawberry."

He looked baffled. "What did that have to do with *you*?" he said. Then, "Wait, because of your *name*, is that it?"

I just stared and stared at him. We were out here in the wind and he was saying he didn't love me and never had. Even the jar of jam wasn't about me. Nothing was.

Reeve Maxfield had never loved me. He'd said it, and he couldn't unsay it, and I could never unhear it either. And now the world turned instantly sharp edged and unlivable.

So in that swift moment of epiphany, forty-one days after we'd first met, Reeve became dead to me. It was just easier that way.

If he wasn't in love with me, then I could make myself certain that he could never be in love with anyone else.

He didn't love me, so I closed my eyes and killed him in my mind. It was as violent as anything, as shocking as a plane exploding midair. It made a *boom* sound that shuddered inside me and sent my image of Reeve lurching and pinwheeling through empty space.

Being rejected by him was the worst feeling I'd ever known. But now in my mind he was dead, which was traumatic too. But it was the only way to cope.

I felt the sensation of his death rip through me, and almost instantly it felt as true as anything. Even though, of course, I knew that it was just a "story" I was telling myself because the truth was unbearable.

I turned around and walked away in the wind. And as I did I heard Dana say, "Good-bye and good riddance, you psycho loser."

At which point I turned back and screamed, "I'm the psycho loser? That's hilarious coming from *you*, someone who feels good about herself only when she's being cruel to other people!"

I didn't even stick around to hear what she said in reply. Her words were swallowed up by the wind, and Reeve was already dead and swallowed up by my humiliation and then my grief.

I went home and lay in bed with the light off and all my clothes on, even my Vans. My parents were still at work in the gloom of this windy fall afternoon. Leo stood next to my bed and said, "What are you doing?"

"What does it look like I'm doing?"

"Lying in bed in a dark room. Can you start dinner? Mom left a note saying you're supposed to make couscous. And preheat the oven for the chicken. And that you're supposed to spend time with me."

"I can't," I said.

"You can't what? Make the couscous or preheat the oven or spend time with me?"

"Get out of my room, Leo," I said.

But my little brother just stood there, and he began to look worried. "Are you sick?" he asked.

"No," I said. "I'm in shock."

"Shock? Why?"

I paused. "My boyfriend died," I said, trying out the words, and I began to cry all over again.

Leo was confused. "I didn't even know you had a boyfriend," he said.

"Well, I did, and he *died*, okay? And I can't get out of bed and start dinner and spend time with you. I'm sorry, Leo, but I just can't."

"Should I go?" he asked. He was hovering there in the room, almost as if he was afraid to leave me alone.

"As opposed to *what*?"

"I don't know." Then he said, "Maybe I should call Mom and Dad."

"Maybe you should."

"And what should I tell them?" he asked.

"Tell them my *boyfriend died.* And I am inconsolable."

Then I lifted up the blanket so it covered my head too, and the world went dark, and basically it stayed like that for a very, very long time, until the first day I went to Belzhar.

And now here I am in Belzhar once again, confronting Reeve and Dana the same way it happened in real life. It's just as terrible as ever, the way Casey warned it would be. My tears are already starting.

But then I think of Sierra clinging to her brother in Belzhar when the sky began to get dim. She held on to him tightly, and she stayed with him, and she's still with him now.

Reeve and Dana are just staring at me coldly, and I reach out and do something I didn't do in reality behind the school. This was not part of what actually happened. But even so, I take Reeve's hand, and he doesn't resist.

"What are you doing?" Dana says, but by the end of the sentence her voice has gotten puny and insignificant, just like her. I can barely even see her now; she's basically evaporated. It's just Reeve and me, and his hand is cool in mine at first, but as I continue to hold it, it gets a few degrees warmer.

The sky begins to dim—it's time—and if I keep holding on to him, then I can stay here with him and go back to the way we once were in my mind, when he loved me and I loved him, and we were together.

But now I imagine Casey and Marc breaking the news to Griffin. And in a distraught voice Griffin says, "She *stayed*? But she said she wouldn't."

And I have the predictable, clichéd thoughts: I picture my parents coming up to the hospital in Vermont, where I'm sitting in a bed attached to an IV and a monitor, unresponsive to human voices and staring at nothing, my hand rapidly moving in the air as if I'm possessed. My mother whispers, "Babe, oh babe." And Leo's in the doorway, trying hard to focus only on the game on his little handheld, so he doesn't have to look at me.

But this is self-indulgent. How much everyone would miss me. There's also what I would miss. And again, I think of Griffin, and how he wants to be with me, genuinely.

Reeve, though, loves me *here*, in this limited way. And

he only loves me here because I can't bear the idea that he doesn't. He's a boy from London with an ironic smile, clever words, sleepy eyes, and a scrape to his voice. He's a boy who's kind of a player. Kind of a douchebag, maybe, but not terrible. Just a teenage boy who came to the States for a few months, wanting to have a good time.

That's all he is.

That's all he was, and I can't stay here with him.

Without realizing it, I've let go of Reeve's hand, and he's receding along with Belzhar itself, which slides away from me like water pulling back from a shore.

Somewhere out in the world—in London, England, specifically—he's back at his old high school. And maybe another girl, not Dana, but someone with an English name, like Annabel or Jemima, is flirting with him right now, wanting him to pay attention to her. And maybe he will.

I killed him once, in order to tolerate knowing that he didn't love me. Maybe Dana was right; I am a psycho loser. I killed him and preserved his "love" inside me in a little bell jar. I don't know why I needed to do this. Why I had such a big reaction to a boy not loving me back. Why it felt like a tragedy, even though it wasn't. Dr. Margolis said the mind plays tricks on itself in order to stay in one piece.

"It was self-protective for you, Jam," he'd explained in one of our sessions. "And we can take a closer look at that." But I didn't understand a word of what he was saying.

It wouldn't be the worst thing in the world to see Dr. Margolis again sometime, like maybe when I'm home on break.

Maybe I should buy myself another journal one of these days. There are other things I could write down; I don't have to be ruled by this forever. I might even try writing a few song lyrics; ever since joining the Barntones I've been listening closely to the words in songs. Song lyrics have a lot in common with poetry, at least good song lyrics, anyway.

I can do whatever I want, because it's over now. I am done with it. Done with him.

"With who?" someone asks.

I look up, confused, and I'm back in my dorm room. Above me in the darkness stands DJ, her long black hair hanging down. "What?" I say.

"Who are you done with? You were talking in your sleep," she says. "But you were also writing in your journal," she goes on, holding up my journal. "It was very peculiar."

I snatch the journal back from her and quickly flip to the end, peering down at the last line on the last page, which has been all filled in. This is what I see:

> *And I let him go. So I guess that's the end of him and me. Which isn't the worst thing in the world.*

I close the journal. "What time is it?" I ask DJ.

"Two a.m.," she says. "Can we go back to sleep now?"

I try to orient myself. It's the middle of the night near the very end of the semester at The Wooden Barn. I just saw Reeve for the last time. "DJ," I say, "I have to go somewhere." I get up and grab my down coat from its hook, and shrug it on over my nightgown.

"Where?"

"To Griffin's room. It's important."

"In the boys' dorm? Why don't you just go paint a giant *E* for *Expelled* on your nightgown? That was a *Scarlet Letter* joke, in case you didn't know."

"I did know."

"You guys only had to read Sylvia Plath, unlike the rest of us, who were forced to read Nathaniel Hawthorne and other equally hip and cutting-edge writers."

"Just let me go, okay?" I say quietly. "I need to see him. I think you know what that feels like."

"Yeah," DJ admits. "I do. Well, good luck," she says as I head out. "Don't get caught, Jam. That would be a shame."

Silently I descend the stairs and head past Jane Ann's room, hoping to escape her light-sleeper antennae, and then I push out into the night, the air cold on my blazing face. In the stillness I make my way down the path to the boys' dorm. I've only been on the first floor of that building before, in the common room where girls are allowed, but when I climb the stairs it's easy to find his room. The nameplate reads JACK WEATHERS AND GRIFFIN FOLEY.

I push the door open and slip inside. Jack is curled in a fetal position in the bed by the door, a lacrosse stick resting against the wall. In the bed by the window is Griffin, and his eyes immediately open when I appear, and he says, "Jam?"

"Should I leave?" I whisper.

He doesn't answer, but just draws back the blanket. All I can do is get in, and we lie squished together, side by side, in absolute silence. He's waiting for me to say something. "I went to Belzhar," I tell him.

"How bad was it?" he asks. "The death, I mean."

I don't reply at first. I know that when I tell him, he'll

have every right to think I'm an awful person for having been such a faker all semester. He'll think I'm someone who just wanted everyone's sympathy. But I have to tell him, because otherwise the story about Reeve and me might drag on forever. Griffin could keep bringing it up, thinking he's being respectful of the memory of my boyfriend who died.

"The thing is," I say, "it only felt like a death."

Griffin doesn't understand. He looks at me, trying to figure it out, and then he says, "Wait, he didn't die, this guy? Not . . . back then?"

I shake my head. Griffin just keeps looking, and then he shifts his body away from me. I don't know if this is the signal that I'm supposed to leave, and that he's done with me. He doesn't say anything for a long time, and I realize he's going to reject me now. I don't think you ever get used to that.

But finally he says, "You know what? I'm glad."

"What do you mean?"

"Well, that you didn't have to live through something like that."

"You are?" I'm just astonished. "I'll tell you all about it sometime," I go on. "The whole thing, how it happened. I mean, only if you want to hear. There's a lot more to say."

"I'm sure there is," he says.

And I'll tell the others too," I say. "I understand if you feel like you've been ripped off. You've all been through so much worse. I didn't want to hurt anyone, especially you. But it all just sort of happened. If you want to get out of this, Griffin—"

"I don't," he says.

"You don't?"

"No."

And then, for the moment, there's nothing more I need to say or do, no action I need to take and nothing I need to prove. I feel extremely tired, as if I'd been splitting logs for a year. I lean my head against Griffin's chest and we're silent. Just two hearts ticking away.

At some point we must have both fallen asleep, because a phone rings in the distance—who here has a *phone*?—and wakes me up. I open my eyes and the unfamiliar room is starting to fill with light. It's morning, and right away I understand that I'm about to get caught and be expelled from school. I've ruined everything, and it *is* a shame, as DJ said.

Without saying good-bye, I flee the room. As I race down the hall, Dr. Gant strides toward me. All I can do is skid to a stop, waiting for the inevitable.

But he only says, "Jam," his voice vague and distracted.

"I know I shouldn't be here—"

"True," he says. "But I just got a call. I have to tell somebody." He lifts his eyeglasses and rubs his eyes, then looks at me. "You're good friends with Sierra Stokes, right?" I nod. "So you know about her brother."

"Of course."

"That phone call was from the chemistry teacher. He was watching the news, and there was a breaking story about André Stokes."

I stare at him for a moment, feeling something flood through me, unsure what it is. I feel dizzy now, and afraid, but I ask him, "What did it say?"

"He's been found! He's alive and he's okay. It's the most amazing thing."

For a moment I can't really take this in. He's waiting for me to respond and I'm just silent. "Is that really true?" I finally ask. I immediately think, *I have to tell Sierra.*

But I know I can't. She's unreachable.

André has finally been found, but Sierra won't ever know. She can't be with her brother in the fullness and uncertainty of the real world. Deep inside herself she's on a bus with him in Belzhar, just riding and riding.

"Yes, it's true," says Dr. Gant. No wonder he doesn't care that he caught me in the boys' dorm. This news makes everything else momentarily irrelevant.

"How did they find him?"

"The detective was interviewed. It was a new detective; he'd just started. And he saw some notes about . . . a lead? And he looked into it. Something like that, I can't quite remember. André was being held by a man in a house not too far from DC. They made an arrest. I don't know many details yet; no one does. It will all come out." He shakes his head, distracted. "Poor Sierra," he says.

CHAPTER 21

THE VERY LAST SESSION OF SPECIAL TOPICS IN English ought to be a kind of celebration, but it's not and it can't be. Though we've gotten through the semester together, in a class like no other we've taken, and though our lives have been transformed, we're missing someone. And now that André has been found, Sierra's absence is unacceptable. On the last day, it can be felt powerfully around the oval oak table. I think maybe I feel it most powerfully of all.

Mrs. Quenell knows how upset we are. She's upset too. But still she's brought a bakery box with her, and she places it on the table and says, "Red velvet cupcakes for everyone, to match your red leather journals." When she opens the box, there are only four cupcakes inside. One for each of us.

"Thanks, Mrs. Q," Casey finally says, because she doesn't want us to come across as rude.

"I do know how you feel," says Mrs. Quenell. "And believe me, I feel it too."

André Stokes has been a big story in the news. Over the phone my mom and dad have filled me in on what they've read online and seen on TV. Obviously none of us here has had access to any of that, except for the newspaper, which is delivered to The Wooden Barn first thing every morning.

"She should be home with her brother," I say in what comes out like a wail.

"Yes, she should," Mrs. Quenell agrees.

They need each other, André and Sierra. Whatever he went through in his captivity was dark and frightening; I can't even imagine how frightening. He will have "a long road ahead of him," as the experts always say. But at least there's a road. His family loves him, and that's got to help him over time. Of course, I don't know anything about this at all, but I know that he and Sierra were always so close. If they were together at home they could help each other; I'm sure of it.

Then Griffin says, "You know what, Mrs. Q? This being the last class and everything, I'm just going to come out and ask you something. No one is going to want me to do this, but sorry, guys, I have to."

"Hey," says Marc. "What—"

"She can think what she likes, Marc. I really don't give a shit anymore," Griffin says. "Sorry for the language," he adds quickly. I sit there waiting to see where he's going with this. Griffin speaks so much more freely these days. "Mrs. Q," he says, sitting up straighter, "do you know what happens when we write in our journals? Do you *really* know?"

A pulse jumps in the side of Griffin's face, and I get the feeling he's as shocked as we are that he's asked her this. It's reckless. But we're all out of ideas now, and this is it, crunch time, the zero hour, whatever cliché you want to call it. Class is about to be over for good, and Sierra's still in Belzhar.

The silence is elongated and feels endless. No one takes their eyes off Mrs. Quenell's face, which at first looks kind of neutral, then as if it's trying to harden itself, then suddenly it looks softer. Then finally it collapses.

"Yes," she says. "I do."

We can't quite believe it. I'm still not sure we're talking about the same thing.

"And you planned it?" says Griffin.

Mrs. Quenell plays with her watch, turning the band around and around on her narrow wrist. Griffin has unnerved her. "It's not like that," she says. "You make it sound devious, Griffin. It isn't. It wasn't. That's not it at all."

"So what can you tell us?" I ask. We're begging her, really. We're actually begging Mrs. Quenell, an elderly woman we know very little about except that she's a great teacher and has integrity. She wouldn't let us fall under the weight of our problems. She wouldn't baby us. She had respect for us, even as we hated ourselves and everyone else, and thought nothing would ever feel good again.

Now here we are, on this last day. In under forty minutes she'll leave us for good, but before then, we have to know exactly what she knows, and what it means.

So she tells us. "It's actually kind of a personal story," Mrs. Quenell says. "I've never told it to any of my students before, though they've often asked me what I know or don't know.

"First of all, I can't say that I exactly 'know' what the experience of writing in the journals is like. It's your experience, not mine. And I didn't want to get too involved, because it might have ended up calling attention to the class, and hurting my students. So I did an exhausting balancing act for a very long time. But I'm leaving here tomorrow for good. And before I go, against my better judgment

I'll let you know what I do know, which isn't all that much, I'm afraid.

"I'll start with a little history that I think is relevant." She abruptly stops talking, and the pause goes on for so long that it seems as if she's changed her mind. But then she says, "When I was about your age, I went through a very difficult time. I suppose you could call it a breakdown."

Oh. *That* kind of difficult. The kind that some people at this school know something about.

"I was sent to a psychiatric hospital near Boston," Mrs. Quenell goes on. "And while I was there, I was very withdrawn. I talked to no one. Then one day a somewhat older patient, a college girl, was admitted. I rarely heard her talk, but every day, when it was time for medication, the nurses called out to us by our first and last names, and I took note of her name, because I thought it was unusual. We never really spoke, except once, when we were sitting at dinner and I passed her a platter of food and she said, 'Thank you, Veronica.' She knew my name. And for a split second she looked at me the way an older, wiser person sometimes looks at a younger one. With kindness, and without condescension."

Right, I think. That's the way Mrs. Quenell often looks at *us*.

"Do you know what became of her, Mrs. Q?" I ask.

She turns to me, seeming to force herself to focus on the here and now. "Yes. She got better. And I got better too. And I would probably never have known that, or thought of her again, for I really didn't like to think about that painful period in my life.

"But then, years later, when I was newly married and a very young teacher here at The Wooden Barn, I came upon a poem in the *New Yorker*, and something clicked. It was *her.* I was so pleased that she'd come out of that dark time and done something with her life. Become a writer." Mrs. Quenell pauses. "And then, several years after I first saw that poem, I read that she'd died, which made me quite sad. She was very young. Only thirty. That may not seem young to you now, but one day it will."

Listening to Mrs. Quenell tell us this, I feel a stirring of recognition, but at first I think I'm just confused, and I tell myself to wait, to just try to take it in.

"And then," she says, "after a while the details of her death came out—that it was a suicide—and over time the story got much more attention, and then so many people were affected by her life and her tragic death. And mostly, of course, by her work."

"Plath," Casey says quietly.

Mrs. Quenell nods and looks out the window again, into the snow-blurred distance and the lucid past. "Yes," she says. She seems much older all of a sudden. "She was an extraordinary talent. As all of you are well aware."

No one says a word. We're shocked, thinking about how Sylvia Plath, the writer we so casually refer to around this table as "Plath," was not only someone we've studied and feel like we know, but was also someone our teacher did know, at least a little, a long time ago.

"But she suffered from the disease of depression," says Mrs. Quenell, "and they didn't have the knowledge or the medication then that they have now. Though even now, so many people are still lost. Everything was different then, and the subject could barely be discussed in public. People thought it was a sign of weakness.

"Eventually her journals were published. And through

them, it was clear that she believed in writing everything down. It was as if her motto was 'Words matter.' And I believe that to be true too. Anyone who becomes a Plath expert, as you all are, realizes that what she had, first and foremost, was a voice."

Yes, that's what Sylvia Plath had. I always hear it in my head when I read her.

But she couldn't come back from what she went through; from where she went. And it makes me ache for her, this writer stopped in a long-ago time. This person whose voice I hear, even as I move away from what I went through myself.

"One year," says Mrs. Quenell, "I thought to give my students their own journals to write in. I was off antiquing with my late husband, Henry, and I bought a box of them in bulk at an antique store near here that no longer exists. I hoped that writing their feelings down—in addition to all the reading and essay writing that I required—would help them."

"And did it?" Marc asks.

"You know, it seemed to," Mrs. Quenell says. "The students said the journals changed their lives. They burst into class and chattered on about how *powerful* the journals were. At first I thought they were just speaking metaphorically. But after a while I became convinced it was more than that. I took one of the empty journals home and wrote in it myself, to see.

"But nothing unusual happened to me, so I was confused. Perhaps I didn't *need* the journal in the way my students did. In the way that you all did.

"I started to think that the journals only release their so-called power under the right circumstances. Of course, believing in any of this goes against everything I've ever been taught. The practical ways of the world.

"And yet, and yet," she says. "One after another, my students tried to explain that something was happening to them. At first I was skeptical, and then I became afraid. But then I saw that they were getting better. Writing in the journals really did seem to be a form of release. And so what was the harm? I couldn't quite understand what they were going through, but they all assured me the experience was life-changing, and in a good way. So I let it be."

"Unfuckingbelievable," says Griffin. He's really pushing it here, but it hardly matters now. "How do you choose who gets into the class?" he asks.

"Every year," she says, "I look over the students' histories, trying to put together a group who all seem to have . . . similar kinds of stumbling blocks. And then I match them with a writer who might help them. One year we had a very anxious, alienated group, and we studied J. D. Salinger. That was a good class, though they all talked *way* too much, and no one really listened to anyone else.

"Another year, the students needed to be more self-reliant, so we read Ralph Waldo Emerson. And all of you were in the middle of a million things, and yet were isolated. Plath seemed a very good choice. But it's never just been the journals that have made the difference, I don't think. It's also the way the students *are* with one another . . . the way they talk about books and authors and themselves. Not just their problems, but their passions too. The way they form a little society and discuss whatever matters to them. Books light the fire—whether it's a book that's already written, or an empty journal that needs to be filled in. You all know what I'm talking about, I think," she says.

"Yes," I say. And then I remember Sierra. "But sometimes," I add tentatively, "the class—or at least the journal—isn't safe for everyone."

"You're referring to Sierra," Mrs. Quenell says, her voice suddenly weary. I nod. "That was definitely the journal?" And I nod again. "I was afraid that was the case," she says.

"She's *stuck* there, Mrs. Q," I say. "See, she found a way to *stay*, and at first it was a choice we respected—"

"But *now*," Casey says, "we can't get her back to tell her that André's safe."

"No one has ever stayed before," says Mrs. Quenell in the barest whisper.

It's the first time I see that she truly does understand. She knows what it might mean to "stay." She fully believes now that there's another place, accessed only through the journals. She *gets* it.

"In the entire history of Special Topics in English," Mrs. Quenell says, "everyone has handed back their journals on the last day, and has gone on to thrive." She looks extremely pale as she speaks. "But this time, I'm afraid I've caused something terrible to happen. I should tell Dr. Gant right now." She stands unsteadily. "Inform him of what I've been doing all these years while I was entrusted with young minds. I should turn myself in. There can be . . . a tribunal. Or whatever they want to call it."

"No," we all say. "*Stop.*"

Everyone is alarmed. Mrs. Quenell was all set to retire, to travel, and now her plans are potentially ruined. I can't bear for her to feel guilty about what happened to Sierra. "It's not your fault," I say quickly. "You've been trying to do good. And you did do good, Mrs. Q. What happened to Sierra is a freak occurrence, I guess. You're an amazing teacher. Don't tell Dr. Gant. It won't make a difference. It won't help Sierra. He's not part of this. This is . . . ours," I say.

And it is. It's our story and no one else's.

Mrs. Quenell calms down and agrees that she won't say anything to anyone. "You know," she says finally, "I've always had an idea in the back of my head that I would teach Sylvia's work to my very last class of students. I would teach it, and then I would be done. There were some years when I *almost* considered teaching it, but it wasn't exactly right, and besides, I truly wanted to wait. And then this year, all of you came along, and I knew this was the right class, and the right moment."

Special Topics in English is about to be over for good. I feel choked up, because I know that we will never all sit here together like this again, and that Mrs. Quenell will soon be gone. And I feel this way because of what's happened to me, because I've let go of so much. Because I've changed.

And I also feel this way because of Sierra. Leaving her in Belzhar isn't acceptable, but we don't have a choice.

At the end of class, after we've eaten the red velvet cupcakes, and handed back our own journals, including Sierra's, and after we've even played a round of Sylvia Plath *Jeopardy!*—a slightly ghoulish thing to do, but fun—Mrs. Quenell checks her watch and says, "I'm afraid it's just about time for me to release you." She looks at each of us in turn. There's that *attention* again, as though no one else exists other than the person she's looking at.

"I want to say how proud I am of all of you," she says. "I'm so sorry that you're leaving here with a certain sadness. What happened to Sierra is my sadness too. But you're leaving stronger than you were. And somehow, I think you know things you didn't know before."

What exactly do I know now? In my head I try to make a list, the way Marc would probably do.

I know the truth about Reeve; that's one huge thing. I mean, I always knew it, but I couldn't take it.

And I also know that pain can seem like an endless ribbon. You pull it and you pull it. You keep gathering it toward you, and as it collects, you really can't believe that there's something else at the end of it. Something that isn't just more pain.

But there's always something else at the end; something at least a little different. You never know what that thing will be, but it's there.

I learned all of this in Special Topics in English. Mrs. Q taught it to me.

"And I also want you to know," she says, "that despite what it says in that awful brochure the school hands out for reasons I cannot *fathom*, I don't view any of you as 'fragile.' Highly intelligent, yes. Emotionally fragile, no. I think there are better words to describe you.

"You're all equipped for the world, for adulthood, in a way that most people aren't," she continues. "So many people don't even know what *hits* them when they grow up. They feel clobbered over the head the minute the first thing goes wrong, and they spend the rest of their lives trying to avoid pain at all costs. But you all know that avoiding pain is impossible. And I think having that knowledge, plus the experiences you've lived through, make you definitely *not* fragile. They make you brave."

I wish I could go over and cry against her silk shoulder, thanking her and reassuring her. I wish I could tell her everything I've lived through this semester, and everything I've lived through over the past year. She's read my file, but it's hardly the whole picture. I want to tell her about Reeve. And about what I know now that I didn't know then. But she's an old woman who's been teaching high school English for a very long time, and she's tired, and proud of us, and so concerned about Sierra. She deserves a calm and dignified send-off.

So all I say is "Thank you, Mrs. Q." And everyone else thanks her too.

"I want you all to have a marvelous vacation," she adds as she slips on her gray wool coat, "and a marvelous rest of the school year. You're all terrific young people. I look forward to seeing what you do with your lives."

Then she clicks shut the brass fastener on her briefcase that now contains our journals, and stands up. She nods to us one final time, this gracious woman with the perfect white bun and the tiny gold wristwatch, and then she slowly walks out of the classroom. It's the only time she's ever walked out ahead of us, but somehow that's the right move today.

We sit stunned for a few minutes, and then Marc says, "So I guess that's that."

"No, it's not *that,*" I say. "What about Sierra? We're just going to leave her there?" I know I sound kind of pathetic and repetitive. Nobody has any fresh ideas. Nobody knows what to say. Casey does that thing that girls do to each other to be supportive: She squeezes my hand. It's like she wants to tell me, *I'm here for you, Jam.* And I appreciate it, but the only way she could really be here for me is if she helps get Sierra back. And neither of us knows how to do that.

Finally we all leave the classroom too. Casey reaches up

from her wheelchair and swipes a hand over the light switch. Though we're all going to be at The Wooden Barn for another semester, Special Topics in English will be over. The whole experience will close up like a fault line in the earth, and it will be as if this huge thing had never even really happened.

We'll just be four kids who were in the same class first semester. Maybe we'll get together once in a while, or we'll pass one another and say things like "Hey, how's it going?" "How's history class?" "How are the Barntones?" "Are you trying out for the play?" But it won't be the same.

Even Griffin and me—there's no way to know what will happen to us. Everything is very new and tentative, and so much hasn't been revealed yet. Are we good for each other? Are we compatible? Who knows? We just love being together, though; that's indisputable right now.

On the path outside the classroom building, after everyone else is gone, he and I stand together a little longer, and I put my head on his shoulder. "You go on ahead," I finally tell him. "I just want to walk a little."

He doesn't question this, but kisses me, then nods and heads off down the path. He still lopes when he walks, as if he might be about to break into a run. I could watch him for a long time. But there are things I have to think about right now.

Other than the list I've made in my head so far, what else did I get out of Special Topics in English? People are always saying these things about how there's no need to read literature anymore—that it won't help the world. Everyone should apparently learn to speak Mandarin, and learn how to write code for computers. More young people should go into STEM fields: science, technology, engineering, and math.

And that all sounds true and reasonable. But you can't say that what you learn in English class doesn't matter. That great writing doesn't make a difference.

I'm different. It's hard to put it into words, but it's true.

Words matter. This is what Mrs. Q has basically been saying from the start. Words *matter.* All semester, we were looking for the words to say what we needed to say. We were all looking for our voice.

I stop on the cold path to squint up at the trees, which are thin and still against the bright sky. Uncovered, hanging out until their big budding moment, which won't happen for months. It's like they're hibernating now, waiting for spring. Off in some kind of waiting place, just like Sierra.

She needs to be able to burst out too, to shoot out all green again, and have a life. She needs that as much as the rest of us. But how can I give it to her? How can I find the words?

I'd so much wanted it to work when I asked the nurse at the local hospital to go shout to Sierra to come out of Belzhar, just the way it had worked when Griffin called to *me* to come out of Belzhar, and then I'd tumbled out of that crazy, goaty version of the place and returned to him. But of course it hadn't worked with Sierra.

I found what I needed to say at The Wooden Barn. But maybe it isn't just the words that matter. It's that other thing, which Mrs. Q was talking about today. The voice. It doesn't just matter *what* you say. It matters *who* does the saying.

It matters whose voice it is.

Quickly, I pivot on the path and head back to the dorm as fast as I can go, my breath visible in the air, my feet thudding loudly. Luckily, no one is on the pay phone now. That same miserable phone I spoke into long ago, begging my mom to let me come home. I hadn't known anything then. I hadn't known that if you hold on, if you force yourself as hard as you can to find some kind of patience in the middle of all your impatience, things can change. It's big, and it's always incredibly messy. But there's no way around the mess.

I have Sierra's home number, which she'd written on a scrap of paper before Thanksgiving break. I press the numbers, and the phone rings for a long time before someone answers. A man. Tired, guarded. No doubt the Stokes family has been getting phone calls from reporters and crazy people constantly since André was found.

"Is this Mr. Stokes?" I ask in a rush. And then I plunge ahead. "I'm Sierra's friend Jam up at The Wooden Barn in Vermont. Maybe she's told you about me?"

I hear a sigh. "Yes," he says. "I know who you are. She liked you."

"Mr. Stokes," I say. "I am so incredibly happy for you about André; I mean, that is the best news in the world. But I know it's like Sierra is gone now too. And maybe you think she'll be gone forever. But I had a thought. I can't explain it, it'd be too complicated, but I wondered if there's something I could try. Something to say to Sierra, to see if it reaches her. Well, it wouldn't be *me* saying it."

"What are you talking about?" says Mr. Stokes.

"Can you put André on the phone?"

He pauses for a very long time, and I hear a murmured discussion in the background. Finally Mr. Stokes gets back on and tells me he knows Sierra thinks so much of me, so, okay, hold on.

And then the phone is put down, and a long time passes, and then it's picked up again, and a flat teenaged male voice says, "Hello."

"André, this is Sierra's friend Jam, up at her school? I'm so unbelievably glad you're home." I'm speaking quickly, making sure I get a chance to say everything. "Listen, you don't know me," I go on, "but I have a very weird favor to ask you. It's important. I know it's going to sound crazy. But I need you to know I'm *not* crazy."

"Wait," he says, "don't you go to the school they sent her to in Vermont? The crazy school?"

"Yes, I go to The Wooden Barn. But it's just that most of us at the school have *issues,* that's all. I had to call you because I know something. Something big that can maybe help." There's silence from him, and I keep talking over it. "You have to go to her, André," I say, "and let her know some things. Please. She thinks that it's best to just stay where she is. But it isn't. It can't be best just to . . . you know . . . stagnate. I mean, even if you hadn't ever been found—and oh my God, thank God you were—she still could have come back and faced the world. It's better that way. I know this for myself. If she comes back here, yes, I know it's all uncertain and sometimes terrifying, but it's other things too. And she has you. You have each other. And whatever else is there for her in the future."

I pause. He doesn't say a thing. I'm sure he has no idea what I'm talking about. "André, do you have a pad and pencil handy?" I ask. "Because you have to get the pronunciation right. She needs to really *hear* every word clearly. Just go stand over her hospital bed when you're alone with her—do it soon, okay?

Like, right away if you can. Like, *really* soon?—and say these words: 'Sierra, it's me, André. I'm here. Come out of Belzhar.'"

His terrible silence continues. "You got that, André? Do you want to repeat it back to me so we can make sure you have it right?"

There's silence again, and it goes on for so long that I finally have to say, "Hello? Are you still there? André?"

But there's no reply. He's gone, and I don't know when he hung up, or if he heard what I said.

CHAPTER 22

IT HAPPENS FAST. THE VERY NEXT MORNING, ON the day we're all supposed to leave for winter break, someone bangs on my door at 6:00 a.m. When I open it Jane Ann stands before me in her pink shortie robe, crying.

All I can think is, What now? What can possibly have happened now?

"I wanted you to be the first to hear," she says. "Sierra woke up very late last night." Jane Ann is definitely crying, but she's also laughing.

André did it. He did it.

I'm allowed to make the announcement about Sierra at breakfast. There's shrieking and applause all around. I'm desperate to talk to her, of course, but I don't want to push. I imagine she'll be in touch with me soon, though I don't know how soon. I picture the Stokes family huddled together in their home in DC, not wanting to be apart at all, ever.

Later today I'll be with my own family. I try to eat breakfast after I make the announcement, but I'm so overcome by the news about Sierra, not to mention the accumulation of everything else that's happened to me and to all of us in our class, that I can barely eat. I've made Jane Ann swear she will make sure that Mrs. Quenell learns about Sierra waking up before she drives away from her house for good.

I sit in the dining hall feeling very much the way I did the first day I arrived at The Wooden Barn. All around me now come the clinks and clanks of dish, glass, and spoon, and the *sproing* sound I've heard at dozens of breakfasts, as the industrial toaster pops out another six slices of bread. The room smells seriously of egg and butter and coffee. It's too much for me right now, too much stimulation and brightness, requiring too much thought, and I sit with Griffin's hoodie on, clutching a mug of strong tea.

I realize that I'm anxious about my parents coming. They'll be here to pick me up soon, I know, and Griffin is planning to swing by my room to meet my mom and dad and Leo. "I just think they ought to know who I am," he's explained, and I agree with him, though I have a legitimate reason to be nervous.

What if they think I've *exaggerated* his interest in me? What if they don't believe that we're even involved?

No, I'm different now. All they have to do is spend five minutes with Griffin and me, and they'll see the oversize hoodie that I like to wear, and the way Griffin and I give each other looks that have nothing to do with anyone else in the room. They will see.

On the phone the night before, my mom had told me that if I wanted to come back to Crampton for spring semester, maybe it would be worth a try. But no, I told her, I really want to stay on at The Wooden Barn, at least until the school year is through. My friends are here; my life is here. I've already gotten my skedge for next semester, and a couple of my classes look pretty good, including a music theory class with a new, young teacher. And, of course, Griffin will be here.

Maybe I'll come home for senior year, though; that's possible. The Wooden Barn can feel pretty airless. Since I've been living here, I haven't thought much about what's going on in the world.

I miss roaming around on the Internet late at night too, and I miss the texts that used to fly back and forth between me and my friends. I even miss those friends. I never did find out why Hannah and Ryan broke up. I hope she's doing okay, and I feel sorry that I wasn't there for her when that was happening in her life. I don't know that she'll ever really get over the way I distorted everything so badly. I don't blame her if she never gets over what I did. But maybe, somehow, we can work our way back to being friendly again, if not actually friends.

It wouldn't be easy going back to Crampton for senior year. Dana Sapol will still be there, and Danny Geller, and all those kids except for Reeve, of course, who's back in England. No one will ever forget how I fell to pieces so publicly over a boy I hardly knew. And I will never be able to explain it to them.

But maybe, if I do go back eventually, and if anyone comes up and asks me about what happened, I might cut the conversation short by calmly saying, "People change."

Yes, I'm definitely finishing out the rest of the school year at The Wooden Barn, but as for next year, I'll just have to see.

DJ will be flying home to Florida later in the afternoon. Now, in the middle of the day, she and I are sprawled on our beds, nervously trying to kill time. My suitcase is all packed and zipped, and I'm waiting for my parents' car to pull up outside the dorm. I'm listening like a dog for the crunch of tires over snow.

"So what are you going to do over break?" DJ asks.

"Sleep late, for one thing," I say.

"Oh, me too," she says.

"And buy clothes that aren't made of flannel," I add. "Hang

out with my little brother." Leo, fellow other-world traveler. "Talk to Griffin and Sierra. Eat pizza. That kind of thing."

"Sounds nice," says DJ. "Speaking of pizza, I'm starving."

"Is that code for 'I'm about to have a binge emergency'?"

"No, it's code for 'I'm starving.' I barely ate breakfast," she says.

"Me either."

"I'm kind of jangled," DJ tells me. "Rebecca and I had an emotional farewell. I just know her parents are going to try to brainwash her when she's back home. They're going to tell her being queer is only a phase. I just hope she stays strong. Strong and queer."

"She will."

"Anyway, my stomach was all clenched during breakfast, which is why I hardly ate."

"Don't you have some crackers hidden somewhere, DJ?" I ask.

"Yeah."

"So go get them."

She extracts a box of crackers from deep under her desk, and I go to my dresser drawer and root around, and then I pull out the jar of Tiptree Little Scarlet Strawberry jam that I decided I was never going to open as long as I lived.

I study the label now, and feel the jar's cool, smooth glass surface.

"This stuff is supposed to be pretty good," I say, and then, trying to look casual, I grasp the lid of the jar and give it a turn. It makes a surprisingly sharp *pop,* as if it were releasing not just air, but something else that's been dying to get out for a long time.

Then I sit cross-legged on my bed, leaning against the study buddy, facing DJ, and with a slightly bent knife stolen from the dining hall, I spread some of the dark red jam on a couple of crackers—one for her, and one for me. When I put mine in my mouth, the sweet taste startles me. I let it linger.

ACKNOWLEDGMENTS

I AM FORTUNATE TO HAVE BEEN SURROUNDED BY wise and generous people while writing this book. I consider myself particularly lucky to have been the recipient of the advice and expertise of Courtney Sheinmel, a wonderful writer, reader, and friend. It was Courtney who also introduced me to her friend, the writer Julia DeVillers, who not only made helpful suggestions, but also introduced me to her exceptional daughter Quinn DeVillers, who had a lot to say, all of it incredibly smart and useful.

Emma Kress, an extraordinary teacher and writer, offered her own wisdom; and Adele Griffin, a writer I truly admire, was an early and very thoughtful reader. Thanks are due to Delia Ephron for her perceptiveness, support, and friendship; and to Kaye Dyja, for giving me an honest and thorough teenager's perspective. And to Jennifer Gilmore, for her sensitive eye, kindness, and all else. And to Martha Parker, for being present every step of the way. And to my mother, Hilma Wolitzer, for teaching me everything she knows about writing novels. And, of course, to my husband, Richard Panek, for his support and love. Thanks, too, to Laura Bonner at WME, for all her terrific work and unflagging enthusiasm.

I am also grateful to Michelle Kutzler, DVM, PhD, DACT, who gave of her time to talk me through the finer points of goat delivery. My agent, Suzanne Gluck, while not (to my knowledge) versed in that particular field, knows everything about how to help a writer bring a book into the world. Through Suzanne, I made a very happy home at Dutton and Penguin Young Readers, where I have been the recipient of the great kindness and care of the terrific Don Weisberg.

Finally, I owe a large debt of gratitude to my editor, Julie Strauss-Gabel, whom I cannot thank enough for her thoughtful suggestions, patience, and overall brilliance. Without Julie's counsel, neither Belzhar nor *Belzhar* would exist.